Wildwood

Softly he let the trousers slip down from my hips and pool on my feet. There I was, standing against the door frame, naked but for my wine-red knickers, yet it was the desire in my expression that was the most shamelessly naked thing about me. His fingertips brushed my hip and he caught his breath. As he lifted his eyes to mine I saw my longing mirrored there, its edge as keen and cruel as my own.

'Avril.' The word was inaudible; I saw only the movement of his lips.

Oh God – I was on the verge of begging and I mustn't do that. 'I dream about you,' I told him, and something flickered in the depths of his eyes.

'Do you?'

'Do dreams matter?'

'Depends what you dream.'

'I dream we're in the wood. It's always the wood. Why's that?'

By the same author:

Cruel Enchantment
Divine Torment
Burning Bright
House of Dust (In the Black Lace novella
collection Magic and Desire)
Bear Skin (In the Black Lace novella collection Enchanted)

www.janineashbless.com

Wildwood
Janine Ashbless

Black Lace books contain sexual fantasies.
In real life, always practise safe sex.

First published in 2008 by
Black Lace
Thames Wharf Studios
Rainville Rd
London W6 9HA

A catalogue record for this book is available from the British Library.

www.black-lace-books.com

Typeset by Palimpsest Book Production Limited, Grangemouth, Stirlingshire
Printed and bound in Great Britain by CPI Bookmarque, Croydon, CR0 4TD

Distributed in the USA by Macmillan, 175 Fifth Avenue, New York, NY 10010, USA

ISBN 978 0 352 34194 5

The Random House Group Limited supports The Forest Stewardship Council (FSC),
the leading international forest certification organisation. All our titles that are
printed on Greenpeace approved FSC certified paper carry the FSC logo.
Our paper procurement policy can be found at www.rbooks.co.uk/environment

1 3 5 7 9 10 8 6 4 2

The poem that Ash quotes from in Chapter 6
is 'Lights Out' by Edward Thomas (1878–1917)

Dedicated to D.F. –

who was far too good for the students he taught.

I can only apologise.

Contents

Prologue: Oak King, Holly King

I climb the gate and go into the wood.

It's the high end of summer, the last few weeks before the tints on the leaves overhead start to change. The foliage around me is at its darkest and thickest and greenest. Underfoot there's no trace of damp, but I almost feel as if I'm moving underwater. I take one of the winding paths at random, knowing that it will switch about and fool me and steer me into unfamiliar and dangerous places.

They – the People of the Wildwood – emerge from between the trees and fall into step with me; at first I see them only distantly or from the corner of my eye and it's easy to pretend it's all just my imagination. Soon, as I leave the safer margins of the wood and sink deeper, they grow bolder and I can look straight at them, but always there's something ambiguous about them, something that suggests that the flicker of shadow and the glow of sunlight, the chance nod of a branch or the startled flap of a bird's wing is not something that simply confuses my eye and makes it impossible to bring them into focus, but something intrinsic to their nature. They are impossible to define but they are there: hunched elder-tree witches and wrinkle-faced apple-men, trolls bearing crusts of leaf mould upon their shoulders from where they've been sleeping, spindly bramble-urchins with sharp eyes and sharper teeth, horses of yellow bone, and boars of mud and withered leather. Hybrid things from a place where chitin and bark and skin and earth are interchangeable, and hair is grass or reeds or mats of phosphorescent mycorrhizae.

Things that look, so long as I'm smart enough not to pay them close attention, like scarecrows, and things that look like road accidents and things that look like nothing I have analogues for. Some are even beautiful. They whisper in languages I've never heard and their ancient eyes are full of sorrow and promise and need.

I carry on walking, my heart in my throat, my blurring eyes fixed on the path. There is no way back from here. I must find what I'm looking for before they close in on me. And close they do, from the sides and the rear, until they're right at the edge of the path. They smell of wet compost, of earth and old leaves and fungus. It's not unpleasant. But as they close the smell grows stronger and the light greener and the creak and crunch of their steps louder, until I'm hemmed in on all sides and they tower over me. Their expressions are variously cunning and wise, vacuous and gleeful, but none of them are kindly.

Eventually I am crowded to a halt. I feel like I can hardly breathe. Then just as I'm sure I'm to be torn apart, two of them step aside and, in the gap, is revealed the first familiar, human face among all that crowd. It's Ash, and he looks at me with a smile that is both pleased and surprised and it goes straight though my breastbone to lodge in my chest. My heart thumps with relief and a warm, tingling wave brushes my skin from top to toe.

'Avril?' He's wearing what I take to be a grey coat, and a wreath of oak leaves. He is king in the wood, I tell myself. From my right an elder-witch, the eyes in her grey face holes full of rot, reaches out and plops a wreath upon my own head. Raising my hands I discover a crown of birch, the triangular leaves still fresh.

My entourage draws back a little, forming a circle around us.

'We bring the queen,' says a voice over my shoulder, a voice that rumbles like rocks in a barrel and originates at a point several yards over my head.

Ash looks around the crowd, frowning. 'Oh no,' he says. 'I'm sorry. You're mistaken.'

'Your queen,' thunders the voice, and a huge hand catches me in the back, slamming me forwards. Ash opens his arms just in time to grab me and I end up against his chest, half the breath knocked out of me. His coat feels solid, like armour.

'You don't understand.' He says it gently, like a traveller anxious not to give offence in a foreign land, and under the copper arch of his brows his greenish eyes linger regretfully on mine. But he still says it. 'She can't be.'

'Yours!'

'No.'

'No,' I chime. 'Please realise. We can't.'

'If not yours, then ours,' says the voice.

That shuts us up. Through the circle ripples a low murmur of anticipation and greed. I glance hurriedly at the hulking mob and then back at the man whose arms are round me. 'Ash . . .'

He blinks. His eyes are darker than normal, his pupils wide in this dim green light, and he looks suddenly uncertain.

He wouldn't turn me over to them, surely?

'We could, you know,' I say, and it comes out high and shaky.

'Could we?'

I nod, frantic.

'Well, we could.' His breath is shallow.

'So as not to upset them.' My arms are around his neck. His dreadlocks are heavy on the backs of my hands.

'That would be polite,' he admits. He brushes aside a birch twiglet that has come astray from my crown and is lying against my cheek. My skin seems to catch light from his touch. His other arm is holding me very close indeed. 'It's an understandable error they've made.'

'Perfectly.'

'Yours!' thunders the voice in satisfaction.

'So long as you realise that,' he murmurs. His lips are perilously close to mine.

'Of course.'

'Mine,' he agrees, an edge of hoarseness to his raised voice.

'Yours!' they chorus, scores of inhuman voices lifted together. Then they retreat from us, fading back into the wood as they go, and we're left alone in a narrow clearing hemmed in by trees. Ash and I pull back slowly to arm's length.

'Are we safe?'

'Are we ever safe?' he answers ruefully. 'They're watching, if that's what you mean.'

'Oh.' I've realised that his coat is made of tree bark interlaced with ivy, and my wandering fingers find a coarse edge of the strange garment. 'Then I suppose we have to . . .'

'I suppose we do.'

I try to slip my fingers under the edge of the coat, but I jerk with shock as a bark plate breaks off and falls, revealing a patch of chest about the size of my palm. The rest of the bark seems to be stuck to his skin. 'Did that hurt?'

'Uh.' He looks just as shocked as me. 'No.'

I touch his warm skin with my fingertips. The bark has left no imprint. Carefully I prise off another piece and Ash watches curiously. I find that the ivy does not come away so easily; its tiny flat rootlets cling tenaciously to his skin. Instead of the tribal tattoo at his shoulder he has green and jagged leaves growing there and I trace the tendrils with my fingertips. Green on cream: the colour contrast is dizzying.

'What about you?' he asks, running his hand down the curve of my waist. My own dress is composed of curls of papery white bark and they fall effortlessly beneath his touch, leaving a wake of smooth skin that's a deep golden brown at this time of the year. Ash makes a noise in his throat that I take to be appreciation and I feel suddenly self-conscious. He's right: it doesn't hurt. Instead each piece falls away with a tingle of nerve endings that is pure pleasure.

'It's not as if we're attracted to one another.' It's hard to keep my voice steady.

'Not in the least,' he says, his hand shedding birch-bark curls like confetti as he runs it round and over my breast, spiralling in. 'We've never been like that, Avril.'

'I know.' I'm finding it hard to speak as he closes on my exposed nipple. 'Oh God.' My fingers scrabble clumsily at the oak bark, revealing swathes of ivory flesh.

'You're not enjoying this.' His voice is teasing, his breath warm on my ear.

'Neither are you.'

His next pass bares my right flank and hip. I lift my thigh against his to allow him access all the way down and I feel his response – a surge in the plated region of his groin. Ash winces.

'It's OK,' I tell him, gently stripping him of his armour and exposing the warm velvet flesh beneath, inch by inch. He moves in my hands like a hatchling struggling from its shell and I cup his balls and caress his cock, urging it erect. It jerks between my palms, flushed and proud. 'I can see how reluctant you are.'

'Yes.' He looks dizzy. 'That's quite obvious.'

'Very, very obvious,' I say with appreciation. His glans is glossy like polished wood. I trace fingertip paths up the solid length of his shaft and feel obliged to remind him, 'This doesn't mean anything.'

'Of course not.'

'We're acting under duress.'

Ash pushes up against me so he can get his hands round my waist and down to the swell of my arse. 'Naturally.' He cups the twin mounds, his fingers daring and possessive. 'I don't want you – you understand that, don't you?'

5

'Yes.'

'You're not beautiful.'

'I know,' I gasp before he clasps the back of my head and kisses me with ravenous kisses. My body is pliant against the hard length of his and I can feel his thick erection trapped between us. It excites me beyond measure. He eats my soft whimpers of distress.

'Avril,' he groans as we break for air at last. Then he sinks to his knees before me, his hands on my hips. His only clothing is the living ivy and his prick stands like wood. He stares up at me with an expression so intense I'm almost lost. While he stares his hand travels to the inside of my thigh, brushing aside the last few curls of bark there and, as he presses his lips to my belly and his thumb describes circles on my mound, his fingers slip inexorably into the crease of my sex. My folds are plump velvet like the petals of an overblown rose, and at the heart of the rose I am wet and waiting for him.

'You smell like summer,' he mumbles, his tongue sweeping my skin.

Oh good God, he's inside me – two fingers, scissoring to open me, stirring. The rest of his hand rubs against my sex and my clit, firm and easy. He stoops to kiss my hip, my belly, the crease of thigh and crotch, his lips fervent as his fingers slip in and out. I lay one hand on his bare shoulder to feel his muscles working, one hand on his hair. He is oak, I am birch, and my sweet sap is welling out and running down his fingers, oiling his palm. His teeth nip at my mons, tugging on the skin, sending sparks straight to my clit. I start to make frantic little noises. But just as my orgasm is so close that I can taste it he pulls out from me and rocks back on his heels. I nearly lose my footing and I have to grab at him to steady myself.

'Ash!' My cry is soft but my whole body is screaming with frustration. I push my fingers against his lips and he bites down on them – the pain reassuring, something to cling to. Lovingly he touches himself with the hand he's had inside me, smoothing my honey onto his hard cock, making it shiny with my juices. He's so aroused that there's no give to that stiff column, but he strokes it a couple of times anyway.

The look in his eyes would be frightening in any other context, so strong is it, so charged with such implacable intent.

Then he takes me by the hips and pulls me forwards, right off balance, so that my body slides down the length of his. I straddle his thighs as I sink into his lap. He spreads me, settling my sex right over the head of his cock, and holds my weight effortlessly as he pushes deep into the space he has prepared so well. My body, tight though it still is, is starving for him and swallows him in one hot wet gulp. It only takes a couple of thrusts to seat himself to the hilt and, as he does so, he groans my name. Face to face again, I find his lips. My arms are round his neck.

'Ash . . .'

His kisses silence me. His hips surge under my thighs and, as I grind my pelvis upon him, part of me thinks that this must be an incredibly uncomfortable position for him, but I've once again forgotten how strong he is. The muscles of his arms bulge as he lifts most of my body weight, sliding me up and down on his impaling shaft. I try to help, pushing with my spread legs, but it's not really necessary. Ash can fuck me. Ash is fucking me and I'm riding him. Brought already to the very edge, my sex responds at once and I arch my back and spit out incoherent, urgent cries.

Ash mouths at my throat and words are wrung from him like drops of blood. 'Avril,' he groans: 'Oh God, Avril. I don't want you. I don't want you. I don't love you.'

I know I need to hear those words properly but right now I'm too frantic with my own need and my mind is like a blizzard of golden leaves and everything, everything is dissolving and turning to light.

In the midst of rapture something touches my arm lightly, like fire.

I open my eyes and find Ash's own are closed, his skin flushed and damp as he thrusts. Every one of those thrusts sends an aftershock of orgasm through me, rendering my mind to pulp, and I can barely focus on his face.

The light has dimmed.

Pain stings along my left thigh.

I look down and see a holly leaf with its spines embedded in my skin. There's a red line scored down my left forearm too. A dark mass moves in the wood, over Ash's shoulder. Blinking, I try to focus.

The mass is a wall of vegetation – dark, shiny leaves like a storm front on the move, and at its apex a man with a look of thunder and in his hands a spear of blackened wood. He strides into the clearing, the gale of holly billowing around him, and draws the spear back to thrust.

'It's Michael! Michael's got into the wood!' I cry, but Ash can't hear me. His arms are around me and his thighs are like slabs under me and he's deep deep inside me; Ash is in the last throes of his agony and he can't hear, only feel.

As the spear impacts between Ash's shoulder blades I scream, and wake.

Sliding out of bed, I land on my arse on the rug. It takes a long time before I can truly believe I'm safe in my own room, and longer still to stop trembling. My body is aquiver from the orgasm I've just experienced – one of those aching belly-deep orgasms you get in sleep – and frantic with adrenaline.

The fear goes first. It was only a dream after all, and I should be used to them by now.

Getting to my feet I go to the window. My bedroom is in the converted attic of the old cottage, with quaint sloping roofs on either side of the centre beam and only two small windows, one on either side of the bedhead. Kneeling to draw back the curtain I look out into the night. Part of me expects to see Ash out there in the long grass, silver with moonlight, looking up at me. It wouldn't surprise me in the least. But the night is moonless and the meadow is empty. All I can make out is the black bulk of Grange Wood against the horizon, like a living darkness.

Dropping the curtain I turn back reluctantly to my bed. The light from the landing illuminates the room softly. Michael sleeps on his back down the centre line of the mattress, hands resting on his chest. His black hair is a crisp outline on the pillow and the sheet covers him only to the waist. Jenny, the girl from the pond, lies on his far side, curled into a ball near the foot of the bed. Neither of them stirs. I can hear Michael's even breathing, though not hers.

My tongue feels like a piece of carpet. A pulse still beats in my clit like the tick of an old-fashioned watch and my thighs are wet and sticky. I need a drink of water, desperately, and there's a carton of orange juice in the fridge so I head down the stairs. A glance out of the landing window gives me another look across the estate grounds towards Grange Wood. Somewhere out there under the dark oaks Ash lies asleep, I presume. I wonder if he lies alone.

I shrug off the last shreds of my dream. It's all due to the wood, of course – those dreams that crowd my sleeping hours, night after night, powerful and vivid and exhausting. I live too close to the ancient trees. Dreams seep out from under the shadow of the wood edge and they cross the old orchard and the lawns and crawl in at my window. They fill my head with confusion and my body with heat.

It's all the fault of the Wildwood.

1: Something Old, Something New

'Now what kind of woman brings a knife along to a wedding?'

I jumped, but it was too late to conceal anything. The cut had already been made. I straightened to meet the gaze of the man who'd accosted me. It wasn't, thank God, the vicar: that would have been too embarrassing. 'I didn't actually bring it to the wedding,' I explained. 'I keep it in my coat. In the car.'

'In the car, right.' He made it sound just as wicked. Standing on the churchyard grass with his hands in the pockets of his beautifully cut suit, he was clearly relishing the thought of my lawbreaking. Under his black brows there was a complicit glint in his eyes. 'So, what sort of woman keeps a knife in her coat pocket? International assassin, perhaps?' He looked pointedly at the thick black strap in my hand. 'Rubber fetishist?'

I could feel the blush warming my face. 'I'm an arborist,' I said, folding the clasp knife safely away. I touched the trunk of the young rowan I'd been tending to. 'This tree's been staked for so many years that the strap's cutting into the bark and choking it.' I poked the rotten base of the tree stake with my foot. If I'd been wearing my steel-capped boots like I did for work I'd have given it a solid kick and knocked the piece of wood away, but in strappy open-toed shoes suitable for an August wedding I had to be a little more cautious. 'Anyway, by now the tree's supporting the stake, not the other way round. So I was just cutting it free.'

'I see.' He was still smiling, which I found disconcerting. Men that good-looking didn't usually smile at me.

Not that many men I'd met were quite that handsome, I corrected myself mentally, taking a moment to look at him properly. And usually I was wearing combat trousers, a reflective waistcoat and a safety helmet when I did meet them.

'You're a tree surgeon.'

There was a hint of doubt in his tone, which made me bristle. I knew what he was seeing when he looked at me, though he kept his gaze just focused enough on my face to be polite: a tall young woman in a fuchsia-pink summer frock which showed off her tan and clashed just a little with the jacket, betraying a lack of expertise when choosing clothes. A big mouth. A silk flower in my hair that stood in for the wedding hat I'd refused to buy, and a rather amateurish attempt at make-up. It was not my normal look and I was horribly certain that the effect was less than flattering. The dress hid my toned thighs and the jacket hid the muscles of my upper arms – the long flat muscles of a keen swimmer or climber and in my case both – and left me looking simply rangy. 'I'm a landscape gardener,' I said, drawing myself up taller, 'with a specialisation in trees.' Damn it, I wasn't going to let this man embarrass me. 'I work in a National Trust garden in Cumbria.'

'Sounds lovely.'

'I think so.' He really was unusually handsome; it was something about the eyes, the way those black lashes contrasted with the blue of his irises so that they flashed every time he moved. His hair was dark too, growing thick and a little unruly. It added up to what I thought of as Irish looks. And I was willing to bet a suit like his cost more than my monthly wage. Maybe several times more.

'And even at a wedding you just can't resist a little tree work?'

'Well, you know.' I shrugged. The way I see it, looking after trees is more than a job. 'Obviously the churchwardens here don't know what to do with them.'

'They knew enough to plant a rowan near the main door.' He plucked a leaf from a low branch and rolled it negligently. 'It's supposed to protect buildings from lightning and fire and witches.' He smiled. 'Doesn't work though, not any more. Alas, the Church must resort to insurance like the rest of us.'

'You know your trees then,' I said, surprised.

'I know their virtues.'

It was such a strange phraseology that I was temporarily at a loss. 'Anyway,' I said, 'they've been taking forever with the photos...' I waved towards the church where the bride and groom were still posing. 'I had to find something to do before I passed out from boredom.'

'They've certainly been taking their time. You're a friend of the bride?'

'Emma's my cousin. We grew up together.' I smiled ruefully, not about to admit that we'd spent most of our childhood fighting. We were really quite fond of each other now that I lived on the other side of the country. 'You were in Chester's half of the church, I expect?'

'Yes. I met him through work.' Not, 'He's a friend,' I noted.

'He seems a nice guy.'

'He does. Your arboricultural work...' He trailed off with a gesture that conveyed that he was fishing for my name.

'Avril Shearing.'

'Avril...It means "boar fighter", did you know?'

'Really? I thought it was French for "April." Friends have sometimes told me I look a bit French; it's my Mediterranean complexion and the burnt-honey colour of my hair. So far as I knew I wasn't of Gallic ancestry, though family legend had it that Great-grandmother had been naughty with several visiting GIs during the War, so the exact composition of the

Shearing bloodline was an unknown quantity. The women in my family have never been conventional.

'It's a common misapprehension.'

'Boar fighter?' I grinned a little. 'I like that. What language?'

'Old English. Language of the heathen Saxon.' There was a twist to his smile now.

'Right ...'

'You're fully qualified?'

'Uh-huh.'

'Do you have a business card?'

This time I laughed out loud. I didn't move in the sort of circles where people swapped cards. 'No – what for?'

'Well, in case I need to contact you again.'

This brought me up short. I stayed smiling, not sure if he was hitting on me. From his expression he could be, easily, but I didn't quite believe it. Men like him did not go for women like me. 'Contact me?'

'To deal with my trees.'

Again I hesitated. 'Sorry, I've got a full-time job. I don't do contract work.'

'You misunderstand. I'm in the process of buying some property, and it's quite heavily wooded. I may be looking for someone to manage it for me, on a full-time basis.'

Several trains of thought ran through my head simultaneously, most of them doubtful, some outright cynical. 'OK,' I said cautiously.

'Don't worry about the card.' He turned away from me as an usher called 'Michael!' from the church porch. 'I can find you if necessary.'

'Find me?' I was starting to feel dazed.

'Information is what I deal in. Don't fret, you'll be quite easy to get hold of.' He started back up the slope.

'I'm sorry ... You haven't ...' I stuttered at his retreating figure, and he paused to flash me a coruscating smile of enquiry that simultaneously made me want to grab him and to give him a slap. 'What's your name?' I finished weakly.

'Michael Deverick.' He said it as if he expected me to know exactly who that was, and strode off without another word.

Nor, I noted, had he offered me *his* business card.

'You could have just asked for my phone number,' I muttered under my breath. But I had the distinct feeling that he was not the sort of man who bothered to ask for anything.

Taking an ambling route between the gravestones I returned to the wedding party, which was still waiting around for the photographer to finish. Emma seemed tireless as she alternated posing and chivvying others into position, but Chester's smile was beginning to look forced and most of the guests had broken off into weary little knots of gossip, wondering how long it would be before they'd get a glass of champagne or something to eat. A number of those lucky enough not to be related to the bridal couple had already left to make their way to the reception at the Waters Hotel. I was jumped by Chester's sister Miranda, who worked in an academic publishing house and had distinguished herself at the hen party by removing the stripper's jockstrap with her teeth. I liked her a lot.

'Avril! How are you?'

'Hungry.'

'I could kill for a drink,' Miranda admitted. 'You know they're going to do this all over again when we get to the hotel?'

'Oh God,' I said in quiet despair. 'I know Emma hasn't eaten anything in six months, but she should have mercy on the rest of us. Why has it got to be such a marathon?'

'Weddings always are. That's why I want to get hitched in the Maldives, on a beach, me in a white bikini and a veil, and all the guests can go swimming while they wait.'

'I'll get married in a hot-air balloon,' I said. 'And we'll bungee jump after saying our vows. That should cut things nice and short.'

'Hmm.' Miranda's smirk grew teasing. 'And was that Michael Deverick I saw you talking to? Isn't he gorgeous?'

'Do you know him?'

'Oh yes. Chester started off working for him when he first went into the City.'

'He doesn't look that old.'

'He isn't old, just talented. He's made an absolute killing on the stock market – he's worth a not-very-small fortune. They say he's got an almost uncanny ability to predict the markets.'

'You mean he's a crook?'

'Avril!' She smacked her lips. 'So what were you two talking about?'

'Trees.' It was the only thing I was prepared to admit to. In retrospect, I was fairly sure the man had been mocking me.

'Oh come on! Was he checking you out?'

I shook my head. 'I'm not his type, Miranda.'

'But I bet he's yours! Couldn't you just eat him up?'

The phrase brought rather stirring pictures to mind and I couldn't help giggling. Admittedly I'd already wondered whether his cock was of the same superior quality as the suit it was kept in. 'Don't start! Blokes like that aren't interested in chicks with chainsaws. His type is . . .' I looked around for inspiration and found it walking across the grass in teetering heels: no one I knew, but then there were a lot of guests at this wedding. The blonde wore a slashed lime-coloured dress that made the most of her slender frame and her hair was swept up into an elegant twist to display the line of her neck. Her sculpted collarbones were visible and her shoulders were so fine that they came to points. 'Her: the anorexic one. Two grapefruit on a skeleton.'

Miranda, curvy and brunette like her brother, sighed in sympathy. 'She is a very pretty skeleton.'

'Lovely. I expect she lives on white wine and appetite suppressants. That's the sort that men with money want.'

As if to prove me right Michael Deverick appeared round the corner of the church, his path converging with the blonde's, and as he held out his arm she took his elbow and draped herself gratefully over him.

I rolled my eyes. 'See? She's too weak to stand up unaided.'

'Jealous?' Miranda asked slyly.

'No!'

Miranda pulled a face. 'I bloody am.'

By the end of the evening I was a little the worse for wear. I'd danced for hours and I'd done the rounds of the relatives and eaten at the buffet too, so by the time the bar closed I was still steady on my feet, but perhaps not as wary as I should have been. My first clash with Simon, earlier in the evening, should have been a warning of what was to come.

Simon was an old boyfriend from back when I lived in the village. In those days he'd been merely the sporting darling of the parish and was the lad to whom I'd eagerly surrendered my virginity in the bowling alley at the back of the pub. Nowadays, big, blond and beefy, he looked exactly like what he was: a county cricketer. We'd parted badly, and he's always been a bit snide whenever I've met him since.

Simon had cornered me as I was going with Miranda to the toilets. As we turned into the downstairs corridor we found Simon there, lounging against an occasional table with a drink in his hand.

'Avril!' he said brightly. His face was ruddy from the spirits and his bow tie hung loose around his neck. 'Nice dress.'

I stopped. It was a nice dress, now that I'd taken the jacket off. It had spaghetti straps at the shoulder and was made of soft, rather clingy cotton. 'Thanks.'

''Scuse,' Miranda said, making a bolt for the ladies'.

'Didn't think you'd be in dress,' he continued. 'Thought it'd be dungarees or something. For, you know, your gardening.'

'Right,' I said. 'Well, some of us are advanced enough to have a change of clothes, Simon. And I even washed my hands after work.'

He put his hand on my waist. I should have pulled away right then but I'd had enough alcohol to take the edge off my caution. And it wasn't as if I really disliked Simon after all those years, or as though he were physically unattractive. 'Nice dress,' he repeated, looking down my front. 'But looks as if you're a little cold.'

He was referring to the way my nipples were sticking out through the fabric, hard little points of fuchsia pink. I wasn't wearing a bra. I giggled.

'Remember that time,' he said, dropping his voice to a murmur, 'we went out in the snow looking for squirrels?'

I did, and my body did too, my flesh warming instantly to the memory, which was why I didn't stop him when he put his hand to my left breast and brushed the nipple very gently with his fingertips. My skin tightened, shivering.

We'd gone out across his father's fields from spinney to spinney, looking for squirrels on the pretext that they ate pheasant eggs and chicks. Simon had carried an air rifle. At the time I had no particular grudge against grey squirrels and didn't match his eagerness for the hunt – they weren't my pheasants – although ironically nowadays I know the damage they can do stripping tree bark and I'm far less sentimental. I remember the spots of blood bright against the snow under the bare black trees, like the start of a fairy tale: *Skin as white as snow* . . . I remember how Simon had laughed at the disgusted faces I'd pulled when he flipped over the little corpses with his toe. I'd got so grumpy that he'd broken off, still laughing, and backed me against a sycamore sapling to kiss me into a better mood. As I melted into compliance he'd slipped out of my embrace and round the back of the tree, drawing my arms out behind me. I didn't struggle as he lashed my wrists with his leather belt, pinning me to the tree, though I'd laughed and scolded him. When he'd finished trussing me he'd returned to face me and slowly unzipped my coat.

'Simon!' I'd yelped, but he'd ignored my protests and peeled open my fleece liner and my cardigan and finally, button by button, the blouse beneath to reveal my bra. It was a still day, but it was the middle of winter and there'd been an inch of snow on the ground. 'Simon, it's cold!' I'd protested, wriggling against my bonds but weak with laughter.

'So I see.' He'd eased my breasts gently from their lacy cups, exposing them to the chill air. My nipples were as hard and cold as bullets, but they'd radiated fire through my body as he pinched them. 'Bet I can get them colder, though.'

He'd bent to scoop some snow and I'd realised then how exposed I was. The farm was private land and there shouldn't have been anybody wandering around, but the spinney provided no cover from prying eyes should anyone have been out checking on the stock. My tits were there for the entire world to see. When Simon rose with a lump of compacted snow in either hand I'd squealed, for fear of the cold and for shame, but there'd been nothing I could do to stop him rubbing each pinky-brown nipple with ice until I was gasping.

'Someone might see!' I'd moaned, rocking my head back against the trunk, my tits jiggling helplessly. The snow was melting from the heat of my flesh and the ice-water ran down my breasts and ribs.

'Good,' he'd said brutally. 'I'd like that. You're beautiful.' And so saying he'd wiped his last melting clots of snow down my skin and opened the front of my jeans, kneeling to drag them down over my bum cheeks, knickers and all in one swoop. Then he'd thrust his face into my bush and begun to eat me out in great hot licks. 'Nothing cold down here!' was his one comment.

Standing in that hotel corridor I remembered the sharp bite of the winter on my breasts and the icy slipperiness of the sycamore bark on my buttocks as Simon's face ground into my crotch, the chill on my naked thighs contrasting with the boiling of my sex, the gusts of his warm breath through my pubes, the way the juices running down the inside of my legs felt hot enough to scald me.

It's got smooth, algae-covered bark, has young sycamore. It's a bugger to climb and leaves you covered in a green stain when you've done it. I'd learnt that for the first time that day with Simon, when I went home with a green arse. It was the first thing I learnt about trees.

The experience also left me with a permanent kink for sex in the open air.

I was so hypnotised by memory and by the whisper of his fingers over my breast that I wasn't thinking what I was doing, there in the hotel. Until the moment he pressed up against me.

'God, you've got lovely little tits,' he breathed.

I could feel his erection through his trousers, butting me. With a sharp intake of breath I thrust his hand off. 'Stop it, Simon!'

'I heard you split up with wossisname, that surfer bloke.'

'So?'

'So come on, Av,' he said, grabbing my arse.

I gave him a shove and he sat back hard on the corridor table, skewing the little tablecloth and sending the vase of dried flowers rocking. 'I always knew you'd turn into a dyke,' he growled.

'Oh grow up!' I snapped and flounced off into the ladies'. By the time I came out with Miranda and we headed back to the wedding marquee there was no sign of him.

Chester's friends, mostly City types, had long since faded from the scene by the time I headed across the hotel lawn towards Reception and my single room. Only the old country crowd were still resisting every polite attempt by the hotel staff to make them vacate the marquee and let them clean up or, if they'd drifted outside in the warm evening, were now talking and laughing under the stars. There was a group of them hanging out around the fountain. This sat in the centre of the lawn and it wasn't playing, but it was big enough to be a natural focal point and as I strolled past I could see that several people were sitting on the rim of the lower basin, paddling their feet in the water. Light was provided by submerged lamps and by the moon. From the crowd someone hailed me by name. I turned and saw that it was Simon, dishevelled and clinging to a bottle of champagne.

'What now?' I asked with a sigh.

'Av! You're a climber, right?'

I tilted my head, waiting.

'Reckon you could climb that then?' He gestured at the fountain, and I followed the line of his arm. It was a monstrous construction, built when the Waters Hotel was a private residence and its owners had serious pretensions to grandeur. The round basin was occupied by an enormous bronze triton, reclining in a bronze shell. He held aloft another scallop shell that formed a second basin, and tipped a conch to his lips as if blowing a signal blast. All around him smaller Nereids disported in the water.

'What for?' I asked when I'd taken all this in.

'No but, could you?'

Several of the crowd with him sniggered and I looked warily at their faces. Some were familiar from the village, years back, though none were among those I'd counted as friends. Others were strangers, but from the same mould: all young, none sober, with taunting looks upon their faces. I looked again at the fountain. The whole thing was maybe thirty feet high. The metal wasn't wet but it looked polished smooth. On the other hand there were so many rococo details – foaming waves and cherub heads and the like – that there should be no difficulty finding holds for hand and feet.

I shrugged. 'No problem. Why?'

There were more sniggers.

'Well, we've got this bet on, like,' said Simon, grinning with undisguised slyness. 'What with you being this big-shot lumberjack so you say –' He broke off to allow space for several derisive snorts from his audience.

'I'm not a lumberjack,' I said, wincing at the word.

'Whatever. An *arborist* then.' He executed a clumsy, mocking bow of apology. 'We were wanting to see if you could climb this, to the top shell there.'

Actually almost all tree climbing is done with rope and harness, but I'd done plenty free-climbing on rock faces too. That didn't worry me. 'And what would I get for winning the bet for you?'

'Oh,' he said, 'I'm betting against you.'

'Really.'

'But if you win I'll buy you . . .' He pulled a face. 'A crate of bubbly?'

'A new climbing rig,' I countered. 'With ropes and ascenders.' That would set him back a bit and was currently beyond my pocket. I don't exactly earn a fortune.

'Fair enough.'

'OK then.' I don't have an excuse. I wasn't drunk – not really. I was just stung by the group's air of derision. I was pissed off with Simon. I thought it would be a bit of fun. It's no excuse really. Turning my back, I kicked off my shoes, crouched to shimmy off my tights from beneath my dress (to whistles and catcalls) and finally shucked the stupid jacket again. After considering my very inappropriate climbing attire I finally tucked one side of my skirt up into the waistband of my panties to free up my legs. That was received with appreciation too. What the hell, I thought.

They made way for me at the lip of the basin, and I tried not to recoil when I found out how cool the water was. Luckily it came only to my knees as I waded across the slippery basin to the statue, feeling the hard discs of coins shift beneath my toes.

Make a wish, I said to myself, teeth gritted.

My audience was yelling advice and encouragement as I started the ascent, but I wasn't listening. When you climb, concentration is everything; the world shrinks to include only you and the surface you're battling. I laid hold of the beak of a sea monster, my first point of grip, and felt the metal chilly beneath my fingers. Getting my foot up onto the monster's tail I pushed myself up, seized the arm of a flailing sea nymph, and suddenly was clear of the water. So it went on: from fish to shoulder to head to triton's hip, my bare toes gripping the bronze scales. I had to grab his raised arm from beneath as if it were an oak branch and swing both legs up from below, hanging monkeylike before getting a thigh up so that I could haul myself up onto his massive bicep, then sitting astride it to catch my breath. That was the only tricky bit, really. My skirt rode right up to my waist as I hung there, and there were loud whoops from the watchers.

I squinted into the triton's huge, bearded face, wondering how he'd react if he could feel a human sat astride his arm. My pussy, separated from his skin only by the flimsiest cotton strip, must feel red hot on his bronze. 'Sorry,' I said, grinning. Then I knelt up, found my feet and, using his conch shell as a last stepping stone, scrambled into the high scallop shell. It was full of water, just as cold as that down at the bottom. I stood upright cautiously, ankle-deep, and looked down at my audience. I raised one hand to punch the air.

Amid the chatter a loud whistle rang across the lawn. I looked around, wondering if we'd been spotted by an angry hotel manager.

Then the water started up. It came out of the conch and struck me in the face, such a shock that I staggered and hunched to my knees. All around my scallop shell little jets sprang up vertically. From the figures below, from pursed lips and gaping fishy jaws and even the breast of one amply endowed Nereid, long plumes arced into the night, all converging around the highest point of the edifice, all gushing over me before falling in a curtain from around my feet. In seconds I was absolutely drenched, and it felt icy cold. The only thing I could hear over the splash of the water was the howls of laughter from the crowd below.

I realised what had happened at once; this whole thing had been a set-up arranged by Simon. He must have got some of the hotel staff in on it too, to time my humiliation so precisely. I spat water, speechless with shock and rage. I realised that my soaked dress must be translucent, that the cotton was clinging pore-close to my skin, that my body was exposed before a score of shrieking drunks as if I were a contestant in a wet T-shirt competition.

And as I ground my teeth I realised something else too: that I could shriek and attempt to cover myself and submit to the humiliation and become the victim they wanted, or I could face up to them. So I straightened my back and stood up tall, my back taking the blast of the main jet of water, my hands clenched at my sides, my body held proudly. I looked down on them with my hair – which always goes to rings when it's wet

– hanging around my face and all the contempt I could muster in my eyes. My gaze swept the crowd.

It fell on Michael Deverick. He hadn't been in the audience to start with, I was certain of that, for I'd have noticed him. But there he was, a little way across the grass, alone now, watching me. He wasn't laughing. His expression was watchful and intense. I forgot the others for a moment as my eyes met his. My chest was heaving with the strain of drawing breath. I must have been one hell of a sight.

The laughter died away to muffled giggles.

'Enjoying your shower, Av?' Simon called.

I wrenched my gaze back to him. 'It's fine,' I declared. 'Have you got the balls to join me?'

He must have been a lot drunker than I was. He passed his bottle to friend, dumped his jacket in one motion and scrambled into the water without a word. I could see the furious determination in his face as he approached: I'd really got his back up. It took him two attempts to find a footing on the statuary, which was ten times more slippery now that it was running with water, and that just made him madder. On the third attempt he scrambled as high as the triton's waist, reached out to grab at the arm and struggled to his feet.

The triton shrugged. That's how it looked to me, watching from above. The metal flesh rippled and danced under the cascade of water and Simon lost his grip. He lurched, trying to make up for lack of balance with his feet, but the fool had kept his shoes on and the surface was too slick for purchase. His feet slid from under him and he fell face forwards. I heard the wind being knocked from his lungs as his stomach made contact with the bronze, then he was suddenly sliding away, arms spread wide. He bounced off the lowest tiers, tumbled sideways and clipped his head as he hit the pool. When the splash settled he did not get up. From where I was, looking down on his body floating there limply, I could see a mist of dark blood spreading out around his head.

Several people in the crowd shrieked. Others started to climb into the pool.

I made no cry. I don't remember there being anything in my head at all, not a thought. I just began to climb down. It should have been much harder because of the water, but I have no real memory of the short journey. My body simply took over where my mind could not cope, and it must have been done in less than a minute. Even so, by the time I splashed down knee-deep into the water the others had reached Simon and dragged him to the bank. People were scrabbling for their mobile phones and running to get help from the hotel.

'He's still breathing!' someone yelled.

I stopped where I was, halfway across the pool, suddenly lost. The scrum around Simon was thickening and there was no room for me. Probably it was best that I keep well clear. I turned away and waded to another quadrant, slopping out onto the lawn, shivering. My nipples were so stiff with the cold that they ached.

There, at the edge of the dim circle of illumination cast by the pool, stood Michael Deverick. Our eyes met. He raised one brow and smiled, very faintly. I thought – I hoped – for a moment that he might drape his jacket around my shoulders, but he turned and walked away into the dark.

No one was more surprised than I that nine months later I was working for him. Fairy tales are supposed to end with a wedding, not start with one.

But then, the fairies in this tale weren't exactly what I'd imagined either.

2: Into the Woods

The night before I drove down to Devon to start my new job, I had a dream that woke me shaking.

At first I took no active part in the dream; I simply saw. There was a dark space, huge but crammed because within it fought two dragons. One was red like ripe hawthorn berries and the other as white as birch bark; both were scaled and winged, though their wings couldn't have been much use there in such tight confines. They fought coiled around each other and rolling over, claws scrabbling for purchase and teeth clattering as they slid and interlocked, their yellow eyes protected behind cloudy nictitating membranes, their hot breath coming in roaring gasps while barbed tails lashed. Neither seemed able to make any impact on the armour of his foe, but the ground shook. I felt the vibration running up from my feet into my belly. I felt the heat radiating from their writhing bodies. And as I became aware of myself, so did they become aware of me; the struggling ceased and two pairs of amber eyes turned in my direction, flaring bright as the protective membranes rolled back. I felt my heart galloping in my empty chest as, tiny and vulnerable, I met those terrible stares and all the blood seemed to drain down my body, paralysing my legs and swelling my sex.

They came for me, forgetting their struggle in their eagerness to lunge for my flesh. The red one closed its jaws about my chest, knifelike teeth sinking deep. The white one took both my legs in its long mouth, grinding down. It was a dream and

I felt no pain, just the incredible pressure of penetration and the lubricious heat of their wet mouths. Helpless, I was lifted between them, splayed and gasping. First one then the other tugged my limp body.

I woke just before they pulled me apart, wet with sweat and excitement.

Knocking the chain brake on with the back of my wrist, I switched the engine off and dropped the saw to my side. It caught at the end of its short tether and swung below me while I leant back in my harness, relishing the sudden hush. The rope lashing me to the fork high overhead wanted to send me swinging back towards the main tree trunk, but my heavy boots kept purchase on a branch, holding me steady over the forty foot of clean air that separated me from the road verge. Tony, my groundsman, moved in across the grass to clear away the dead branch I'd just dropped. I smiled down at the orange blob of his plastic helmet and gave him the thumbs up. That was the last of the hanging snags in this lime, and we'd had to get it cleared so that the builders could pass safely up the drive in order to work on the Grange.

Slowly the petrol fumes cleared and I could breathe the clean air and the scent of the cut wood. It was June and the lime was in its first bright green flush of leaves. I tipped my mesh visor up and rocked gently on my heels, enjoying the light through the stippled canopy, the sense of space below and around me, the sensation of being held by the harness like a child on a swing.

I love working with trees. I love their size – it's like working with giants. I love the challenge of climbing up into them, and the incredible sensation of working at height, when all the rest of the world shrinks away beneath me and there is nothing else that matters, no problems, no one else, only me and the rope and the wood and the basic questions: Where next? Will this branch hold my weight? Can I reach?

I love using my skills to bring down those vast structures, when it's necessary to fell them, with clean precision. I love the fresh air and the weather in my face, rain or shine. I love being out on a frosty morning but feeling toast-warm from the heat generated by my own labours. I love the fact that I have to work hard, pushing my muscles to the limit, over and over. I love working up a sweat and an ache and then going home at night to relax into a bath with a favourite bath bomb fizzing around me filling my world with rose petals and perfume. I love watching the plants change with the seasons and slowly grow, knowing that the trees will be there for far longer than I will. And I love too the roar of the saw in my hands and the bite of a newly sharpened chain into the wood and the smell of sawdust and two-stroke mix. I love the fact that I do a job most other people couldn't attempt. I love being good at this.

There is no way you'd catch me working in an office all day. I'd go crazy.

I stared out through gaps in the canopy, drinking in the view. From here I could make out glimpses of the grounds that were my new realm: the lawn hacked roughly from a pasture of waist-high weeds, the ruined glasshouse, a corner of the pond, and the tips of exotic trees planted in Victorian times and now coming into their full stature – great Douglas firs and monkey puzzles and tulip trees, the dark spires of a grove of wellingtonia, the golden foliage of ginkgos and larches. Further off, outside our boundaries, a hazy patchwork of fields stretched out to the grim line of the Dartmoor plateau. When I turned to look in the opposite direction my line of sight was blocked by the green bulk of Grange Wood, just coming into leaf, but I knew that Exmoor lay beyond that. We were sited almost perfectly in the centre of the vale between those two wild moorlands, but down here the land was lush and the climate sheltered.

It was time to descend. There were more limes all along the drive to the Grange that needed attention. I took one last look around me and it was then that I saw her, perched on a branch to my left: an old woman with a hooked nose, wrapped in a shawl.

I gaped.

She winked one golden eye at me. The shawl was flecked brown wool, and from beneath it her bare feet stuck out, bearing the most incredibly filthy curved nails. She spread her arms wide and dropped off the limb, gliding away on wide wings.

I nearly choked. It had only been a trick of the eye, but for that brief moment the illusion had been perfect. 'She' had been a bird all along: a big one, OK – maybe a buzzard – but only a bird. A twisted branch behind her had been conflated with her outline, and I'd completely mistaken the scale of what I was looking at, but it had been enough to fool me. I laughed out loud.

When I'd recovered my poise and felt a bit less like an idiot I kicked off from my station and swung in to the trunk, catching myself on springy legs. From there it was a simple matter of abseiling down the length of the rope all the way to the ground. As I touched earth it felt like gravity had claimed me again, and I stretched my back, as always half disappointed and half relieved to be back. I unhitched the climbing harness and dropped it to my ankles. I'd found that if I walked about in one then the thigh straps tended to press in places that were, well, unprofessional.

I glanced towards Tony, meaning to tell him about the buzzard, but he was talking on his mobile phone. Tony was a local man, Devon born and bred, and grizzled like an old

Labrador. Despite his years he seemed, to my silent relief, to have no problem working under a woman's instruction.

Another builders' van rattled past us as I carried harness, saw and rope to the back of our Land Rover. There were a lot of men at work on the Grange, converting the Victorian shell into a state-of-the-art conference centre. What Michael Deverick was thinking of building a conference centre in rural Devon, I wasn't sure, but it was hardly my problem. I had nearly thirty acres of overgrown garden to worry about restoring instead, not to mention the woodland beyond that.

Tony stuffed the phone back into his pocket. 'That was Mr Deverick,' he said. 'He wants to see you.'

'Me?'

'Up at the house.'

I was a little surprised. I hadn't known our employer was actually on site. I hadn't even seen him since Emma's wedding; my somewhat perfunctory interview had been handled by one of his project managers. I scratched at the back of my neck, trying to cover for the confusion I was feeling. 'Now?'

'He said as soon as you got down from that tree.'

As I walked up the drive, I realised I was actually feeling a little nervous. I'd dumped my helmet but a quick check told me that my hair was tangled into elf-locks by sweat, so I just hoped that by a small miracle it would dry to sleekness as I walked. The rest of me wasn't in much better condition; it had been hot work up there. The dust and little insects and flecks of bark that always sift down from a tree canopy had stuck to the bare skin of my face and neck and arms, and would stay there until I had a bath. I was wearing heavy boots that made me clump and padded chainsaw trousers that, being cut for the male waist, tended to slide rather low down my hips. The sleeveless vest I wore under an equally sleeveless khaki jacket had a distinct damp patch positioned just over my breastbone.

I wasn't ashamed of the way I looked, but it certainly wasn't respectable. And respectable was what I needed if I had to face Michael Deverick.

It wasn't just that I wanted to make a good impression on the man who'd given me a job, although I could hardly imagine a job that I'd want more. It had been a difficult decision leaving the National Trust just when I'd got my foot on the ladder, but there I'd only been one in a large tree gang while here I was in charge of my own, with two other full-time gardeners and carte blanche to engage casual labour when I thought it necessary. I had been given almost free rein to do to the gardens what I thought fit, a generous budget, no deadline and, on top of that, a wage rise and a rent-free house of my own on site: the former head gardener's cottage. Thankfully that building was in better condition than Kester Grange itself, boasting such necessities as electricity and an immersion heater. Plus I was close enough to Cornwall to get to the surfing beaches early on my weekends off.

I'd fallen on my feet here.

What worried me was the way I'd got the job. I hadn't applied for it, or seen it advertised anywhere; the invitation to interview had simply arrived by post. There'd been no sign of any other candidates and my interview had consisted of a check of my certificates and a walk around the gardens with the project manager. It was as if it had already been decided that I would do fine. And what sort of man would employ anyone after the kind of debacle Deverick had witnessed at the hotel?

A creep, that's who, said my better judgement. But had I listened?

He was there at the front entrance of the house as I approached, leaning against the bonnet of his black Range Rover to look over some plans. The building manager was with him talking earnestly so I hovered, my gaze casually sweeping the Portakabins and the scaffolding and the pallets of bricks, resting anywhere but on Michael Deverick, who was tieless but wearing a blinding white shirt. Without his jacket on the trim shape of his torso was obvious. He probably went to the gym three times a week and had a personal trainer and a masseur and a Swedish dietician, I told myself with a secret smile.

He didn't keep me waiting, calling me over almost at once. 'Avril. How are you settling in?'

I made myself meet his eyes confidently. 'Great, thanks. We've nearly finished on the lime avenue.'

'I read your management plan for the garden. It looks excellent, though I have a few questions.'

'It's just a preliminary document,' I said, then cursed myself silently for being so defensive. 'I'd be happy to talk it through.'

'Perhaps we should go round to the rockery. I think there's a bench there.' He waved me on, steering us out of the bustle of human traffic that was constantly passing before the front door. I sneaked a sideways look at the crisp cotton of his shirt, the clean leather of his shoes. He made me feel hot and grubby. In more ways than one.

'What do you think of what I'm doing to the Grange?' he asked as we walked.

I looked up at the red-brick bulk towering over us. The original Victorian construction, all gables and chimneys and turrets, had been stripped back to a shell, and within that the builders seemed to be filling the space with glass and stainless steel so that the new oozed out from the old like flesh from a tightened corset. 'It's radical,' I said, not wanting to commit yet.

'You think so? Nothing is constant but change, Avril.'

We entered the overgrown ruins of the old rockery, but the

bench we sought was buried beneath a pile of lumber so we had to remain standing. Deverick flicked through my management plan. 'You mean to drain the lake?'

'Not completely. But originally it was only about a third the size. The outlet's been blocked by fallen trees, so I think if we remove those the water level will fall back to its original boundary. And then we'll have a lot of mud to plant over.'

'Fine. And the lawn needs returfing completely?'

'Well, it's too late for mowing to restore it. But what I'm suggesting is that we keep the far stretch there long for the moment, and manage it as a wildflower meadow, see...'

'Fine.' He flicked the file shut. 'Whatever you feel is appropriate. As long as it looks good from the house.'

I got the impression he really wasn't interested in the landscape, but I was to be surprised.

'Have you been into Grange Wood yet?'

'Uh, no.' I blinked. 'I mean, I went as far as the old gate on my first walk-through, but not beyond. It looks very overgrown. There were no conifers that I could see, so I guess it's probably ancient oak coppice. I haven't had a proper look.'

'It's certainly old.'

'I assume it's not urgent. I've been prioritising the areas nearest the house, mostly safety work so far. We had a couple of wind-broken cedars round the terrace at the back...'

He held up his hand and I fell silent. 'I'm afraid I'm changing your priorities,' he said, blue eyes fixing me. 'I want you to get into the wood and do me a proper survey. I'm intending to have the place under a management regime within the year. I want footpaths, I want the undergrowth cleared, I want any features mapped – you know, follies and the like. Caves. Extra big trees. You can take a first look this afternoon.'

I was stunned. 'OK,' I said slowly. 'What's this in aid...I mean, what's it for? You have plans?'

At once he switched off, indifferent again. 'Oh, I don't know. Paintballing maybe. There would be plenty of room for a paint-balling area. Do you think conference attendees would enjoy that?'

My knowledge of business conferences is about equivalent to my knowledge of the far side of the moon. I puffed out my cheeks and blew a sigh of helpless incomprehension. 'Well. Yes. Maybe.'

'That's fine then. You can get started. And I want you to report back to me about anything unusual that you find. Anything.' Once again his eyes were on me, cold and commanding.

'What sort of thing?'

Suddenly he smiled and his face lit up with the sparkle of it. He was the sort who could charm the birds out of the trees, my gran would have said. I wasn't exactly immune. 'I don't know,' he said ruefully, as if confessing a terrible lack. 'Anything.'

'OK.' You're the boss, I thought.

'Thank you.' Then he changed tack abruptly: 'Do you know what this plant is?'

I glanced at the one he indicated, with the splayed leaves and the hooded purple flowers in tiers. 'Monkshood. That one's flowering early. And it doesn't belong in the rockery – it must have self-seeded.'

'It's very attractive. I think we should have a bed of it by the front door of the Grange.' He snapped the top off a spike of flowers, and I winced.

'Don't! It's poisonous – I mean, really poisonous. You should wash your hands.'

He seemed amused by my reaction. 'Oops,' he said without a hint of dismay. 'How unfortunate.' He tucked the flower into the breast pocket of my open jacket and I froze like a rabbit in the headlights. His fingers strayed close but never quite brushed against me; I could not mistake the threat though. My nipples, ever traitors, tightened. 'It's a good thing you know your stuff, Avril,' he said, stepping back to admire his work.

I could feel myself colouring. I've never reacted well to being teased.

'And how are you finding your new house?'

'Oh . . . fine, thanks. I mean, it's small, but then I haven't got a lot of stuff.'

'It doesn't bother you, being alone on site at night?'

'Not at all. I like the quiet.'

'Most women would be afraid to be so isolated,' he said, watching my face. I shrugged: what could I say to that? 'But then, you're not like most women, are you Avril?'

I decided that this was meant as a compliment, or at least to take it that way. 'Uh, thanks.'

'And I suppose having the place to yourself might have its attractions. You can run naked round the whole site if you like.'

Oh, now he was definitely teasing. 'Um,' I said witlessly, scratching my hair and unable to meet his gaze.

'It must be a little lonely though,' he concluded, 'even for you. Perhaps you'd like to join me for dinner this evening? I'm staying at the County Hotel on the main road.'

I'd sort of braced myself for this. He'd steered me away from the builders so we wouldn't be overheard. 'That's very kind of you . . .' I began.

'It's not exactly lively there either, so I'd appreciate the company.'

'Listen,' I said brightly, 'if you're bored, there's a pub in the village. The Red Knight. It's nice, not rough or anything. Tony and Owen and the local boys drink there. You could join us. We'd be happy to see you.'

He wasn't fooled, not for a moment. 'Safety in numbers, Avril?'

What was I supposed to say? 'The County's not really my sort of place,' I hedged. 'I mean, cut-glass decanters and fancy food, it's not my thing. I haven't even got anything suitable to wear for dinner.'

'I seem to remember a rather fetching pink dress,' he said, deadpan.

'I threw it out,' I growled. 'It was ruined by the water.'

We glared at each other. I was trying not to bite my lip, or show the dread I was feeling.

'You seem a little nervous, Avril.'

I'm just useless at this pussyfooting around. Fools rush in, as they say. 'Can we be honest for a moment?'

'Feel free.'

'I'd like to know why you hired me. I mean, I'm good at my job, don't get me wrong, but you know, given the circumstances . . .'

He smiled. 'I hired you because I like what I saw.'

I gritted my teeth.

'But on the other hand, what I see is not always what others see. Does that make you feel better?'

I was perplexed. 'I don't know.'

'Well, Avril, since you're keen on honesty perhaps I might clarify a couple of points. First, I need someone to do your job. If you want to do it, and I want you to do it, I can't see that we have a problem.'

I nodded, waiting for the caveat.

'Second, if you're implying, which I think you are, that I might be considering using our professional relationship as leverage to get you into bed with me –'

I winced.

'– then I'm rather insulted.'

'I'm sorry.'

'Why should I need to resort to methods that crude?'

I'd been on the verge of feeling relieved, but those last words kicked the rug out from under me. I searched his face for signs of humour but found only amusement, which was not the same thing at all. There it was again, that enigmatic arrogance. That absolute certainty. And, undisguised this time, a promise. 'I see,' I said.

'Good. I'm glad we understand each other.'

'I have a rule,' I said in a low flat voice. 'I don't get involved with people I work with.'

'Ever?'

'Ever. That's the rule.'

'Sounds like that one came from bitter experience.'

I shrugged, but my mettle was up. 'You live, you learn.'

'And yet,' he said, breaking into a slow, sweet, chilling smile, 'even though you suspected me of the lowest motives, still you took the job.'

I had no answer to that one.

'Hh.' He nodded, satisfied. 'Well, I'll be getting back. I'm sure you've plenty to be getting on with.' He was doing it again, I realised: walking away and leaving me thrown completely off balance. 'Think, Avril,' he advised as his parting shot. 'Rules are for the weak, to keep them safe. Is that what you are?'

I waited till he was out of earshot, then I ran my hands through my hair and swore a blue streak.

After lunch, as instructed, I left the others trimming a laurel hedge and set out to explore Grange Wood. I took with me only a clipboard and pencil, intending to sketch a map and make a few notes. I knew the wood was walled and that it blanketed a low hill and dropped away to the river valley and public road beyond, but that was about all. I was still wearing my chainsaw trousers and my helmet, since the padding of the former gave good protection should I have to wade through brambles and the latter was useful when ducking under branches. Passing through the old orchard, with a pause to shake my head wistfully at the cankered apple trees so shamefully left to waste over the last decade, I climbed over the gate in the stone wall and entered the wood. Within ten minutes I was in love.

Woods, like people, vary in character, from lofty cathedral-like beech woods to grim, pitch-black western hemlock plantations. But Grange Wood was one of those western-seaboard oak forests that seem to have been crafted by goblins, purely to enchant. Overhead, the first flush of leaves was turning from salmon pink to light green. Beneath my feet the spring flora was in full surge, seizing every last hour of sunshine before the shade grew too dense. Pink spires of foxglove were in flower and, in the middle distance, a mist of bluebells hung over the ground. Unlike the main garden where the earth was deep and rich, here the ground was rocky and the boulders covered in moss, and ferns grew in abundance. The trees themselves, twisted oaks bearing great twiggy burrs and piebald birches grown fat on the wet soil till their swollen boles seemed ready to burst, were splotched in lichens and mosses. Many of the trees had fallen. Some of these had died and their rotting trunks provided new footing for the ferns, their former places now clear patches where saplings had sprung up and were engaged in a furious race for the light. Others of the fallen trees were still alive even with half their roots jutting into the air and from a recumbent position were reaching up branches of their own. There was dead wood everywhere, underfoot and hanging overhead and poking up from banks of bracken. There wasn't a tree in sight with a straight trunk. From a forester's point of view it was a horrible, mismanaged mess. I couldn't help think it was beautiful.

There were some faint paths, tracks made by rabbits perhaps. I followed one winding between the boulders and the tree trunks, hoping it would take me to the crown of the hill, but it soon peeled away and began to circle the flank. There were birds singing all around, though I couldn't see many, only little flickers of movement at the periphery of my vision. A grey squirrel hung head down on the bole of a tree and stared at me until I pointed a warning finger and mouthed a silent gunshot, at which it fled and I grinned. The smell of damp wood and moss was intoxicating, overlaid with the very faint sweet smell of the bluebells. I didn't write anything on my paper after 'acid oak–birch woodland'. I just let it all sink in, in a daze. It wasn't as if there were any of the noteworthy features Michael Deverick had been looking for, not even any very tall trees. From a timber point of view this place was a dud, and in fact anyone trying a paintball game here was likely to break a leg.

'Wow,' I said to myself.

Something shiny hanging from a branch caught my eye. I left the path and crossed down towards it. To my surprise, I found it was a glass ball, crimson coloured and as big as my two fists, strung up and spinning slowly on a length of fishing line that was almost invisible. I frowned and tapped it. A strange thing to find in a wood, I thought. Like a giant Christmas bauble.

It wasn't the last. As I switched to another path and resumed my same general drift northwards I caught sight of others glinting in the sunlight, some red but others blue or yellow or green. And there were other decorations too: little bundles of twigs tied with red wool. The more I looked, the more of them there were.

'Someone's been watching *Blair Witch*,' I muttered. Those signs of human presence made me feel less comfortable, though not because they were sinister in themselves. There shouldn't have been anyone in these woods, that was all. Nobody had lived in Kester Grange in years. When Michael Deverick bought it the house had been near-derelict and the estate gone halfway to wilderness.

I crossed the rocky bed of a stream. There was a big boulder in the centre of the course, and straddling that a hawthorn bush. Multicoloured rags had been tied to its twigs and hung, some faded and some still fresh, among the last of its white blossom. I gnawed my lip, hands on hips. Then I turned to follow the clearest path, down beside the water, away from the hill. I marked the stream tentatively on my sketch map, but I had no idea where it was flowing from, or to, and was beginning to think I'd have to buy a compass. I made an attempt to scramble up the bank but a branch of sallow I was pushing back slipped from my hand to smack me hard across the top of the thighs and I slid back down and decided to continue downstream to a clearer patch. If I'd not been wearing padded leggings, or if I'd been a bloke, the blow would have been really painful.

I remembered the slap of the plastic ruler on Scott's skin as I rubbed my stinging legs.

God, it was long time since I'd given my ex much thought, at least by daylight. I didn't miss him and our break-up hadn't been particularly painful as these things go – or at least not for me. I grinned at the thought.

I'd driven down to the house he shared in Norwich as usual that Friday, except that after three weeks of serious overtime clearing windthrow I'd wangled an early departure and I got to Scott's place a couple of hours early. When no one answered the doorbell I wandered through into the overgrown back garden, where I half-expected to find him and Alex and Stacy knocking back beers and contemplating the algae scum on their pond. No one was there, but I did notice that lights were on in the high windows of the detached garage where they all kept the wetsuits and boards ready for the weekend. The side door was unlocked. They'd be packing the car, I assumed, and called, 'Scott?' as I entered.

No one replied. The smell of board wax and seaweed was strong and comfortable. I looked down the garage and there was Scott all right – about two-thirds of the way down, stark naked, his arms and legs spread wide. His wrists were roped to the metal brackets on either wall that held the surfboards. His ankles were held apart by the broom pole taped between them.

My first thought was that he hadn't got himself into that position.

Scott hadn't seen me; he was wearing a blindfold. He hadn't heard me either, though I'd made quite a bit of noise getting the swollen old door open, because there was an MP3 player clipped to a bracket too, the earplugs pumping out what sounded to me like a tinny wasp buzz of music. Old school metal, I'd have guessed; it was what he liked to drive to when he got use of Alex's car, or mine. It was what he'd been listening to when he totalled his own, the idiot. But he must have felt the draught from the door, because he said 'Stacy?' in that loud voice people use when they can't hear themselves properly. 'We'd better hurry up; Av will be here soon.'

My second thought wasn't really a thought at first, just a wave of relief that it was all over. No more insane drives on a weekend down some of the most choked motorways in Britain trying to snatch a few hours with a boyfriend on the other side of the bloody country. No more waiting in Penrith station for his train. No more half-assed explanations on the phone that he'd been forced to stay on too late at the office and that he wouldn't be with me until tomorrow morning – make that lunchtime, probably. It was over. At least I'd be able to use my vibrator and fantasise about other men with a clear conscience from now on.

'Stace? Come on.'

I walked down towards him, fists bunched, wondering what

exactly I was going to do now. He looked very vulnerable, spreadeagled like that. And just a little bit silly. The black hair beneath his arms stuck out in wild tufts. His nipples were hard from the chill of the concrete garage and I could see the gooseflesh around them. His cock stuck straight out like a short peg, stiff but not distended. His balls were bunched up high. I put out my hand and stroked that fat pouch, stirring the hairs. He did have really hairy balls, did Scott, even though years of wearing a neoprene suit had rubbed the hair off his arse and legs where you'd expect to find it.

He reacted to my touch, squirming in his bonds and making appreciative noises. The headphones pulsed: zing, zing, zing. I tickled his fancy a moment longer then passed under his arm to take at look at him from behind. Lines of dark hair marched up the unguarded nape of his neck. His back was narrow and strong, his hips lithe. Those familiar buttocks, muscular yet bald as a baby's, sported a red mark like the imprint of a bar across their fullest swell. I didn't understand what it was until I looked down. Arrayed on the beach blanket on which he stood – and he was still wearing his socks, I noted, with a contemptuous wrinkle of my nose – was a ruler, a table-tennis bat and a bright-yellow kitchen glove.

I couldn't really be sure what the rubber glove was intended for – Flicking him? Wanking him off? Sticking a finger up his butt? – but the other two seemed pretty obvious. I picked up the ruler, twelve inches of transparent plastic of the sort we used to use in school, and laid it across the welt to see if it fitted. Which it did perfectly. Scott felt the chill.

'Stace!'

I bent the plastic back with my other hand and let him have it, stingingly. He jumped and quivered and gasped, 'Ah! Yes! Go on!'

He was a gobby bugger for someone who was tied up so

submissively, I decided. I'd had no idea that he got his jollies doing this. He'd never once asked me to spank him. I checked his cock and saw that it had grown in response to the stimulation to become a proper erection. It needed teaching a lesson, just as Scott did. Moving back round before him, I slapped his cock sideways with the ruler. Then I slapped it back. Its moist eye winked as his foreskin eased back from the swelling glans. Scott rolled his own head from side, exposing his throat.

A good job for him I wasn't really vindictive, I thought viciously as I slapped his cock back and forth, my smacks getting harder. His tool lurched and lolled like a tree in a storm and he gasped and bit his lip and bared his teeth, strung between the pleasure and the pain. I struck at the tops of his thighs too, as I gained in confidence and ire, and that made his pinioned legs thrash. I laid a couple of strokes across his lower belly, just over his bladder, ignoring his protests. In fact the only target I avoided was his full scrotum; I wanted to punish him, not castrate him. When his cock was bright red I stopped and inserted the ruler between his thighs though, beating up with measured, warning taps on his spunk-bag, letting him know what I could do, if I wanted to. He spread his knees as much as he could and groaned, sweat running down the inside of his thighs, his prick dancing.

I got irritated with that. He was enjoying it too much. Abandoning the torture without warning I crossed back behind him to pick up the ping-pong bat. The rubber had been removed from one face revealing the plywood, and holes had been drilled through the paddle. Well, experimentation was the only way to find out the effects of this one, so I brought it across in a resounding smack on his arse. I was delighted to find that the unclenched male bottom is just as capable of a delightful wobble as the female one.

I spent some time appreciating the subtle difference in

sound and vibration I got from the two different faces of the paddle and, by that time, Scott's bum was flushed red all over. I could hit his buttocks a whole lot harder than I could his prick, too, which gave me great satisfaction. Scott, I could tell, was trying not to sound too wimpy, but his grunts were coming out as half yelps. My own breathing was coming hard from the exertion.

But my other hand was feeling left out. I decided the only way forwards was to stand at Scott's side, right under his straining arm, and, with the familiar perfume of his deodorant and his sweat in my nostrils, to punish him fore and aft at the same time: one jouncing blow on his pert buns with the bat, followed by a lighter stinging slap on the shaft of his cock. Over and over, until he was red in the face and gasping and crying out, 'Stace! Suck it! Suck it please!'

I wasn't going to stoop to that. I gave him three really hard smacks on the behind, enough to make my own arm ache, then turning the ruler I scraped its narrow edge up his prick from root to bulging helmet. It was like squeezing a bag of icing. His spunk shot out in a long sticky line at the first spasm, falling through the air to bespatter the concrete floor. A second gobbet followed. The weaker aftershocks just splashed and oozed down his cock. Scott pitched forwards in his bonds, babbling like an idiot.

At that moment the door opened and Stacy walked in, saying, 'Scott, Avril's car's out the front –'

She stopped when she saw me and went red to the ears. Stupid cow. She didn't even remember that he couldn't hear her. I stepped back, raised the bat one last time and let him have it on the arse with everything I had left in arm and shoulder and chest. I nearly lifted him off the floor. Scott wasn't expecting an epilogue and certainly nothing that hard; this time he let loose a scream of pain. Flicking out one earplug

I told him, 'You're dumped, dipshit!' and marched out past a cowering Stacy.

I hadn't had a proper boyfriend since.

I came out of my reverie, surprised at myself and more surprised by the effect it'd had on me; I was tingling and a bit flushed. This wasn't great timing for the female equivalent of a rogue erection I told myself and, for a moment, I was tempted to stick my hand down my waistband and work it all off. There wasn't anyone to see, I reasoned, and I'd feel a lot more comfortable if I released some of the pressure. Then I finally spotted my first real landmark – an outcrop of particularly large boulders off to my left – and I pushed thoughts of sex firmly away as I turned to it.

The trees seemed to be thinner there, the bracken higher. I hoped in vain for a path, but none came into view and eventually I just breasted the ferns. The damp from the leaves started to soak into my clothes and the smell of the bruised stems was curiously unpleasant. Just before I reached the rocks I broke out into clear ground – a wide patch of trampled bracken. The smell here was worse. A cloud of flies rose buzzing. There was something lying on the crushed leaves, something red and black, thin like stripped branches and twisted like driftwood. I stared at it for a long moment before I realised what I was looking at.

It was the remains of a deer. A big one, with a burgeoning rack of antlers. There wasn't much left of it but bone.

I made a face. Then movement caught my eye and I looked up at the rocks, straight at a huge dog that had appeared on one of the boulders. As I hesitated another jumped up next to it; both were watching me with ears pricked. They were dark grey with amber eyes. The muzzle of the first wrinkled into a snarl. My head told me I must be looking at a couple of German shepherds, and I'm not normally at all nervous of dogs. Ancient instinct from somewhere deep inside me had a very different theory: I felt like I'd been punched in the stomach.

'No,' I said, starting to back off, trying to keep calm. The big canine gathered itself to jump. Instinct won: I turned and fled, crashing through the bracken. I had a good head start and I'd turned downhill, but there was no way I was going to win that race. Within seconds I heard it rustling through the leaves behind me. I redoubled my efforts, completely reckless now, my feet catching on the bracken stems and nearly tripping me flat. I had a vague idea of climbing a tree, and I fled towards the only one that promised spreading branches I could catch hold of and jumped for the lowest branch. My fingertips grazed painfully across its underside. I landed heavily, realised that I wasn't going to have a second chance because the animal was crashing through the ferns nearly at my heels, and just managed to put my back to the trunk, throwing my arms up to shield my throat and face. I caught a glimpse of the beast, jaws gaping, in mid-leap, and I shut my eyes.

It hit me full on, sharp teeth and claws raking my skin. But there was no real weight behind the attack. It exploded around me and when it had passed I was still standing, my back crushed to the bark of the oak, gasping in the sudden silence. I looked down and saw piled up against me a great shapeless mass of dead holly. Some of the dried leaves were still falling away, snapped by the force of its impact. I pushed it off and the clump collapsed onto its side amidst the bracken.

There was no sign of any animal.

I ran my hands down my forearms, feeling the sting of many tiny cuts from the spiny leaves. My fingers came away bloody. I put my hands on my knees, clawing back control over my ragged breath, still staring. By the time I'd straightened up I was starting to shake. I walked right round the tree looking in vain for any further sign of threat, then set out, blindly.

I think I'd lost my bearings a while back, but at least there'd been a chance of retracing my path. Now I was really lost. It doesn't take much to do that in a wood, where the horizon is hidden and the land folds in unforeseen directions. Little hillocks that wouldn't even show up on a map become huge obstacles, and tiny valleys promise to lead places but peter out to dead ends. I stumbled around aimlessly, switching between rabbit tracks. As the shock of my flight wore off it gave room to shame and confusion and finally an unfocused anger. I had no clue what had just happened to me and that made me want to lash out even more. I felt just as I had done standing on the fountain, hearing the laughter and realising for the first time that it was all a joke at my expense, and that everyone but me was in on it.

When I finally stumbled onto a track – a proper earthen track, wide enough to drive a Land Rover down and carpeted in pale grass – I was none the wiser about where I was, but I did feel some relief. It didn't stop me snapping at the first person that I saw coming round a bend in the path, 'Excuse me, this is private property, you know.'

He stopped dead, taken aback. His hands were thrust into the pockets of an army-surplus jacket. Everything about him was army surplus down to the boots on his feet, and all of it looked worn out and hung baggily. 'This is a public bridle path,' he replied. 'I've got a right of way.'

I took a better look at him and noted he didn't look the squaddie type at all. He was a redhead, and red hair is so criminally unfashionable on men that there are only two options: shave the lot short and let your scalp shine through, or go the other way and flaunt it defiantly. This guy had chosen the latter course, sporting long dreadlocks tied back loosely. There were two gold rings through his right eyebrow. More student than soldier, I told myself.

'There's no bridle path through Grange Wood,' I insisted, already regretting being so rude.

'Oh there is,' he said, not rising at all to the aggressive tone of my opening gambit. I'd realised he was somewhat older than his style of dress indicated: not a student but a real neo-hippie. His stubble glinted red gold where the sunlight caught his cheek. 'Look on your county map; this is an ancient greenway. It's been used since at least the Middle Ages by local people, and was said at one time to stretch all the way to Dartmoor. Supposedly the fay ride from Yes Tor down this path on moonlit nights.'

In the face of this excess of information I just repeated dumbly, 'Fay?'

'I'd avoid them if I were you. They like young –' He tilted his head, glanced sharply from my helmet to my leggings, and suddenly his expression, which had been quite relaxed, grew much colder. 'Hey, you're not one of Deverick's stooges, are you?'

This wasn't how I wanted to hear myself described. 'I work for Michael Deverick, yes,' I said stiffly.

He swore under his breath and looked about him sharply. 'He's not in the wood, is he? No, I'd have heard if he was.'

'No, he's not.' Christ, he was a bit too intense.

'He's got more sense, I'd assume. He sent you in though. Got someone to do his dirty work for him, as usual.'

'I'm just starting a survey.' Now that he was the one being unfriendly, I was quite uncomfortable. 'I'm not doing anyone's "dirty work". Have you got a problem with him?'

Swampy – or whatever his name was – pulled a face and pointedly ignored my question. 'And did he tell you what he was looking for?'

'What d'you mean?'

'Did he tell you how dangerous it was?'

We glared at each other. A blackbird rustled around noisily in the undergrowth. 'There's ... you should be careful,' I admitted awkwardly. 'There're dogs or something loose in the wood.'

'Or something,' he agreed.

I refused to use the word lurking at the tip of my tongue. 'You've seen them?' I demanded. My head was whirling. I couldn't even make up my mind if I had imagined those ... animals, whatever they were.

'There are lots of things in the woods. Some of them are there to keep people like Deverick – and you – out.' There was no mistaking the hostility now.

'You put the Christmas decorations up, did you? Are you trying to scare people off?'

He squinted, half-contemptuous, half-irritated.

'What have got in there? Your squat? Your caravan? This isn't your land, you know.'

He laughed out loud, but it didn't sound like he thought it funny. 'You think it's Deverick's? People like you make me sick.'

'I'm damn sure it's Mr Deverick's land. And all I'm doing is my job.'

'I can see that. Kill trees, do you, to make more room for little boxy houses and executive golf courses? Congratulations. You should be proud.'

That was so unfair. Nine times out of ten I was on the side of people like him – ignorant, impractical, self-righteous pricks as they were. 'It's not exactly that simple, is it?'

'You work for Deverick. Sounds simple enough to me.'

'You have no idea what he's planning,' I protested. 'He's very positive about enviro–'

'*I* have no idea?' He'd gone really pale; it was a strange reaction. 'Who do you think you're kidding? I know exactly what he's up to! And you can tell him from me that he's not getting his hands on these woods. So go on, you can piss off now.'

Well, that certainly brought the conversation to an end. He folded his arms, waiting for my next move. I gritted my teeth, looked around me, and finally admitted, 'I don't know which way's out.'

He didn't laugh at me. Good God, a man who didn't laugh. He just nodded, very slightly. He had hazel eyes, I noticed, fractured green and brown. 'The track behind you will get you to the bank at the wood boundary. Don't worry, the bridle path is safe, even for you. Go through the gap in the hedge, down the farm track and you'll be on the road to the village.'

I blinked. 'You're sure? That doesn't sound like the right direction at all.'

'You got yourself turned round. It happens here a lot. It's the witch balls.'

'The what?'

He sighed. 'The glass balls.'

I shook my head. 'What do they do?'

'They deflect witches,' he said, as if it were obvious. 'And similar sorts.'

'Hey,' I said, trying to make light. 'My sister reads the tarot, but I'm not a witch.'

'No,' he said. 'You're not.' And reaching out, he plucked something from my jacket pocket before I realised he was touching me. I saw the object in his hands: a hooded purple flower. Then he dropped it to the floor and crushed it underfoot.

The monkshood. And then I remembered its other common

name: *wolfsbane*. I nodded dizzily and turned away, confused into acquiescence. Only after I'd started walking down the track did I think to ask my eco-freak acquaintance about the flower's significance. I span round, but he had already gone, vanished from the public right of way into the forbidden depths of the wood.

3: Ill Met by Moonlight

That night there was a full moon. I switched off the TV, grabbed my climbing harness and headed out across the rough grass-land behind my cottage.

I love the night, out in the country. Taking away my vision seems to bring all my other senses to life – my skin prickles, my ears pick up the faintest sounds, even my sense of smell seems more acute. Stick me in an urban alley after midnight and I'm as jumpy as the next woman, but not out here where the furtive noises that can sound so ominous to city-dwellers are familiar to me: the scream of a fox, the clatter of a pigeon in the treetops as it settles itself, the creak of branches. There's no harm in the English night, so long as you're away from other human beings.

I intended to climb the big old low-branching beech in the middle of the meadow. It wasn't cold and the sky was clear enough to show the Milky Way like a band of gauze across the sky, something you'll never see from a city. My heart was racing. Michael Deverick's words, like seeds planted in my mind, had been putting out pale, irresistible shoots; I was on my own in the grounds, the whole of the estate locked down behind its high wall and its new electronic gates and, like I said, I enjoy sex in the great outdoors. Getting my kit off in the countryside gives me one hell of a buzz. I like the feel of the air on my skin and the sense of being in intimate contact with the landscape around me. I'd never tried combining it with climbing, mind you, but that idea once it had occurred to me had bitten and niggled and burnt until I had to scratch it.

This wasn't like me. OK, it was like me to think of it, but not to act so recklessly on an impulse. I felt light-headed, almost high.

With one last look around, I pulled off my top and dropped it on the grass, relishing the whisper of the breeze across my skin. My nipples tightened as if in anticipation. I stretched my arms up and jiggled my boobs, bathing them in starlight, intoxicated with my own daring. I dropped my trousers next, leaving them where they lay, creating a trail across the lawn from my back door towards my goal. Grass stubble scratched my ankles. I shook my behind playfully at the moon. Scents of flowering woodbine and cow parsley and elderflower flowed over me, washing from an area of longer grass and shrubs beyond the tree: a perfume of early summer that I adored.

My knickers were the last item of clothing to go and then I strode forwards naked but for my shoes. I kicked even those off when I got under the canopy of the beech, feeling the husks of last year's mast prickly beneath my bare soles. I cinched on my harness more by touch than sight and tossed the rope end over a branch. Climbing naked, I then discovered, wasn't nearly so comfortable as in padded trousers. Luckily it was a well-furnished tree and after the first scramble I didn't need the ropes. I kept the harness on though; I liked the feel of the tight belt about my waist and the leg straps that fitted snugly about my arse cheeks and between my thighs. The torch I had hanging from a side loop slapped against my right cheek as if in appreciation of the way the straps framed my backside.

By the time I got right into the high crown I admit I wasn't just flushed from the exertion, I was feeling wickedly horny too, adding the thrill of vertigo to the dizzy surge of sexual arousal. Adding to the scents of the night was the perfume of my own body. I found a place where I could plant my feet wide apart on two radiating limbs and hook one arm over a branch near my head. My back was to the trunk and my legs were spread wide, beneath them nothing but a drop of fifty feet to the ground and the cool air which licked at the inside of my thighs. It was as if I were inviting the whole of the night into my open sex.

Go on, touch me.

I let my free hand drift down to my clit, stirring the wet itch there to further torment. My lips needed little coaxing to part; I was a night-flowering blossom, heavy with nectar. Shudders of pleasure mounted quickly through my body. I imagined what would happen if I should let go and slip; how they would find my body in the morning stark naked and legs spread. How shameful that would be, I told myself teasingly. Perhaps Michael Deverick would be the one to find me. I imagined his face stooping over mine, his eyes blazing with dismay and frustration. I imagined what it would be like to be working in the shrubbery alone one day, and then to turn and see him watching me with that lancing gaze. How he'd step forwards and peel the tight Lycra up my breasts and bend to bite my salty, grateful nipples. How he'd wrench my jeans down and slam me up against a tree trunk and fuck me long and hard. Sex with him, I was sure, would be deliberate and prolonged; he was a control freak. My bare arse brushed the bark. Maybe he'd make me get down and lick his cock clean when he'd come. Maybe he'd tie me to the tree with my own ropes and screw me as I strained against my bonds. Maybe he'd bend me over a fallen trunk and fuck my splayed pussy while my hands clawed at the leaf mould and I screamed for more until the woods rang and everybody on the whole estate knew I was finally getting it, getting it, getting it.

I came then, riding the storm surge of chaotic imagery.

'Woah,' I breathed, blinking. An owl hooted its wavering call from the wood edge.

Glowing with pleasure, I worked my way back down to a larger branch and settled myself comfortably. The smooth beech bark felt cool against my hot pussy. I flicked away a spider that had the cheek to run across my thigh. My feet dangled in space and I swung them idly.

From here I could see through a broad gap between the leaves, down onto the long weeds that had once been a lawn. The moon had turned it silver, but the shadows beneath the shrubby elders and the far tree line were jet black. When someone came into sight wading through the grass he was clearly visible, and left a dark furrow of bent grasses in his wake.

I held my breath. For a brief moment – my head addled with moonlight and sensuality – I thought that I'd somehow summoned Michael Deverick. Then I recognised my army-surplus tree-hugger from Grange Wood. His dreadlocks were unmistakable. He was shirtless and, under that moonlight, so pale that he seemed to glimmer, except on his left shoulder where there was a big dark patch.

'What are you up to?' I muttered under my breath, leaning forwards to get a better look. His hands trailed through the flower heads caressingly. Then my eyes widened as I realised that he wasn't just shirtless; the waist-high foliage had been hiding the fact that he was naked. At this distance I couldn't make out any details, but a momentary glimpse of the unbroken line of flank and hip made me certain.

Bloody hippie, I thought, with tolerant disdain. Of course, it was Midsummer's Eve, wasn't it? No doubt he was indulging in a bit of pagan nudity for the occasion. If I kept him in sight then I might spy on a bit of sky-clad morris dancing or what-ever it was these people did. Of course the fact that I was butt-naked myself made it difficult to feel really superior. Then I caught sight of his companions, and I forgot to feel superior at all. My spine crawled.

They came through the grass as he did, many of them, on either side, but they left no tracks behind them. Some danced, some skulked and some slithered along barely cresting the grass. They were the same colour as the moonlight on the dappled foliage and it was hard to make them out; my peripheral vision caught the flicker of their movements easily enough but the poor light made them difficult to focus on if I looked directly. I thought some were doglike, some hunched and muscular as buffalo, some slender as gibbons. My eyes itched as I strained to pick them out against the silvery froth of the meadow and through the gaps between the clumps of beech leaves. I could only be certain of glimpses: the scimitar curve of a horn, the flick of an angled ear, the green glint of a pupilless eye. Only Swampy himself seemed to be truly solid. They were absolutely silent, not even the grass whispering as they passed.

I'm dreaming this, I told myself.

As they reached the edge of the long weeds and slipped out onto the shorter grass I lost sight of most of them behind the banks of beech leaves, though I was certain that one was a bear with a ruff of grizzled fur. It lifted its blunt muzzle to the air and sniffed and grunted before lumbering onwards, out of sight.

There've been no bears in England for centuries.

The man with the red 'locks seemed in less of a rush than his companions, or perhaps it was only his own crude materiality that caused him to lag behind. One shadowy form dawdled to stay with him, dancing around him in circles that left no trail of bruised grass. She was easier to see as she came close to him, as if he loaned her some focus: a naked girl, whip thin, with wild hair down to her shoulders and something twiggy protruding from that hair over her temples. I thought it might be a tiara until I realised it was branched horns she wore on her head, like the horns of a roebuck. He laughed and brushed her face with his fingertips. She twirled for him, head thrown back, blocking his progress with her slim body, twining her arms about his neck then turning her back to bump her arse against his groin. The invitation was unmistakable and he put his hands about her waist. She wriggled up against him, arching her back and grinding her bum into his crotch, writhing her head back against his shoulder. What man could resist that sort of offer?

I felt warmth flicker into renewed life in my own sex. They were up to their hips in grass and I couldn't see any detail, but from the set of their bodies it was clear enough what was going on. He braced his thighs and took what was being offered to him, hoisting her hips so that he could sheathe himself in her from behind. I squirmed on my branch. She arched forwards and he had to lean back to balance her, his hands gripping hard on her hips, his thighs working with deliberation. She made a noise like the yawn of a cat and writhed her bum in ecstatic circles. I drank in the sight with furtive, guilty fascination: the shimmy of her tiny breasts, the gape of her lips, the smooth hollow between his hip and thigh, the hunch of his strong shoulders as he pumped into her.

Bereft of those baggy clothes he was a lot more toned than I'd given him credit for. Good, strong arms, I thought. He was almost beautiful.

She was bent right forwards now, nearly double, her arse thrust high under the moon. I'd never hope to be so lithe myself. It gave me a good view of his naked torso though, and the sheen on his taut belly as he thrust. He shifted one hand from her hip to clap it against her bum cheek, clearly relishing the sound of skin on skin.

Dirty boy, I breathed. My pubic mound was pressed against the unyielding branch and leaking onto the bark. This voyeurism was entirely new to me, and the fact that spying on them was making me hot filled me with delicious shame. I could actually hear both of them panting. I watched each thrust and imagined what it might feel like as he quickened towards his goal, his movements jagged and frantic until he groaned and lurched, grabbing her tight, his muscles locked.

He was one of those blokes who really show it when they come. I like that so much in a man.

Then she changed. I didn't see the moment of transformation; I only know that when she lifted her head next there was nothing human about it. It was the head of a hind on the long neck of a deer, her fur as white as her skin had seemed only a moment before. Her velvet-tipped antlers tossed skittishly. For a moment he froze – as shocked, I assumed, as me. I forgot how to breathe. She kicked and bucked and danced out of his grasp so that he staggered and nearly keeled over, skipping around him in ever-widening circles, and from one spring to another I couldn't tell if it was a deer or a woman tossing her antlered head and laughing at him in great silvery peals.

I shut my eyes and pressed my forehead to the tree, clinging to its solidity.

When I looked up next he was alone, hands braced on his thighs, his head hanging. The meadow lay silent once more except for the distant call of the owl. I lay flat on my branch, hearing my heart hammering under my ribs and feeling my mind whirl around and around inside my empty skull like a moth trapped in a lampshade.

It seemed a long time before he moved, but as he stepped out onto the coarse sward of the cut lawn I glimpsed his cock for the first time. It drooped now in a pale elegant curve, spent but still engorged, and I couldn't help wondering what he'd look like close up. I swivelled on my perch, trying to keep him in sight as he passed from one window in my tree canopy to another. He moved with an easy grace. I liked that too.

But I didn't like what happened next. He stopped abruptly and bent to pick up something from the ground. Whatever it was, it was small enough to fit in his hand and dark in colour. Only when he lifted it in both hands up to his eyeline did I realise that he'd found my knickers.

I went cold. He stretched them across his hands, examining them. They were my after-work panties, bright aquamarine and a bit lacy, not the ones I'd sweated into all day, but there was still something horribly humiliating about having a strange man handle my most intimate clothing. They would carry the perfume of my sex, the proof of a whole evening's horny anticipation of the pleasure awaiting me as soon as it grew dark and I was sure I would be alone. Outrage flared in my breast, sending a blush roaring up my cheeks.

He looked around him carefully.

I knew I was being hypocritical. Hadn't I shed those knickers so that I could climb a tree naked and have a wank? Hadn't I fantasised about being used mercilessly by a man I really didn't like that much? Wasn't my pussy wet and swollen with my own unsated longings after watching this man fuck someone else? Who the hell was I to condemn him?

He spun slowly on the spot, searching the landscape. His gaze lingered for a long time on the lights of my cottage, the only lamps in sight. Almost absently his hand drifted up towards his face.

I realised that the real reason I was angry was that I was afraid. It would only have to occur to him to come under the beech canopy and look up, and then he would see the ropes hanging from the low branches and me stuck up here like a big featherless pigeon, unable to hide or escape.

He was stroking his cock with his other hand, I realised. Again, almost absently, his gaze on the shadowy landscape, his mind far away. My mouth went dry. Was he thinking of me? He had no idea those were mine, did he? He couldn't know I was living on site? The thought made me squirm inwardly. Then he turned his face to my tree as if looking straight at me, and my heart gave a great kick of fear under my breastbone.

Then he strode away, headed I don't know where – the same direction as his shadowy friends, anyway. He took my panties with him. I put my hot face to the beech bark and cursed myself for a fool.

The moon drifted behind a cloud. Descending as quietly as I could I abandoned my ropes and ran back towards the house still wearing my harness, my clothes balled up in my hands. My heart raced to a beat faster than my bare footfalls.

Partway there something big and solid loomed out of the night. I stopped in my tracks, embarrassment turning to real nervousness. It moved with a lumbering heaviness. There was a loud snort of breath and I quivered, then a waft of distinctly bovine aroma reached my nostrils. A cow? I wondered, feeling the first gush of relief. What's a cow doing here?

Then the moon came out again and my relief shrivelled away. It wasn't a cow. It wasn't even a bull, though it had the thick forward-swept crescent horns, because it stood on two legs and had the body of a muscular man, as heavyset as a wrestler. I couldn't make out much detail. Against the grass he just looked very dark, but the whites of his eyes flashed. He must have stood a good seven foot tall, and he was between me and the house. He took a shambling step forwards, swinging his head from side to side. A great thick semi-erect pizzle hung against a scrotal sac that looked as big as my two bunched fists.

'Oh God,' I said, shrinking away, dropping my clothes.

He struck a fist into an open palm either in threat or antici-pation, and took another few paces forwards. I could hear the hard noise his hooves made on the ground. My guts seemed to turn to mush, my legs to rolls of wet newspaper. The tip of his cock bobbed, rising.

Then someone grabbed my belt and yanked me roughly backwards. I nearly fell over. I flailed about a bit, but the back of my hand only slapped warm flesh and I couldn't stop him unhooking the battery torch from my flank with his free hand. Then he released me. With a snap yellow light sprang across the night, aimed straight at the bull-man.

'Look!'

I turned my head and saw, picked out in the circle of the torch beam, an old tree stump covered in ivy. Two jagged branches crowned it, making horns of a sort. A rotten branch jutted out of the leaves about halfway up its length. The ivy shivered a little in the breeze.

Had it only been a trick of the moonlight then, adding animation to a dead object? I turned back and saw my counter-culture chevalier holding out the flashlight at arm's length as if it were a rapier. He grabbed my hand and clapped it to the plastic cylinder. 'They don't do well under artificial light.'

The moment he let go of the torch it drooped in my grasp and the beam wobbled away across the grass. The great black bulk of the ivied stump stirred to life and shook its horns, lurching forwards.

'No!' He grabbed me and redirected the torch on its target. It was only a tree stump once more. I braced my arm, and only when I was sure of my aim turned to look at my rescuer. I had no idea what to say. My inner voice was howling in protest. He glared at me and I stared back in agony. Two of us, completely naked under the moonlight, except for the straps of the harness that neatly framed my pubic area and were far more sluttish than mere bare flesh. Oh, and that small scrap of cloth wrapped about his right hand.

The memory of his touch seemed to set my skin on fire. He was still close enough to touch me again, anywhere. His expression was unreadable under the moonlight and I didn't dare turn the torch on him. For a long long moment we just stood looking at one another. The black patch on his shoulder was matched by another on his opposite hip, I registered dimly, but my brain had stopped working properly.

'Keep the torch on it,' he said at last, harshly. 'All the way back home.'

I nodded like an idiot.

'Then turn the lights on. Keep them on at night until the dark of the moon. He'll have lost your trail by then.'

I nodded again. I didn't want to be the one to walk away and leave him staring – not at my naked arse. 'Thanks.'

He shook his head. 'You make a habit of running around naked at night, do you?'

'Hey.' My head was so stuffed full of shock after this evening that it felt like it was going to explode. 'You can talk – you and Bambi.' I was rewarded by wince of surprise and – perhaps – dismay. He exhaled slowly.

'Listen to me. You have to be careful here.'

'I was careful.' That came out sounding sulky. 'Well, I thought I was.'

'It's the wood,' he continued, ignoring me. 'It gets under your skin. It affects your judgement.'

'The *wood*?'

'It can open up ... doors. In your head. Doors to old dark places. You'll understand what I mean if you're around for long. Be careful, that's all.'

I gaped. After everything I'd just seen, was he implying that the real problem here was *myself*? 'Right,' I said. I think he caught my oh-my-God-they're-all-nutters-what-do-I-do-now tone.

'OK. Just remember,' he said, retreating into the dark.

So I sidled all the way back to the cottage, holding the wavering and increasingly diffuse beam on a harmless dead-wood stump as if my very life depended on it.

Michael Deverick rang first thing next morning.

'How did it go yesterday?'

I was eating toast and marmalade in my kitchen and still trying to work out what had happened last night. My mind was numb. 'Uh ... sorry?'

'The wood. Did you make a start on the wood?'

I blinked heavily. 'Yeah. Um, yeah ... sort of. I walked through to the bridle path.' I wasn't going to admit getting lost. 'It's not easy terrain.'

'You went in?' His voice was sharp. 'How far?'

'A mile or so. To the path. I could do with picking up an OS map, you know ...'

'But you got in?' I couldn't work out why he was repeating himself, or why he sounded so agitated. 'What happened?'

What happened? I thought about the holly wolves and my voice dried up. 'Uh. I, uh, met this bloke,' I admitted grudgingly. 'He didn't seem very pleased about you buying the estate. He was quite –' I hesitated: *threatening* was too strong a word to admit to '– unfriendly. He warned me off out of the woods.'

There was a silence on the line.

'Uh, you still there?'

'What was his name?' My employer's voice was gravelly.

'I don't know, sorry. He was tall ... coppery hair ... looked like he'd been sleeping rough, maybe. Looked like a New Age Traveller.' I heard an exhalation of breath.

'I'm coming to pick you up. You're at the cottage, are you?'

'Yes.'

'I'll be with you in twenty minutes.' The line went dead.

Fifteen minutes later I heard the grunt of his big four-wheel-drive vehicle outside and I came out, keys in hand. He'd already emerged from the driver's side. 'Come on,' he said; 'let's go.' From his manner on the phone I'd expected to find him in a bad mood, but there was a smile on his face. He was impatient certainly, but he looked pleased with himself.

'To the wood?'

'Oh yes.' He was wearing more casual clothes today but they still looked neat and expensive. In fact a second glance suggested that they were brand new, fresh from the packet. The creases on his cotton trousers were still sharp and his Timberlands were unscuffed. City boy, I said to myself.

I went round and climbed up into the passenger seat and the scent of clean leather and some *parfum pour homme* filled the car's interior. I inhaled with secret pleasure. I checked out the dashboard admiringly, though the vehicle I really aspired to myself was a beat-up Land Rover that stank of two-stroke and collie dog.

'Nice motor.'

'Hold on,' Deverick warned, releasing the handbrake and slamming the difflock. We sprang forwards. He took the car straight across the estate as if it were a paved road, completely indifferent to the terrain and the threat to his transmission, slewing around bushes and lurching up and down folds in the ground, ploughing through bonnet-high foliage which might have hidden rocks or fallen trees or anything. 'Oh God!' I gasped once. I had to grab at the overhead handle straight away and brace my feet; my butt didn't stay in contact with the bucking upholstery for more than a second at a time. My knee-jerk exasperation at his showing off gave way to exhilaration as we careered through the orchard and, with both of us grinning and whooping like teenagers on a roller coaster, finally drew up near the old Wood Gate.

'What do you think?' He turned his dazzling smile on me.

I shook my head expressively; none of the phrases that sprang to mind were the sort you could use on your boss. 'More money than sense' was the politest of them. 'Is that how you drive in London?' I sputtered, laughing.

'I go rallying at weekends. I find it relaxing after a long week in the city.'

Now there was a hobby I could relate to. I warmed to him, just a bit. 'Nice.'

He turned sideways in his seat to look at me. 'So tell me, have you been to the Eden Project, Avril?'

The change of tack took me by surprise. 'Not yet. I mean to, because we're quite close here, aren't we? But I've had so much to do.'

'Well, as it happens I've got a function to attend there shortly. A dinner party, you understand. After hours. I could do with a partner and I thought you might like to come along with me.'

The smile fell off my face. 'I don't think that would be a good idea.' I was suddenly far too conscious of how close we were sitting, of how intimate the space was, of how much the car was his territory.

'Really? I'd have thought it would suit you perfectly. Guided tours of the rare plant collections; behind the scenes in the tropical rainforest dome with trees you've never even seen growing in this country . . . ?'

'Ah,' I said, horribly tempted. He was playing dirty. I shook my head. 'Look, Mr Deverick –'

'Michael.' His eyes twinkled.

Not subtle. It put steel into my glance and my voice. 'Take my word for it, I'm not the dinner-party type. You really don't want me there, believe me. It's just not my thing.'

'What? Good food, fine wine, beautiful clothes, a little conversation?'

I met his eyes, wishing they weren't so blue, wishing my treacherous body wasn't melting under their glance. 'Champagne?'

'Certainly.'

'I can't stand champagne. Rich dull people in fancy clothes talking about share prices and the trials of yachting at Cannes? I'd go mad and bite someone.' I ignored the way his lips quirked in a smile at that and shook my head in despair. 'I'm just not into that sort of thing. My idea of good living is a roast dinner in a pub and a pint of Old Peculier. Don't waste your time, Michael; I'm not your type.'

'Yachting at Cannes? Is that what I do?'

'Tell me you don't own a yacht.'

'No . . . I own a powerboat,' he admitted.

My snort was restrained. 'I stand corrected.'

'You tell me, then,' he said softly. 'What's your idea of a perfect day out?'

My pussy was turning to hot mush. I wondered if I was going to leave a stain on his suede upholstery. I rolled my eyes. 'Mine? I'd like to wake up at dawn and run straight out onto the beach with my board. Catch the morning light on the wet sand. Then spend the day surfing big waves with a whole crowd of mates, maybe stop for chips and a plastic cup of tea from the van pulled up on the slipway, but basically keep going till we're so tired we can hardly wade through the surf. Then get changed and hit the pub for a proper dinner, me and my friends, sink a few pints of beer to wash down all the salt water and just talk and have a good laugh and enjoy ourselves.' I smiled fondly.

'And after that?' said Michael softly. 'Back to your cosy cottage to watch the TV? Or – no – perhaps slipping out into the warm night and over the stile into the field behind the pub. Giggling, a little drunk, but perfectly sure you know what you're doing and how right it is. Lying on the warm grass, listening to the cows munching behind the hedge and the thrush calling, feeling his lips on your throat as you stare at the crescent moon. The taste of the sea salt on each other's skin. The smell of the crushed grass. The warmth of his wiry body on yours, shielding you from the night breeze. His weight between your thighs.'

He was looking deep into my eyes, his expression grave. Mine was frozen, not because I was offended but because somehow he had described in perfect detail the night I'd first got off with Scott.

He relaxed and glanced away. 'Just a guess,' he said, deferentially. 'I'm good at guessing.'

'No kidding,' I whispered. I could feel the pulse in my crotch.

He flicked a smile. 'So what you're really saying isn't that you're not my type, but that I'm not yours. That an evening of my company would be too boring for words.'

An evening in his company would be terrifying. I wanted out of the car. I wanted out before I fell apart like casseroled chicken and let the big bad wolf eat me up. Words clogged in my throat.

'I wonder,' he mused, 'how long I could keep you entertained?' And he slipped his hand gently onto my thigh.

I quivered. His eyes held mine as he slid his fingers up the inner seam of my denims to the point where my thighs brushed together. For a moment he paused there, making a point of not forcing me into anything. Assessing my readiness. I could smell his aftershave and his warm skin. My shoulders were rammed hard into the car seat, my spine taut with alarm. I might have done a number of things at that moment: I might have slapped his hand away or opened my door to jump out or told him exactly how unprofessional I thought his conduct. What I did was allow my legs to ever so slightly part to his touch, letting his fingers continue their journey right up into the hot pocket of my crotch and press against my pubic mound.

His eyes widened slightly as he acknowledged my complicity.

The seams on my jeans were sturdy and it would take a fair pressure to make any friction felt through them. He gave me that pressure. His grasp was firm, his fingers strong. They squeezed my mons and stroked the hidden crease of my sex with long, sure movements. I arched against the seat back, curling my lip to bare my teeth, barely breathing, my outrage and displeasure as undisguised as my submission. I couldn't wrench my own gaze from his face, from those slightly parted lips and those merciless blue eyes fixed in intent concentration on his task. He wasn't smiling but I could read the pleasure he was getting from his control and from my surrender. He caught his lower lip in his teeth as he delved deeper, his wrist working hard, and I writhed my hips shamelessly against the invasion. His thumb ground back and forth across my zip. Control was slipping rapidly away from me, swept aside by wave after wave of pleasurable sensation, each demanding the next. A flush blazed up my throat and cheeks. Oh, oh, oh, I cried in my head, my lips shaping inarticulate monosyllables, my tongue suddenly craving his. The hard edge of his hand mashed into my swollen sex. I arched my back, thrusting my breasts up, and then suddenly my sight was glazing over and I was bucking helplessly and he was hearing for the first time the broken little gasps and moans of my climax.

'That's right,' he whispered as he pleasured me. Then as my last spasms died away he withdrew his hand and glanced at his gold Rolex. 'Not more than a couple of minutes then,' he sighed. 'How tedious for you.'

I threw open the passenger door and staggered out, slamming it behind me. Then I had to lean back against the side of the car because my legs had gone to quivering jelly. Shame was almost overwhelming.

I heard his door open and then close. 'Let me know if you change your mind about the Eden Project,' he said. Then he walked away.

What could I do after that? I followed him up the slope to the eaves of the wood. Inside my jeans my pussy was all squishy with juices and my backside felt swollen, and on my cheeks was a scarlet flag of embarrassment, but there was no other alternative. Anything else would be running away.

When I caught up to him just in front of the Wood Gate he didn't even glance at me. His gaze rested on the mossy bars in much the same way as most people's might rest on a box they knew to be full of snakes. 'Is this the way you came in?'

I was shocked. Was that it? He'd frigged me senseless and now he'd moved on to something more important? 'Yeah,' I mumbled.

'Did you climb it or open it?'

'I climbed over.'

He shoved his fists into his pockets, feet firmly planted. 'Hm. Did you climb the hill?'

'No.' I shook my head, and then wondered at myself. I'd meant to climb the hill, hadn't I, to start with? I'd hoped for a view over the land. 'There's a lot of dead wood,' I muttered. 'I ended up going that way.' I pointed vaguely round the right flank of the mound.

'I see.'

I walked past him to the gate and laid my hand on the top bar, intending to climb. Then for the first time that day I took a proper look into the wood and I frowned. 'That's new,' I said sharply.

'What?'

'Those.' I pointed up into the trees at the ropes and the pallet-wood platforms. My eyes were picking out more details with every moment: plastic-sheathed bivouacs on the forest floor, ladders up some of the trunks, canvas slings hung up like hammocks twenty foot above the ground. 'I swear they weren't there yesterday!'

Michael snorted, then filled his lungs. 'Ash!' he roared.

Rooks exploded from the treetops, cawing. Then figures began to appear, crawling out from their benders and sliding down their ropes. Wiry, smoke-grimed figures clad in khaki and hand-knitted Tibetan woollies. Men and women, all sharp cheekbones and knotted hair. The beards were straggly, the braids long unwashed, the eyes bright with the prospect of confrontation. One woman nursed a baby at her bare breast, one man cradled a rawhide drum under his arm which he began to beat upon. They whistled and called to one another, grinned and lit cigarettes and eyed us up. One young man pranced about painted green and wearing only a loincloth; he turned his back and flipped it up to display for our benefit a pair of scrawny green buttocks.

'Ash!' demanded Michael, ignoring them all as best he could. 'Where are you?'

Ash? He came out last, my tree-hugging animal-lover. Michael knew him already then. I stepped away from the gate, my head spinning. After all, the last time we'd seen each other we'd both been butt-naked and he'd just fucked a ... a ...

Woah. This was way too much for me to deal with, just after getting my button pressed by Michael. I'd hoped to face Ash with some semblance of dignity but right now I didn't know what the hell anyone was playing at, myself least of all.

'Showing your face finally then,' said Michael with a measure of triumph.

'Finally.' The two men faced each other across the gate, jaws set, eyes hard. No love lost there, I thought.

'You look like crap. The country life not suiting you?'

'I can cope for a while yet.'

Michael had a point; Ash looked dog-weary and black shadows lurked under his eyes. He looked, unsurprisingly, like he'd been up all night – and then some. His glance had barely passed over me as he came to the gate and I felt relieved; all his attention was on Michael.

'And what's going on with this lot?' With a jerk of his chin my employer indicated their raggle-taggle audience.

'Like it?' Ash hooked his thumb in his belt. 'There's a camp at every gate now.' He tapped what was presumably a mobile phone in his pocket. 'And I've got every local reporter in the area on this.'

'Just what the hell's that in aid of?'

'Publicity, Deverick. Just in case you try anything really silly involving heavy machinery. You don't like publicity much, do you?'

My eyebrows rose at this. The memory of standing face to face with this man with not a stitch of clothing on either of us was horribly clear. I wished my knickers weren't awash with my own stickiness. Especially when he looked over at me – but then he said coolly, 'And I'll warn you now, we've started spiking the trees.'

'*What?*' I was horrified. Spiking trees is really nasty Earth-First stuff: driving metal spikes deep into the living wood where they can't be seen but cause any chainsaw coming into contact to kick back into its operator's face. 'What d'you think we're trying to do here? Nobody's planning on felling the wood, you idiot!'

'Good. Then you'll be safe.' He looked at Michael. 'Won't she?'

Michael glowered.

'Tell him you're not planning to fell,' I said recklessly. 'Are you?'

He didn't even look in my direction. 'I want access to my wood. By any means necessary.'

'But it's not your wood,' said Ash, his grin more a baring of his teeth.

'Oh, I think you'll find it is. I own this land now, and everything on it. *Everything*. The deeds are in my possession and if you want a look at a copy I shall be delighted to let you know the address of my solicitors. In fact I'm quite certain you and they will be in correspondence very shortly. You and your rent-a-mob are nothing more than trespassers.'

'Bring it on.' Ash looked contemptuous. 'This is wildwood, Deverick; no one owns it. No one ever has. It's never been under human dominion at any time in history. It belongs only to itself.'

'You're wrong,' I butted in, shaking my head. Here at least I was sure of my ground. 'I'm sorry, but you're just wrong. There's no wildwood left in England. Read your Rackham. It's all been used and managed in some way at some time: firewood, charcoal, grazing or timber or shooting. The only reason *any* woodland in this country survives and hasn't been cleared for fields is because it's been useful in some other way.'

Ash's light, fierce gaze rested on me. I felt my cheeks warm. Don't you dare say a word about last night, I cried silently. Don't you dare!

'Not this one,' was all he said.

'I'm sure you're right that it's ancient woodland and it's never been anything else,' I added. I could understand why he was so passionate about Grange Wood; it was a wonderful place. 'But it's not wildwood. It can't be.'

'Listen to the expert, Ash.' Michael was smiling coldly. 'She knows what she's talking about.'

'Not about this place. Have you told her, Deverick? Told her what you're planning?'

I felt a chill.

'I'm planning,' said Michael, 'to get access to *my* land. And if I have to build a four-lane highway to do it, that's what'll be done.'

My own reaction to this must have shown on my face; Ash raised an eyebrow. 'Oh, don't be saying that, Deverick. You'll upset your friend here. Been keeping her out of the loop, have you? Not shown her your bulging development portfolio yet?' His lip curled. 'It's not like you to be so ... reserved.'

'Hey,' I warningly.

'Ms Shearing is a most valued employee.' Michael's tone was so bland it made me wince. 'She's already been able to make a preliminary report on Grange Wood which I'm sure will be of inestimable assistance to me.'

'I bet.' Ash was deadpan but his next words were aimed at me, not Deverick: 'You just can't keep her out of the trees, can you?'

Despite myself I flushed. This whole confrontation was horrible. I was starting to wish the earth would open and swallow me up. No – I wanted it to swallow both of them instead. That would solve all my problems neatly. But Michael only shook his head, smiling a cold little smile.

'Don't piss me about, Ash. You've never won a fight with me yet, and you're not going to win this one. You're just going to get hurt. And I'm going to get exactly what I wanted all along.'

Ash bit his lip. 'Really?' He tapped the top of the gate. 'Well, if you're so sure, why don't you hop over and come in for a stroll?' He made a mocking wave at the landscape behind him. 'Get your shiny new boots a bit muddy, why don't you?' His hazel eyes seemed almost vulpine. 'See how you like the place, eh?'

I waited for Michael to stride triumphantly forwards. He folded his arms across his chest and didn't move. The two men glared at each other, the derision fading away to something much darker. I was forgotten, invisible. The mob of activists at Ash's back stood in total silence, not a muscle moving. The skin on my neck crawled as I watched them both. There was something going on here, some secret struggle that I knew nothing about, but I could feel the hostility and I was sure this was no joke. Their faces were set like stone. I was willing to bet at that moment that either man would willingly have seen the other dead. It made me feel queasy.

The rooks rose again and swept in circles above the treetops, making a racket like they were mourning the end of the world. For a moment the pulse at my temple became a lancing pain and I put my hand to my head. When I looked up again both men were stepping back, contemptuously, and I'd missed who'd blinked first.

'Enjoy your rural idyll while you can,' said Michael. 'You know how this is going to end.'

I turned away with him. What else could I do? I stopped to look back over my shoulder though, and caught one last glimpse of Ash leaning on the gate, head bowed and hands knotted together. He raised his head and for a moment our eyes met. I thought, though I couldn't be sure, that he looked despairing.

'You know him?' I asked, lengthening my stride to catch up.

'I knew him years ago.'

Years? Michael made it sound an eternity. I couldn't imagine he and Ash sharing any social circle. Apart from being of roughly similar ages I couldn't think of anything they might have in common.

Which goes to show how wrong you can be.

'He's a bit of a prick,' Michael added, laughing. 'Tries to make out he's some sort of green Gandhi. Fatuous Disneyfied drivel about living in harmony with the planet, not exploiting its resources, la la la. It's all just envy and spite of course.'

Personally I suspected Michael Deverick rather enjoyed being an object of envy. 'So is this really about Grange Wood,' I dared to wonder; 'or is it about you and him?'

Michael seemed to shake himself. 'Neither,' he replied. He opened his car door. 'Stay away from him for the moment, though. I don't expect you to run that gauntlet to try and get into the wood. They've probably got their wicker man ready and waiting for us.'

I nodded, relieved. 'I'll get back to the limes then.'

'Get in. I'll give you a lift.'

'No.' I set my shoulders. 'Thanks, but I'll walk over. I need the fresh air.'

4: A Woman Scorned

I stood at my kitchen window and looked at the gloom outside. At this time of year it really ought to have been light even this late in the evening but it had rained solidly for two days now; heavy summer rain thrown down from a sky green as an old bruise. Unable to work properly because kit was dangerously slippery and any vehicles just churned the grass areas to mud, Tony and Owen and I had been confined to the workshop in the old stable block, cleaning and sharpening and tuning every tool we owned. I was going stir-crazy.

Owen had been having trouble with his girlfriend and was grumbling about it. He was eighteen, a year older than her, and she wasn't putting out. He'd solicited Tony's opinion on the subject, which turned out to be, 'If you're in a relationship it's the lass that's in charge and the sooner you learn that the better, lad,' followed by a wink at me and: 'Isn't that right, Avril?'

'I can't comment,' I'd answered, waving my combi-spanner in a wise manner, 'on the grounds it might incriminate me.'

Owen didn't ask my advice, for which I was grateful because I had no idea why a seventeen-year-old girl wouldn't want sex with him. If I'd been seventeen I'd have been all over Owen like a rash. Working five days a week on fairly heavy manual jobs, he was all lithe and deeply tanned muscle. His face was ordinary enough but his mousy hair was sun-bleached on top and more importantly he was a good-humoured boy. Working too long in his company made me feel distinctly twitchy. And just a little bit old.

I'd always had a healthy sexual appetite but this was by far the longest I'd been without a steady boyfriend and it was starting to wear on me. My dreams were full of faceless men with bludgeoning erections and I'd woken up practically every night since I'd moved into this cottage and reached for the slim pink vibrator I kept in the bedside drawer. The dragon dream had recurred too. God, I thought gloomily, I need a proper shag. I need to get out this weekend and get laid.

The rain finally overflowed the gutter above my window and ran out in a pale curtain. I thought of the environmental activists camping out in the woods and wondered what they were doing. Smoking dope and screwing like rabbits if they were lucky, or maybe just wedged in shoulder to shoulder in a foetid fug under leaky tarpaulins. Probably couldn't even get a fire lit in this weather to make a brew. Poor sods. Coming to a decision I reached under the sink for my biggest vacuum flask. As I filled it with black coffee I remembered the Christmas cake in the pantry. I also added a bottle of sloe gin to the carrier bag, before donning my thickest set of waterproofs and squelching out into the rain.

Waterproof trousers are horrible to walk in. I'd brought a big rubber-clad torch but I kept my head down under my hood and almost the only thing I saw on the long walk over to the wood were the toes of my wellies poking out from under the frayed yellow rubber of the trouser–cuffs, and the only thing I heard was the rain. When I reached the gate I called out hopefully: 'Anybody here? Hello?'

If they had anyone on watch they were doing a poor job. No lights showed among the trees and no one stirred. I didn't want to appear to be invading their camp but several more shouts produced the same lack of response, so I clambered laboriously over the gate, barely able to swing my rubberised legs high enough, and slithered down the far side. I tramped up to the nearest vaguely teepee-shaped bivvy and shone my torch on it. 'Anyone home?'

It was much less well-constructed than I remembered, just a cone of plastic sheeting really. I lifted the flap and looked inside. There wasn't a groundsheet. Weeds still grew from the earth. The only sign of human occupation was a roughly humanoid form made of dead brambles tied together with orange plastic baling twine. I blinked, nonplussed. 'OK,' I muttered, as rainwater ran dripped off the end of my nose.

The next bender was no better. It turned out to be nothing more than some black plastic bin bags draped over a shrub, and contained only another scarecrow, this one made of wadded bracken. After that I found another, swinging in a makeshift climbing harness from a tree, like a corpse hung in chains. I was starting to feel confused and finding the life-sized scarecrows really quite creepy. It was a relief when my light picked out movement among the trunks and Ash came stomping down the slope, a canvas tarp draped over his head and shoulders and a fluorescent lantern in one hand. My smile wasn't feigned. 'I did shout.'

'I was asleep. What are you doing here?' he asked, reasonably enough.

'I brought you lot some cake. Where is everyone?'

He frowned. 'They'll be here if they're needed. At a moment's notice. *Cake*?'

'It's a Christmas cake my mum made for me,' I explained, presenting the carrier bag. 'But she forgot I don't like walnuts much so I've been saving it until I threw a party at my place or something, and then I thought you guys might like it. It'll be fine; fruit cake keeps really well and she makes them with brandy.' I was aware that I was gabbling a bit. 'There's a bottle of home-made sloe gin too, and some coffee.' I blinked rain-drops from my eyes.

'Coffee.' He was looking at me like I was mad. 'You made me coffee?'

'The weather's that bad and I thought you must be miserable...' I shivered as a stray drop found its way down the back of my neck. His expression was making an uncomfortable situation worse. I decided to get to the point. 'Look, you've got it wrong, you know. I'm not your enemy.'

'Aren't you?'

'No, I'm not.' I sounded sharper than I'd intended. 'I don't know what it is you think Michael's planning or what it is he's done that pisses you off so much, but I'm not here to cut down the wood. I'm a gardener. I'm on your side, as much as I can be. I love the bloody trees as much as you lot.' I looked around, remembering that there was no sign of any others. 'They've gone off to the pub and left you, have they?' My shoulders sagged. 'Well, you'd better take the cake.' I thrust the bag towards him.

Ash seemed to find speaking difficult. 'You think I'd trust you?'

'You think I'd poison a cake?' I countered, disgusted.

'I think Deverick might.'

'You have got to be kidding me!'

'Well, perhaps not. But only because it would be a bit obvious. Do you know him well?'

'Not really.'

'Do you like him?'

'He's a manipulative bastard.' That wasn't the whole truth, but it would do. Ash surprised me by laughing.

'Oh, you noticed that, did you?'

I pulled a face. 'Anyway, Michael didn't make the cake, my mum did. And I made the sloe gin last year.' I pulled it from the bag. 'Want me to prove it's safe?' I twisted off the cap and tilted the bottle to my lips, taking a good obvious glug. Rain washed my upturned face but I hardly felt it as the warmth of the spirit hit my throat and the distilled flavour of autumn hedges engulfed me like an embrace. 'See,' I said, gasping slightly, 'it's fine.' I passed him the bottle. He took it from my hand and put it to his lips, never taking his eyes off my face, as if he were answering some challenge.

I grinned.

'Very nice. Avril, isn't it?'

'You've been asking around?'

'I talked to a gardener. Older man. He said you were his boss.'

I shrugged and nodded. The gin had roared straight to my head.

'Do you know what it is that Deverick's doing here?'

'No.'

'Then be careful. He's using you, Avril. In ways you can't even imagine.'

'You what?'

'Did he tell you what happened to the men he sent into Grange Wood before you?'

I shook my head.

'The first one died. Ask him.' Ash took the bag from my hand. 'Thanks. If Deverick did send it, tell him I've got a bezoar and he's wasting his time.'

'What the hell's a bezoar?'

Ash smiled enigmatically 'Just tell him.' His attention switched to the darkness behind me. 'You came out after dusk after what happened the other day? Do you remember what I told you?' When I didn't respond he added sharply, 'Bull Peter?'

'I wasn't just imagining him then?' I said weakly, trying to make it a joke.

'That'd be one hell of an imagination you have.'

'I brought a big torch.' The alcohol was making my cheeks burn.

He looked me over thoughtfully. 'You've got guts.'

It seemed a dismissal. He watched as I retreated to the gate and climbed over, doing my best to look dignified. Only when I was safely on the other side did the disappointment hit me. It was getting on for really dark now, I was on my own again and not even bribery could thaw the attitude of the best-looking man within miles.

The best-looking man who wasn't my unscrupulous and possibly dangerous employer. 'Bloody hell,' I whispered to myself.

I was nearly home, in fact I was just coming up to the back of the cottage, when above the rattle of raindrops on my hood I heard a snort and round the corner of the building stepped a familiar bull-horned figure. My heart leapt into my throat then crashed back into my stomach. 'Oh Christ!'

He snorted again, softly. I could see the gleam of his rain-slick skin. His dark eyes flashed rings of white.

'Stop there!' I snapped, raising the torch in both hands. 'Don't move or you know what I'll do!'

The threat was pathetic, but he stopped dead. His broad chest rose and fell.

'Oh, you do understand English then?' I should have switched the torch on anyway, but I didn't. The smell of wet cow wafted to me. I took a cautious pace forwards. 'Bull Peter? Is that your name?'

His head tilted, bovine ears flicking forwards to catch my voice. I could see his nostrils flaring and narrowing with every breath. His neck was very thick, his head – apart from the horns and the ears – human but blunt and heavyset, with chestnut curls on his scalp. His skin was precisely the same colour as a ginger biscuit. His expression, which showed only around the eyes, was curious but a bit vacant. A beef breed, I thought, not dairy. Beef cattle are bred more docile.

An arse man, not a tit man then. It was his lucky day.

'Hey now, Peter. You're not going to hurt me, are you?' I took another couple of steps, brandishing the torch like Van Helsing brandishing a crucifix. He scraped the earth with one hoof and looked nervous. 'It's all right. All right.' I was within arm's length now. I reached out with one hand and brushed my fingertips across his chest.

He felt like man, not tree stump. Warm despite the rain. His musculature was that of a man too, except for those feet. He even had nipples. 'Wow,' I whispered to myself. He shivered, his hide dancing under my fingertips. I stroked his chest slowly, still holding the torch between us and angled up at his face, my thumb on the button.

Deep in his chest he uttered a noise, half bovine low and half groan.

'Shush.' I let my hand trail down to his belly, and followed its path with my eyes. He had no pubic hair. His cock already hung big and distended, though it wasn't totally out of proportion for a human. Unlike his bollocks, that is. He really was hung like an animal.

'You're not real, Bull Peter,' I whispered, discovering that he had no navel. 'So what's the harm?' My exploring fingertips circled his prick and he shuddered all over. He felt hot in my cold hand and it thickened at once in response to my touch, so that all of a sudden my fingertip couldn't reach my thumb around its circumference. I stroked him up and down rhythmically. He was like velvet to the touch and, beneath that, hardwood. 'Oh, you're a big boy,' I told him, delighted.

He seemed hypnotised. His head was tilted high. The eye of his cock gleamed, his own lubrication mingling with the rain. I wanted to fondle the big pouch of his balls but I only had one hand free so I had to release his cock. His whole frame surged back to life and he laid his hands on the front of my coat. His fingers were thick and blunt.

I should've switched the torch on.

He tore my waterproof open, pulling the zip from the rubberised cotton with no apparent effort. Then he tore open my sweatshirt and blouse together, exposing me to the sudden chill, and slid to his knees in front of me. I gasped with shock, rocking on my heels. His head dropped to a level with my torso and then his tongue slid out and lapped at my breast as if trying to lick it off. I was overwhelmed by sensation as he mouthed and licked and tried to suckle at my nipples, coating me in his saliva, his brown eyes rolling. Overwhelmed so completely that I didn't notice him rending the front of my trousers until the elastic and plastic and the thin leggings beneath had given way with a sound of tearing. I laid my hand on his face and cried out. Then I lost my grip as he ducked his head and licked right up between my legs, nearly lifting me off the floor. Only his hands, transferred to my thighs, kept me from tumbling. He pinned me in place as, snuffling, he explored my exposed sex and gently butted my clit.

Bloody hell – his tongue was *long*, inhumanly so. He had no problem ascertaining my state of readiness or of effecting entry. And there was no question but that I was ready for him. The torch slid out of my numb hand. As he stood he lifted me, holding me to his chest, and bellowed in triumph. The vibration made my head ring.

In three strides he had me pinned against the rough wall of the cottage and I was sobbing with fear and relief as he entered me with his prick. I was slick with his saliva and my own insane desire and he moulded me around him, rearranging my insides to make room for his pizzle. I'd braced myself for a real battering and that is what I got; his thrusts were deep and heavy and inexorable. They filled me with his fire. They crushed the breath from me and bruised my arse against the stones.

They were exactly what I needed.

When he'd come – and I'd come twice – and a shift of my weight on his hips had released a wash of his seed overflowing my sex and running down my thighs, I rested my head on his hot shoulder and listened to the thundering of his heart until consciousness left me.

It was a sudden draught that woke me, the chill on my newly exposed breasts. I opened sticky eyes and blinked, trying to make sense of things in the grey light.

It was just before dawn. The rain had stopped and a white mist lay over the silent land. I slid my hand through ivy and a small brown bird rocketed out of the leaves and flew away peeping its protests. That woke me up properly.

I was wedged, standing, between the back wall of my cottage and the remnants of a dead tree which had grown up too close to the foundations. My clothes were torn open down the front and my pubes were mashed against an old knot in the wood. Carefully I tilted sideways and slid out from the embrace of wood and stone, then stood, gnawing my lip.

I was quite sure that when I'd first looked around my new home there'd been no tree stump this close to the house.

Ash came to my house a few evenings later. I shouldn't have been so surprised to open the door to him, after all he and I – and perhaps his fair-weather activists – were in theory the only people on the Kester Estate once the gates were locked at night. But somehow I'd assumed it was Michael, calling to try his luck.

'I brought your flask back,' he said, a little tentatively. He was wearing a long green coat this time to keep out the drizzle.

I gaped, then took the flask from his outstretched hand. 'Do you want to come in for a drink?' I suggested after a slightly impolite hesitation.

He nodded.

'Coffee? Tea?' I asked as I led him through to the living room. 'I've got some bottled beer I think. You got the last of the sloe gin.'

'Tea would be great.' He looked around him curiously. I wished I'd had some warning of company and a chance to clear my usual mess. My little dining table was occupied by my dismantled chainsaw, which I was busy cleaning, and a new chain soaking in a margarine tub full of oil. 'The sloe gin was much appreciated.'

Indoors, he seemed a whole lot taller. It was a tiny room and he seemed to fill it. I swept an armful of magazines off the sofa. 'Sit down.'

He sat dutifully. Then as I retreated to the cupboard-sized kitchen he stood up immediately and followed me, stationing himself in the doorway and leaning on the post to watch. I felt rather self-conscious. Was he thinking of that night out in the meadow and my bare body? I wondered.

'Milk? Sugar?'

'Just tea, thanks.'

'How is it going in the woods?'

'Um. Soggy.' He folded his arms.

'I bet. How long have you been living out there?' I asked as I hunted out tea bags.

'Oh, pretty much since the last owner of the Grange died. That's . . . getting on for four years now.'

I stared. 'Winter as well?'

He nodded.

'God. That must be . . . I mean, I like the outdoor life, but four years in a tent?'

He hooked a wry smile. 'Sometimes it's a bit grim. Most of the time it's OK. And there are days I wouldn't be anywhere else.'

'But that's much longer than Michael Deverick's owned the place, isn't it?'

'I had a lot to do.'

'To do?'

'To get ready for him.'

Words failed me. 'Right.' I found the last teaspoon in the drawer. 'What is it exactly that you've got against him?' I thought I might as well hear it from both sides.

'Exactly? The fact that he doesn't give a crap what he destroys in order to accumulate the financial power he's after. You want details? He owns a major investments company and puts money into anything that'll make him a profit. His money's behind exploratory oil drilling in Alaskan wilderness and the Russian Taiga. He makes a fortune from palm-oil plantations in the Far East and soya-bean production in South America on land that used to be virgin rainforest. Companies he's got holdings in are busy right now all across Britain building roads and houses and airports on green fields so that the English can own their own cardboard huts on coast-to-coast identikit estates and escape on their cut-price carbon-heavy holidays every year to places that aren't ruined yet but will be after they get there with their stag parties and their chip shops and their nightclubs. Oh, and he dabbles in armaments exports.'

'Well, that's the Market,' I said dubiously. I had to take Ash's cold litany with a pinch of salt.

'Those are the ones I know about because they happen to be legal. I don't doubt there are others.'

'Well he's not a big fan of rules,' I admitted. 'So that's the guy I'm working for, is it? I'd no idea he was so important.'

Ash raised both eyebrows.

'I mean, I knew he was rich. He's throwing money at this place.'

'Yes.' The word was loaded with meaning.

'And you're going to get in his way, are you?'

'I'm going to try.'

I picked up the hot mugs and ushered him back into the living room. As he took off his coat and seated himself again I walked casually over to the window and cracked it onto the drizzly night. I really had no choice; Ash had brought in with him a reek of wood smoke and clothes that'd got damp and musty and never dried out. I had no great objection to the first – God knows I was used to it – but the mildewy smell was overpowering.

When I turned back his face was pinched. 'Sorry,' he said.

'It's OK . . .' I was twice as embarrassed as he was. 'It's just –'

'I try to get to the public baths and the laundrette in town but it's this weather . . .'

'Uh-huh.' I grabbed for another subject. 'You have a car then?'

'I hitch.'

'Right.' I bit my lip. 'Um, well, if you wanted a bath here there'll be loads of hot water now. I forgot to turn the immersion heater off after mine.'

He looked doubtful.

'And I've got a washer and tumble dryer; I could put your clothes through on a quick cycle if you wanted.' I smiled encouragingly. 'It all goes on Michael's electricity bill.'

The ice cracked. 'OK. That'd be nice. Thanks.'

I showed him the bathroom and climbed onto the chair to pull the biggest towel I owned out of the airing cupboard. He kept his eyes on me all the time, even when my backside was at face height. I felt a bit dithery. 'You've got soap, shampoo, whatever,' I said, wishing I'd been able to hide my razor and the tumbled box of tampons. Why wasn't I naturally *neat*? I opened the cabinet and pointed out the rack inside. 'Bath fizzies here if you like them. That might be a good one for you. It's lime and eucalyptus – not too girly.'

I left him in the bathroom and retreated to the armchair, feeling that I'd made a fool of myself. I didn't have long to collect my dignity before Ash came out again, carrying his clothes in a bundle. He was wearing the towel around his waist and it was long enough to brush the tops of his feet, like a sarong. I fought not to look, and lost. His bare chest was nearly hairless and his left shoulder was covered in a jagged tribal tattoo. I'd expected him to be paper white, being a redhead, but he was tanned to the pale-gold of Jersey cream.

I wanted to lick him.

'I'll do it,' I said, reaching for his bundle, but he carried it to the washing machine himself and loaded it, only letting me add detergent. My machines were kept under the stairs, half-concealed behind the sofa, the only place where there was room for them to be plumbed in. 'Wash cycle three: there,' I said, pushing the button.

'Great.' He waited for the machine to start drawing water, then returned to the bathroom.

He was in there a long time. Long enough for me to tidy the living room, hurl all my clothes off the floor and into wardrobes, straighten the bedlinen, change into a pair of leggings that didn't have a spaghetti stain on them, wash up and finally sit down and give my full attention to berating myself for acting like a fourteen-year-old. I was a grown woman and he was a grown man and he was in my house naked and there wasn't any more simple equation than that, was there?

My eye fell on his mug of tea, balanced on the arm of the sofa. It was cool now. I zapped it in the microwave to bring it back to steaming and carried it over to the bathroom door. Softly I knocked, my pulse racing. There was no sound from within. As it happens there's no lock on my bathroom, so I opened the door and stepped inside.

Ash lay in the milky water under a warm cloud of eucalyptus-scented condensation. Far too tall for my bath, his knees were bent up revealing shins striped with red-gold hair and his dreadlocks dangled into the water about his shoulders. He was fast asleep. Greedily I studied what I could see of his body, but as I looked at the smudges under his eyes I felt a strange flutter of pity. I put the mug down on the corner of the bath. His eyes opened at that small noise and he looked straight up at me.

'Don't forget your tea,' I said, my voice husky. I shut the door behind me as I left.

He didn't take long after that. Through the wall I heard the sound of him rising, followed by the bath draining, the flush of the toilet and then an odd squeaky noise that I only slowly identified: he was cleaning the bath. Wow, I thought, now that's the sort of man there should be more of. When he emerged I was waiting for him with a sweater: a plain white hand-knitted thing that had stretched hugely over the years, it was my comfort jumper and if I tucked my knees up I could pull it right down to my ankles. It was the only piece of suitable clothing I had that I thought might fit him.

He was back in the towel sarong again. I came up close to make my offer: 'Do you want a jumper?' Close enough that I could see the water sheen on his skin and smell the eucalyptus and lime. Close enough so that he could easily pull me to him. Your choice, I thought: girl or sweater.

He picked the clothing. Not swiftly; his eyes were on me the whole time, his expression unreadable but intense. He slipped the sweater over his head and then went and sat back on the sofa, balancing his mug on one knee. It was a good job it was a big towel; like most men he sat with his thighs carelessly apart.

'Suits you,' I said, then went and perched on the lone armchair opposite, dizzy with longing and disappointment.

Ash licked his upper lip thoughtfully. I felt like I was under examination. Why the hell didn't he say anything? The silence was unbearable.

'I asked Michael Deverick about the men he'd sent into the wood, like you said,' I ventured.

'Oh?'

'According to him one of them walked into a wasps' nest and was stung a couple of times. His mate carried him out but he died of the anaphylactic shock.'

'That's right. What about the others?'

'He didn't mention any others.'

Ash took a sip of his drink. 'He's sent a few men to try to get in. One got bitten by "a stray farm dog", I quote. One broke an arm when he fell off a rock pile. Lots of them had problems with the wasps. None of them got anywhere. Are you seeing a pattern?'

'Yeah. Now tell me why.'

'The wood keeps people out. Deverick knows that and he shouldn't have sent you in.'

'But why? Why's it so important that you keep people out? What's he going to do that's so bad?'

Ash thought about answering for a long moment. I could see the doubt in his eyes. 'There's something in the wood he wants,' he said at last. 'It's . . . important. He thinks it's his to take.'

'So this isn't about the wood itself?' I demanded.

'No.'

'But then what is it?' I asked, exasperated.

'I can't tell you.'

'Why?'

He made a helpless gesture. 'You wouldn't believe me if I did.'

'Try me.'

He drummed his fingers on his mug. 'All right. There was a Michael Deverick supplying munitions to the Allies in World War Two. There was a Captain Michael Deverick in the trenches at Ypres. There was a Michael Deverick in the Order of the Golden Dawn back in 1903. He fell out with Crowley, but then who didn't? There was a Michael Deverick sitting as member of parliament for a rotten borough in 1831. Same man. Same man as the one you work for. He's at least two hundred years old and he's a magus.'

'A what?'

'A magician.'

I sat in silence for a while. 'Well,' I said at length, 'he's managed to get British builders to work for him seven days a week. I suppose there had to be some rational explanation.'

Ash looked suspicious. 'You're taking it well, considering.'

'Oh, I'm not bloody stupid! I've seen . . .' The words died in my throat. 'Though to be honest, I'd have had you pegged as the weird one. No offence.'

Ash put his mug down on the carpet. 'None taken. Our methods differ. Nevertheless.'

'So you are a . . . You're one too?'

'A magus. Yes.'

'That bull bloke,' I muttered. 'Bull Peter. What's he? Is that something you did?'

Ash looked nonplussed. 'Ah. I wasn't sure how clearly you'd seen him.'

'Pretty bloody clearly.'

'Right. Well, I think he's a changeling – you know, left once in the place of a human baby. He seems to be imprinted on human women. But I'm not totally sure. It's not as if I've talked to him. He's aggressive with men.'

'He's a fairy,' I said. 'That's what you're saying?'

'Uh-huh. You had any problems with him since that night?'

'Problems? No.' I had a sudden desire to change the subject.

'Good.'

I thought of the things I'd seen flitting through the weeds around him. 'What about the other fairies? They talk to you, do they?'

'Not really. Fay tolerate me better than they do most humans. But they don't talk. You know: parallel lives.'

'OK.' I had to bite back the desire to mention the deer-girl. 'And you're living in the wood and doing your witchy stuff there –'

'Ritual magic.' His tone was very dry all of a sudden.

'Ritual magic, because you want to keep this other magus from getting the thing in the wood.'

'That's right.'

'Then,' I said slowly and clearly, 'what the bloody hell is it?'

I could see the reluctance settling over his face like a cloud. 'Something powerful. Something he could use to control – I don't know – millions of lives. It's something he must never be allowed to get hold of.'

'OK, I get it. You're its guardian, right?'

'Yeah.'

'Can you take it away from here?'

'No.'

'Can you use ... whatever it is, against him?'

'Christ. No.' For a moment he looked really appalled.

'So you're stuck in the wood, and Michael can't get in, and you can't leave.'

'That's about the size of it. For the moment.'

I looked at my nails. 'I'm really starting to wish I'd gone to the pub tonight.'

Ash rubbed gently at the piercings through his eyebrow. 'Sorry. You asked.'

'But you came here to talk to me.' I bit the inside of my lip. 'Didn't you? I mean, bugger the flask. You wanted to talk.'

He sighed. 'Yes. I need ... I mean, I am short of ... Listen, this is how the situation is. I've had four years to build every defence into the wood that I can think of, without Deverick about. But now the estate's in his hands and he's going to be looking for any possible way in past those defences. He's good at that. He'll be looking for any weak point. It might only be a matter of time. In fact, he's found a weakness already.'

'Which is?'

'You. You walked unharmed right through the wood to the bridle path.'

'How come?'

He looked apologetic. 'I set the wards up to block Deverick. They're at their strongest against him, and they draw from the Wildwood. And I assumed that if he were going to launch an attack on the wood itself, with chainsaws and bulldozers and such, that his crew would be male. So, some of the guards are of no use against, say, you.'

'Welcome to the twenty-first century,' I said, with ill-concealed amusement.

'I still think he's not going to be able to find enough women for that job, though I may be wrong. And anyway, the deeper wards will still function. But that was a weakness. He'll find others. He'll think of a way to use them. So I came to ask you if you'd help me.'

'Help you? Against him? What the hell could I do?'

'Well,' said Ash tentatively, 'I can't get into the house any more than he can enter the wood. I'd like to know what he's doing in there.'

'And why should I?'

'That's a good question. Because he's a shit. Would that do it?'

I stared. At that moment the washer came noisily to the end of its cycle. I welcomed the distraction. I stood and crossed the room to squat in front of the machine. Ash half-rose from the sofa and put his hand on my shoulder as I opened the door. 'No,' he said; 'please . . .'

I turned, looking up at him. He was leaning right over me, his face close to mine, and I acted without thought and almost without realising what I was doing, from pure instinct. I put my lips to his in a soft kiss of invitation.

I think he was more surprised than I was though. For a second I thought he wasn't going to respond. Then I felt his sharp inhalation of breath, and then his hand cupped my throat and jaw as he kissed me back – not hard but tentatively and very slowly. Almost as if he were afraid.

For a moment that was all we did. Then I pushed him gently back onto the sofa and followed up, straddling his lap. His eyes were wide with shock, so I kissed him again, challengingly, catching his lip in my incisors. His hands slid round my waist. Our kisses were like strange dogs circling one another, all tension and avid curiosity and barely concealed teeth. Then he slid his hands up the front of my top to cup the bare breasts beneath and I broke away with a gasp, arching my spine as he caught at my nipples. He pulled me up sharply against him, pushing up my blouse and putting his lips to my tits. I felt his wet mouth around my nipple and I cried out in helpless delight. I clasped his head and his long locks were damp under my hands but I was damper, down between my splayed thighs. I love having my tits sucked. Sometimes I can even come that way, they're so sensitive – if the man is right. If he knows what he's doing.

Ash did.

Then suddenly he pulled his mouth away and looked up at me with eyes full of storm. My wet nipples stood out like hazelnuts. 'No,' he groaned. 'I can't.'

If he'd just decided to let on that he was married or gay or something then I didn't want to hear it. I slid out of his arms like water and down between his spread thighs. I pulled his towel open as I went. He was a man and men, I reasoned, are straightforward: pull the lever and you get the candy.

In this case the candy was of the raspberries-and-cream variety. Definitely a natural redhead, I thought as I ran my fingers through his pubic thatch. And I doubted very much he was gay; his erection was like polished rock already and it jerked against my tongue as I wrapped my lips around it, tasting of lime bath bomb, tasting of the salt of his own eagerness. Ash's whole body bucked as I engulfed him and he threw back his head with a groan. I had him now; he wasn't going anywhere. He had a second tribal tattoo, I found, on his right hip and thigh. I traced it with my fingertips. Lovingly I teased his swollen prick head and ran my fingers up his shaft and down and around his balls. Cocks are wonderful. I adore them. I love to feel them urgent and yearning for me, responding to the flick of my tongue and the pressure of my lips and the friction of my throat. I gave Ash's cock everything I had, briefly. Long enough to feel him tense and rock under me. He slid his fingers into my hair, holding me.

Then I pulled away, just far enough so I could look up at him and suggest, 'Let's go to the bedroom.' I planted a kiss right on his cock tip.

His eyes were shining. He stroked my temple. And somehow he still said, 'No.'

No? I blinked.

'No. Finish it off.'

You selfish git, I thought. As I hesitated his hands tightened on my head. For the first time it occurred to me that maybe I wasn't engineering this as well as I'd thought. 'Hey ... ?'

'Finish it off.' Those green-brown eyes weren't shining now; they were burning.

'OK.' I didn't want a fight. Not from this position. Swallowing my disappointment I went back to work. This time I was rougher than strictly necessary. Ash's pelvis twisted as I concentrated on pumping him, forgetting such delicacies as handling his scrotum. I didn't give him a chance to catch his breath or enjoy the journey; I just rode him to the end of the line as directly and brutally as I could. He was too far gone to find it truly painful, but he came with wrench and a gasp that didn't sound like unalloyed pleasure, filling my mouth with his sweet-sour ejaculate.

I sat back, raised my eyebrows and waited grimly.

For a long time he seemed unable to collect himself. Then he blinked and focused on me anew. 'Did you swallow?' were his first words.

'Of course.'

He leant forwards and kissed me. This time I didn't welcome it. I yielded mostly from habit and surprise. His kiss was hard, his tongue invasive. He's checking, I thought incredulously: he's checking to see that I've swallowed it all! I tore from his kiss and he grabbed me by the hair.

'Drink,' he ordered, scooping up the half-empty mug of tea and pressing it to my lips.

'Get lost!'

'Drink!' His hand tightened in my hair until tears sprang to my eyes and the rim of the mug banged painfully against my teeth. I took a mouthful of the lukewarm tea, milkless and bitter, and choked it down.

He released me at once.

'You bastard,' I said, backing away across the carpet. 'Who the hell do you think you are?' My voice was wobbly with shock. 'Get out of my house.' He looked at me speechlessly. There was agony in his expression and anger and shame too, and I didn't understand what was going on with him but he had completely freaked me out. 'Get out!' I shouted.

Ash stood and went to empty his clothes out of the washing machine. He pulled on his wet trousers without looking in my direction, then scooped up the rest and walked out.

I jumped up and got into the hall just as the front door closed, then threw his mug at the door, hard. Tea painted an arc across the wall. After that I retreated to the living room and paced up and down. Then I rang Michael Deverick's voice-mail.

'This is Avril Shearing,' I snapped. 'I want to tell you I've changed my mind about the Eden Project.'

5: Eden

My dress was delivered two days before the dinner party. I hadn't been expecting it; in fact I had other plans about what I'd be wearing. But the boxes embossed with a gold designer monogram changed all that.

I opened the shoebox first: it held cream shoes with delicate beading and heels that were slender enough to be elegant, without being so high as to make me ridiculously tall. They fitted perfectly. I wondered how Michael knew my shoe size. He'd say he was good at guessing, I supposed. It creeped me out a little bit. Of course this was exactly the sort of thing Michael Deverick would do. He was used to being in charge and he liked to spend money on things. Particularly on things that he owned, I reminded myself. I needed to be on my guard.

Then I tried the dress on and stopped worrying about the shoes, because that fitted perfectly too and it took my breath away. Looking in the mirror I could hardly believe the reflection was my own. From the narrow shoulders down the dress fitted like a second skin, all the way to a softly flared skirt with a gypsyish hemline. The cream fabric brought out the warm tones of my skin and hid nothing, flaunting my long lines and my strong shoulders and my flat belly; the sides were slashed to reveal yet more skin. I stared and stared. I haven't got the biggest boobs in the world but they're quite cute and this dress made the most of them. But it was only when I turned my back and looked over my shoulder that I saw the real genius of the design: this dress gift-wrapped my bum, cupping and framing it shamelessly. This dress *existed* to present my buns to the world. Even I was surprised at the effect that so much climbing had had on those pert cheeks.

The only fly in the ointment was that the fabric was so clingy that my panty-line showed up, rather spoiling the effect. I tried on several pairs before settling for the knickers that were least visible through the slashes in the side panels.

I was wearing his gifts when I opened the door to him on the Friday night. He was wearing a dinner jacket cut like a Victorian frock coat. Theatrical, but it looked just right on him.

'Well, hello, Mr Darcy,' I said, letting him in.

He walked around me on the living-room carpet, his eyes twinkling, while I tried not to feel like a doxy he'd just purchased. There wasn't much I'd been able to do with my thicket of hair but I'd found a spray of cream silk flowers – in fact they were left over from Emma's wedding bouquet – to pin there and I was wearing a moonstone necklace which my gran had left me.

'You look lovely,' he said, moving in to take my fingers gently in his. His voice was low and soft. 'But the knickers are ridiculous. Take them off.'

I was speechless. If he'd hit a note just a little bit more peremptory I'd have gone up like a flare and told him where to shove it. But somehow he'd managed to make the order sound so reasonable, so conspiratorial, that I couldn't take offence. Not enough offence, anyway. I swallowed. 'OK. Turn around, then; don't look.' My tone was far brusquer than his had been.

Smiling, he obeyed. I pulled up my dress and pulled down my panties, not daring to take my eyes off him. Then I threw the knickers behind the sofa to put them out of his sight. I couldn't afford to lose too many pairs to the men of the Kester Estate, I reasoned.

'All done.'

When he turned back the smile was still there. He ran the very tips of his fingers down my side from my waist to my thigh, his touch moving feather-light across slivers of exposed skin. 'You're beautiful,' he whispered.

Well, men will say anything when they think sex is in the offing.

'Shall we go?' I asked.

'If you're ready.'

I didn't have a coat remotely good enough for this occasion so I took my red pashmina – a fake one bought from an Exeter street stall – as a wrap and let him steer me out to his Range Rover. My bare pussy tingled at the touch of the cool evening air but I was determined to ignore it.

The journey to our dinner destination was more pleasant than I'd anticipated. Michael drove with a proper respect for the narrow, sunken Devon roads until we hit the main highway into Cornwall. Traffic was unusually light. And we talked for nearly an hour, not about work or the estate or each other, but just casual chat about things in general. It was genuinely nice to converse with him, to my surprise and relief. He was relaxed and good-humoured, and I was enjoying it so much that I nearly forgot where we were going, until we turned off the A391 and down past the Eden Project signboards. We ignored the empty car parks at the top of the slope, dropping in a wide sweep down towards the visitor centre instead. I twisted in my seat but could make out little in the gathering dusk except the glow of lights. The Eden Project is sited in a disused china clay pit and the hole is simply vast.

At the entrance building two stewards in evening dress were waiting to open our car doors. I suppressed a giggle as I stepped out, thanking the young man who was being so polite and wondering what he'd think if he knew I had no knickers on. Maybe he could tell. I felt self-conscious but also deliciously daring. Even the wobbliness of my narrow heels was provoking. And Michael's patronage somehow lent me legitimacy.

As we passed through the building to the door on the far side I looked around avidly, trying to read the banners and catch a glimpse of the exhibits. Michael took my hand and wrapped it round his elbow to encourage me to keep moving. Beyond the far door was a balcony and we stopped to look over. We weren't even at the floor of the pit yet, I realised. The ground fell away yet further. All the lower slopes of the old quarry were planted up in distinct areas, living exhibits in a project telling the story of human dependence on the plant kingdom for food and drink, medicine and clothing and building materials. Artificial lighting added a glamour to the landscape as did the multicoloured pennons fluttered from myriad flagpoles, while overhead the perfect blue twilight was a vast bowl mirroring the earthen one in which we stood. And on the far side of the lowest level stood the two famous biomes – vast polyhedral greenhouses so futuristic that they looked like sealed moon-base environments. One was, I knew, filled with a tropical rainforest created from equatorial plants from all around the Earth's girth. The other was a warm temperate glasshouse where plants from the dry lands of the Mediterranean and South Africa and California thrived. I felt like an eight-year-old waking on Christmas morning and getting her first look at the presents at the bottom of her bed.

The whole landscape seemed to hold its breath.

'Oh, it's huge!' I said. Then, 'Where is everyone?'

There was no sign of any other human being on the site. The only movement was from the flags. I turned to Michael.

'We're here,' said he, leaning on a railing.

'Are we too early? What about the others?'

'Well, you made it clear you didn't really enjoy that sort of party.' He spread his hands. 'So I thought, better just the two of us. I had intended for us to eat in the rainforest biome but apparently there are rather too many bugs there after nightfall, so our table's in the temperate one. We can look around afterwards.'

My face must have been a picture. 'Just us?'

'Just us.'

'You've hired the whole Eden Project?'

'Until dawn.'

My heart crashed into my stomach. 'Are you completely out of your mind?' I demanded.

'Look upon it as a donation to a good cause. I thought you'd be flattered.'

'Flattered?' No, I wasn't flattered; I was frightened. 'Just how far are you prepared to go for a fuck?' I asked. 'I mean, do you draw the line *anywhere*?' I turned back to the glass doors. 'I want to go home. Call me a taxi. You can afford it.'

'Avril.' He stepped between the exit and me. 'Please. I didn't mean to upset you.' I met his eyes and saw that for the first time since I'd met him he looked rattled. 'I'm not trying to bully you or . . . buy you.' He shook his head helplessly. 'I just thought you'd like it.'

'Like it?'

'It's all for you. To do whatever you want.'

'And what if,' I said through clenched teeth, 'that doesn't include sex with you?'

'Well, it's your choice.' He looked pained but contrite. 'I'm not intending to force you into anything. It'll always be your choice, Avril.'

I glared, but he'd drawn all the fuel from my ire. I'd never seen him like this. I didn't know what to say.

'Dinner?' he suggested gently.

'Maybe,' I growled. 'But I'm telling you right now, no sex. You still want to waste your time on me?'

'It won't be wasted.' He was recovering fast and the familiar confidence was back.

'OK.' I clung to my reluctance a moment longer. Then I turned to survey my temporary realm and kicked off my fancy shoes. 'Well, if we're on our own I'm not going to be walking round in these.' Holding them in one hand I set off down the zigzag path, the concrete cool beneath my bare soles.

By the time we reached the biomes I'd more or less forgotten to be mad with him, mollified instead by a night scented with lavender and the awe-inspiring sight of the biomes awaiting us like glimmering fairy palaces. Every step made their huge scale more apparent. By the time we entered the Warm Temperate Biome and I took my first look around at the succulents and the cascading creepers, the bright exotic flowers and the wicked spines springing like fireworks from the dry soil, I had a huge grin on my face. Overhead the huge panes of hi-tech plastic gleamed, reflecting the soft lighting from lamps at our feet.

'Do you like it?'

'It's amazing.'

Michael steered me down a path, past displays on floral perfume and the growing of tobacco, through garden plots laden with gourds and spices and a grove of cork oaks, their rugged bark peeling like roasted pork rind. Then we were walking through a vineyard and I stopped, captivated by a cluster of bronze sculptures which rampaged in frozen frenzy among the low vine clumps.

The one that had really caught my attention was the biggest: a rearing bull, its rugged splendour reminding me strongly of my night encounters with my own bull. But it was surrounded by maybe a score of others, some half-hidden in the landscape. These were human, or almost so: scrawny revellers who beat upon drums and blew trumpets and shook tambourines. They wore animal masks and headdresses, but no clothing. They crouched and leapt and shook themselves, captured by the sculptor in the midst of an ecstatic and completely uninhibited dance.

'What's this?' They reminded me of Ash's mates, actually.

'*The Rites of Dionysus*. What do you think?'

I didn't know what to say. The revellers looked enraptured, but when you looked closer there was a dark edge to their joy. The dancers' genitalia were clearly visible, both male and female, which surprised me in a family tourist venue. And one pair were holding a dog between them, pulling with all their might upon its paws, frozen forever in the moment just before the animal was torn in half. Its jaws gaped in a silent scream. 'Wow,' I said. 'It's ... powerful.'

'Dionysus is the god of ecstasy and the vine. His followers, the maenads, roamed the hills of Greece in packs. Respectable women would join his retinue and in their frenzy tear apart wild animals and any man who spied on them, or who wouldn't submit to them – even their own husbands and children. Those are the gifts of the vine: pleasure and rage; conviviality and madness.'

'I'm going on the wagon,' I said wryly.

'Oh no. You misunderstand the point. Dionysus, like all the gods, must be propitiated in small things if you wish to avoid being destroyed by him.' He pointed down the path. 'His altar awaits.'

His altar was a table laid for two in a grove where ancient, twisted olive trees spread their grey-green leaves. A side table nearby bore the actual food, in heated or chilled compartments. Several wine glasses stood upon the snowy linen cloth. I wrinkled my nose as Michael drew out a cloth-wrapped bottle and began to pour into a champagne flute, but the liquid turned out to be a dark amber-brown with a thick head.

'What's that?' I asked, pulling a face as he handed me the glass, then took a cautious sip. 'Beer?'

'Theakston's Old Peculier,' he said. 'As requested.'

I had to laugh.

'You will drink wine, though?' he chided, pointing back up the path. 'In honour of Dionysus?'

I was glad we were out of sight of those wonderful, disquieting sculptures. 'Only if it's red.'

'Red it is.'

At his request I sat and he served from the side table. The first course was a mozzarella salad, heavy on the basil, which I have a passion for. 'Good guess,' I said, spearing a sliver of tomato. He didn't rise to the barb in my tone. For a few minutes we ate in near silence, the occasional comment passing between us about food. Michael was really only toying with his salad; his attention seemed to be entirely on me, which was disquieting. I started to worry I was going to drop something down the lovely dress. 'What's up?' I asked. 'Don't you eat? You're not a vampire or something are you?'

'God, no.' His face was alight with pleasure. 'I just . . . I'm enjoying watching you eat. That's all.'

I rolled my eyes. 'Can you go ten minutes without thinking about sex?'

'Not around you.'

He was enjoying this, the sod, and it was hard not to smile along with him. 'Well, it's going to be a difficult evening then.'

'I'm particularly looking forwards to the main course.'

'Which is?'

'Sausages,' said he, without blinking. I raised my knife,

preparing to plunge it into his quivering heart. Quickly he threw up his hands. 'Duck! It's duck!'

'Uh-huh?' I was only slightly mollified. 'You're not planning any "fancy a bit of a duck" jokes, are you?'

'Do I look like the sort of man who would stoop to puns?'

'No comments about "breast or thigh", then?'

His gaze settled very deliberately on my breasts and he bit his lip. 'Perish the thought.'

I sat back, dabbing at my lips with my napkin and giggling. 'You're impossible.'

'Thank you. It's something I've been working on. More wine?'

I nodded. 'Is that your Plan B? Get me wellied?'

'Would it work?'

I wrinkled my nose and decided not to answer that. 'Wouldn't be much point. I fall asleep too easily when I'm drunk. Unless you find snoring a turn-on, of course.'

'No, I usually go for fully conscious. The more responsive a woman's body the better, I find.'

My own body reacted to his words with a shiver of pleasure. I was annoyed with myself, but not really surprised. I'd already demonstrated what a walkover I was, after all.

'There's nothing more exciting than the betraying signs of arousal in a woman: nothing. The darkening of the eyes. The way her breath flutters and her blood comes to the skin, and the little involuntary movements she makes...'

My mouth was dry but I didn't dare lift my glass because I didn't trust my hand not to quiver. 'I'd have thought power was more your thing,' I said ungraciously.

'That is power, Avril. Ah...' He was looking at my breasts again, and I knew my nipples had hardened. That dress hid nothing. And the more he looked, the more my areolae tightened and the more my nipples stood out against the cloth. The tiny points of friction were quite uncomfortable. 'I'd have to put you down as really quite responsive.'

I drew the pashmina around my shoulders, biting my lip.

Michael was just gracious enough to make no further comment at this juncture. He cleared the starters and served the next course, moving with an easy confidence and handling the food deftly. I watched from under hooded lids. A previous job as a waiter? I wondered. It didn't seem particularly likely. Maybe he was just good at everything he turned his hand to. The duck breast was perfect: rich and moist and crispy-skinned, and served with creamed potato and sweet red cabbage. The perfect Sunday roast, just like I'd asked for.

Delicious though it was, eating was difficult. I could hardly concentrate.

'Talking of drink,' Michael said; 'there is something I'd like to try.' He brought out a glass bottle with no label and uncorked it. 'You will never have tasted this before, Avril. And I doubt you or I will get many chances to try anything like it again.'

'Oh?' I was dubious.

'This,' he said with relish, 'is wine from the ancient world. In 1982 they found a wrecked ship off the island of Naxos. Estimates put it at about the fourth century BC, a trading vessel from out of Athens. There wasn't much left of the hull, but there were amphorae by the dozen buried in the sands. Some of them still had their bitumen seals intact. And inside was wine more than two thousand years old from the vineyards of pagan Greece. I bought this at auction.'

'It can't be drinkable still, surely?'

'Oh, I shouldn't think it's terribly pleasant.' He tipped a slug into his still half-full wine glass. The liquid looked thin and brown, like vinegar. 'But to have the chance to taste it ... to imbibe a vintage pressed before the birth of Christ, before the rise of the Roman Empire, before the foundation of our civilisation... Isn't that something precious?' He poured into my glass too, without waiting for permission. Then he raised his own in a toast, or a challenge. 'Shall we?'

'Now why don't I trust you?' I asked softly.

He blinked. 'Because you have a terrible cynical mind.'

'Hm.'

'And a very twisted attitude to men.'

'No.' I shook my head. 'I like men. I like working with them and hanging out with them and... I like them in pretty much every way you can like them.'

'You don't trust them.'

I pursed my lips. 'I don't trust *you*.'

Michael laughed, drained his glass right the way down and sat back, eyes closed.

'What's it like?'

'Sharp.'

Sighing, I took a cautious sip. It was sharp, even under the warm and fruity cover of the wine it was mixed with, and slightly resinous. You wouldn't drink it for fun. 'How much did it cost?' I asked.

'That bottle? A little under eight thousand pounds.'

I gasped involuntarily, and felt the rush to my head. I took another sip, just to make sure. Then I started to giggle.

'What's so funny?'

'This. All this.' I waved my hand at our surroundings. 'It's too much. You are completely crazy, you know? I'm not worth all this.'

'So you say.' He wiped his mouth with a napkin. 'Have you got confidence issues, Avril? Because that really surprises me. Of all people ...'

'Everyone has confidence issues. Unless you're a psychopath.' He raised an eyebrow and I rather regretted my words.

'Hm. So what are yours?'

I took a hearty sip of wine and shook my head disparagingly. 'You know, the usual. Not pretty enough. Not smart enough. Not good enough at what I do.'

'That's strange. Because from here you look exquisite.' He didn't wait for me to try to come up with a gracious response. 'And you know you're good at what you do.'

'Yes, well. In my position I can't ever just sit back and relax about that one.'

He regarded me thoughtfully. 'Do you want to know what it is I see in you, Avril? D'you want to know why I've been … interested?'

'You like a bit of butch? Or is it just I'm the only woman in Britain who's ever said "No"?'

He smiled. 'Not quite. You have to understand, in my position I meet so many people – beautiful people, some of them. And almost every one of them is trying to pull just enough weight and to kiss just enough ass to make life comfortable and easy for themselves. But you … you've not gone for easy. You've taken the road beset with thorns and briars. You've gone for something you've had to fight for, tooth and nail. And it's not something comfortable; it simply happens to be the thing you want. Now, *that* interests me.'

I was silent. He'd done something to me with those words that simple flattery could never have achieved. He'd slid past every one of my defences. I couldn't meet his eyes. I'd never felt so self-conscious. 'Well, you know why it is I have to say no to you, then,' I muttered in the end.

'Mm?'

'You'd ruin it all.' I fluttered my hands hopelessly. 'You can't be one of the lads if you're shagging the boss. That's the rule.'

'Is it?'

'Oh yes. I didn't write it, but there it is.'

'Rules are for the weak, Avril.'

I gave him an old-fashioned look. 'Easy to say. But you're not me, and you don't have to work the way I do, and you're not risking anything.'

He smiled, as if looking straight through me to a vista only he knew. 'Imagine a world without rules, Avril. No limits: physical, social, spiritual. What do you think that'd be like?'

'No limits?' I thought about the rite of Dionysus. 'Terrifying.'

'Oh yes. But fear would be a small price to pay. Imagine if you could screw anyone you wanted to, Avril, without *rules* and without consequences.'

I squirmed a little under the table.

'Who's that lad works for you? I've seen him on the tractor.'

'Owen.'

'Owen. Good-looking boy. Have you thought about what it'd be like to screw him?'

I was flushing. 'Look, uh ...'

'Have you thought about it?'

I rolled my eyes. 'Yeah. I mean, he's a nice kid. I like him.'

'That's interesting. Does "I like him" mean "I want to fuck him"? Does one follow on from the other? Or are you simply using a euphemism when you say you like him?'

'I like him,' I said through gritted teeth, 'means I *like* him. That's really important when it comes to fancying a man. I don't *like* you.' The words were uttered from malice; by this point I had no idea whether they were true or not. I'd changed my mind a dozen times during the course of the evening.

Michael's face lit up. 'Yet you want to fuck me. That must be quite disturbing for you.'

I flushed. How was I supposed to answer that? I rattled my fork against the edge of the table in frustration. 'Ash said you were a manipulative shit,' I muttered.

That put the icing on Michael's cake of self-satisfaction. 'Really? You've been talking to the Ginger Rasta, then?'

'When we met in the wood.' I was already so flustered that a simple lie wasn't going to show up.

'And what else did he say?'

'He said you did black magic.' It came out before I could censor myself, a bald accusation.

Michael looked genuinely surprised. 'You astonish me. He's talking even worse crap than he usually does.'

I wished I'd kept my mouth shut. 'He ... He said a lot of stupid things. He's a bit of a nutter.'

'*Black magic*? Are you sure?'

'Uh ...'

'Magic isn't colour-coded! Were those his actual words?'

I stared. 'He said you were a magus.'

'Ah.' Michael sat back again and tapped the tips of his fingers together. 'Well, he's saved me a lot of tedious explanation, at any rate.' Taking up the unlabelled bottle, he held it out at arm's length over the earth and inverted it. As the ancient wine glugged out and disappeared into the dry soil he spoke in a language I'd never heard. I'd take a guess that it was Greek. Then he put the bottle back on the table.

Somewhere a drum began to beat.

'What are you doing?' I asked. The drum was joined by a reedy-sounding pipe.

'I've summoned the bacchanal.'

The music was making the hair stand up on the back of my neck. 'What?'

'The maenads. The votaries of Dionysus.' There was no humour in his expression at all now. 'The rites are begun once more.'

I pushed back my chair from the table. Indistinct figures were visible flitting among the shrubs, like darker shadows. 'What the hell did you do that for?'

'*This* is Plan B.' He said it like his honesty made him irreproachable.

'You prick!'

'Don't worry, they won't hurt you. You're a woman.' Michael stood up and turned, scanning the landscape around us. 'It's me that's in trouble.'

I caught my first clear glimpse of one and was on my feet in an instant. She was small and wiry and filthy dirty, her bare skin blotched with grime and her dark hair snarled with twigs. She loped out from behind a cypress, stared at us, and raised her arms over her head, fists clenched. 'What d'you mean?' I demanded. 'What'll they do?'

'They'll tear me limb from limb,' said Michael. 'They'll eviscerate me and pull me apart at the joints and flay my skin to wear as a trophy.'

I stared at him and then I stared at them – more of them now creeping out from behind every tree – and it was hard to tell which made the less sense to me. The women were universally scrawny and nearly naked except for the odd piece of raw animal hide worn as a cape or a hood. The brown streaks painted up their arms and breasts looked a lot like old blood. I might have dismissed them as bit-part actors hired by Deverick as part of his game, except that I saw their eyes as they came closer. Those eyes were glazed and bloodshot and the pupils so dilated they swallowed all colour.

'Then what are you doing?' I said weakly as they closed in on us. 'Send them away, you idiot.'

They loped around us in a rough circle, heads cocked like curious animals. I caught my first whiff of their scent, a musky odour that was part sex and part the yeasty lees of wine.

'Too late.'

Their nails were long and their thighs scored by the marks

of thorns. Some carried knives, and those looked like they were made from knapped flint. They whined like hungry dogs.

'This isn't funny!'

'You can save me, Avril.' Michael's voice cut through the noise of the women and the wailing of the pipe and the insistent drumbeat. He wasn't looking at them any more; his gaze was fixed on me. 'You can save me.' I stared at him, horrified. They were milling around us in a circle, avid but for the moment still wary, twitching in time to the music. 'Money and power just puts your back up, doesn't it? Well, this is my gift, Avril. My life in your hands.' The boldest of the women came in close enough to snatch at the back of his jacket. He shrugged himself out of it quickly and she threw it away. Two other bacchantes caught it and tore it in two and everyone cried out.

I swore at him, calling him the worst names I could think of.

'Please, Avril.'

'What do you want?' I demanded.

'Claim me.'

A woman stepped in, raking her fingers across his chest before dancing away. Michael winced, but he didn't look at her or try to dodge as his shirt shredded and blood welled up on his skin. 'Oh Christ!' I cried.

'Claim me as your own.' His eyes were bright with pain and urgency. The women were small, but if they attacked en masse they would be overwhelming.

'Go to hell!' The drumbeat throbbed in my skull. I was vaguely aware of the drummers: two naked men who bore the instruments under their arms and hammered upon the rawhide with what looked like leg bones. Their eyes were rolled back so far that only the whites showed. The women stomped and twisted and shook their tits.

'You're the only one who can save me, Avril.'

A bacchante clasped his shoulder and sank her teeth in.

Michael's face twisted. When she danced away, spinning in ecstatic circles, she left a red rose of blood blooming on his shirt. The crowd shrieked with excitement. Two more maenads stepped from the ring simultaneously. They passed on either side of me as if I were invisible and danced up to him, grinding their hips. Their fingernails were ragged and black with dirt. One put her hand to his face. One humped up against his thigh, drawing her claws across the fabric of his trousers.

'Avril!' His eyes blazed, desperate.

I broke. He might have been bluffing, but I couldn't just stand and watch him being torn apart. I stepped in, grabbed the nearest of his assailants by the shoulders and wrenched her bodily to one side. I seized the other by her tangled hair and threw her to the floor. Then I grabbed Michael and because I didn't know what else to do, kissed him hard.

I could taste the bitter old wine on his lips.

The drumbeat stuttered momentarily. I pulled away just long enough to see that the women had fallen still, staring at us, then he answered my kiss with his own and I felt his relief and his hunger and his triumph as he pulled me tight against him. God, his body was hard, and the heat between us was enough to melt my flesh. Our tongues coiled together. I bit at his bottom lip and he caught my hair and pulled back my head, his mouth hot on my throat, all tongue and teeth, while above me through the glass the stars flashed.

'Avril,' he groaned from deep in his chest. His hand was on my arse, crushing me against him, his fingertips biting into my cheek through the soft cloth. The maenads roared and shrieked on every side. I twisted in his grasp, yanking at his shirt, bursting every button as I tore it open; the maenads obliged by ripping it from his back. A perfect hourglass of black hair, broad across his chest and flaring again to a delta at his lower belly, lay close against his skin. I grabbed for his belt buckle and as I ripped it loose the whole garment was snatched down his legs by unseen hands. He wore soft clingy briefs beneath and God knows how he'd managed an erection in the circumstances, but he had, and the cotton was stretched like a tent over his pole. He was so eager that there was already a damp spot marring the fabric. I rubbed my hand up his length and it bucked and pushed against my palm. He caught my face in his hands and kissed my mouth again, sweet and dark like wine, sending my mind into a whirl. The drums roared in my skull. I was so angry with him, and yet so turned on. 'Suck my tits,' I gasped.

He obeyed, bending me back and mouthing at my nipples through the dress, then pulling the shoulder straps down to reveal them. He was a little too impatient with the taut fabric and I heard small fibres tear. He suckled at me again, tugging at my teats with his lips and teeth until my nipples stood out and my tits gleamed all over with his saliva. I arched my back and writhed against him, whimpering. Michael's sapphire eyes were shining as he slid his hands up under my dress. I felt his fingers exploring my bare sex and then, like I was a fruit brought suddenly to ripeness, my juices came seeping out through the split in my flesh. He inhaled sharply, his supporting arm tightening around me. I ran my hands through his hair and saw how my fingers broke through the dark waves. He responded by pushing two fingers into my cunt and, as I gasped at this invasion, my perfume ran down upon his hand.

'You're so wet,' he growled into my flesh. 'Oh, I like that.'

The women had fallen back, licking their lips and beating their hands slowly together.

Gathering all my willpower I put my hands on his shoulders and pushed him down, right over, sprawling on his back and elbows. For just a moment there was a flicker of surprise in his eyes. I noted his hard chest and the way his musculature was brought into definition by his dark hair and the blood trickles from the shallow slices across his breastbone, as I dropped to my knees astride him.

'Like this too?' I asked, drawing up my skirts to my hips, displaying my taut thighs and my downy pussy. We'd collapsed in a patch of wild oregano and the aroma of the crushed leaves rose up around us. The drums pounded through my bones. I gyrated my hips and stroked myself, letting him see what I had to offer, and there was a grin on Michael's face that left no doubt as to his appreciation even if his cotton-sheathed hardness hadn't been stabbing insistently at my backside. Then I slid my fingers between my spread thighs, took the moisture gathering there and painted the gloss of my sexual juices across my lips before leaning in to kiss his, teasing him with stabs of my tongue and nibbling bites. Michael arched beneath me, groaning, lapping at my face until I pulled away again. Then he grabbed my wrist and sucked my fingers, drawing them deep into the hot cavern of his mouth and then biting at their sensitive tips. I ran my fingers over his forehead and eyes, down over his lips and his chest, scribing lines in saliva and sex juices, claiming him for my own just as he'd desired. My fingers found their way right down to the waistband of his briefs.

'Avril . . .'

The maenads had started to sing now: low-pitched interweaving lines of melody that rode the drumbeat. I couldn't resist any more. At last I freed his cock from its flimsy wrappings. Compared to Ash, Michael's member was inelegant and prominently veined, but so solid that I felt a sudden gush of wetness just at the sight. It kicked strongly in my hands. I drew back his foreskin and touched the engorged bulb revealed. 'Yes. Come on,' he urged.

I prevaricated, still revelling in the sight of his body laid out supine beneath me. His body hair blended seamlessly into that at his groin. I'd never actually encountered a man who closely trimmed his pubes before; it made such a deliberate present-ation of his cock that I was awed by his arrogance. Michael ran his hands up my thighs, framing my muff with his fingers before sending his thumbs in, questing for my clit. I twisted in his grasp; this was almost too much. 'Oh God,' I groaned, my breasts shaking as I writhed.

'Come here,' he answered on God's behalf, pulling me down. He gasped my name again and surged beneath me as I sheathed his length deep within.

As I rode him the women closed in, their hands caress-ing my back and thighs as he thrust up from the fertile Mediterranean soil deep into me. I couldn't fend them off and I scarcely cared by now anyway. The primeval melody danced through my blood, tripping along my heartbeat and riding the thrusts of our fused bodies, voices and drums and bodies dissolving into a single rhythmic whole. My last glimpse before I came was of Michael's ecstatic face surrounded by a halo of filthy hands.

We didn't talk as we drove back. I mean, in the circumstances, what was there I could say? In the glow of the dashboard light Michael's face was only dimly visible, but I assumed he wore an expression of satisfaction. His white shirt seemed almost phosphorescent.

He'd had a complete change of clothing and a first-aid kit waiting back at the car. He'd daubed his cuts and bites with antiseptic and they seemed to have stopped bleeding. No marks showed on the new shirt.

As we drew nearer home he broke the silence to enquire, 'Back to your place or to my hotel?'

'You can drop me off at the bottom gate of the Grange.' My voice was raspy with rage.

He didn't reply, but he took the turnings obediently enough and soon drew up outside the locked iron gates, pulling across the road to park in the little lay-by. He didn't switch the engine off. The curve of the wall and the bars of the gate were the only objects visible; beyond the cast of the dipped headlights the night was totally black. I didn't care; I'd far rather walk on my own across the estate grounds than spend any more time in his company.

'You seem angry, Avril,' he said as I grabbed for the handle.

'Angry?' I glared at him as the interior light came on. 'What could I possibly be angry about? Well, I suppose there is the emotional blackmail. That's the sort of thing that might make some people angry.'

His expression was mild. 'You had a choice. I promised you that.'

'Yes.' I slid down onto the road. 'And I should have let them rip you apart.' Then I slammed the door on him. But I was at a disadvantage; the estate gate was over on the driver's side of the vehicle, and the road around here was all loose gravel chippings, so I had to stop and put my shoes back on. By the time I crossed in front of the bonnet he was out too, waiting for me. Half-blinded by the headlights, I nearly walked into him. He caught my wrists. I went rigid.

'Avril.' He was standing very close, so close that our bodies were nearly touching. I could feel the warmth radiating from his torso and smell his skin. He inclined his head so that he could murmur in my ear, and I felt the caress of his breath: 'If you should have, then why didn't you?' His voice was soft and throaty and it made all the hairs stand up on my neck.

I didn't reply. I didn't shrug him off or pull away, though

my muscles were locked with tension. I let him take my ear lobe softly between his teeth and nip at my flesh. I let him put his finger on my cheek and then draw it along my jaw and then down my throat and breastbone, very gently. I couldn't see him at all; the headlights were blinding, but I could feel his excitement. It was like electricity leaping the tiny gap between our bodies. Though I stayed rigid I let him turn me to face the front of the car and then, holding me from behind, put my hands on the warm vibrating hood. He moved slowly, with great deliberation. Giving me time to know exactly what was going on.

See, I had the choice.

'Spread your legs,' he said softly. And I obeyed. I put my ankles apart. My calves were already taut in those unaccustomed high heels. Michael leant into me firmly, spreading my arms wider too, so that I was tilted forwards, my bum sticking out. I could feel the hard bulge of his erection nudging my buttock. Then he stood back, just looking at me. Granting me time to comprehend my surrender. 'Good girl.'

My legs were trembling. My heart was turning somersaults. You bastard, I thought.

Then he lifted my skirt and laid it over my back, exposing my naked sex to the night. I could feel the breeze on my most intimate flesh. I could picture how I must look to him very clearly: all long legs and heart-shaped ass, my face and torso in shadow. Just my pert out-thrust cheeks and the dusky teardrop of the sex that they framed, soft and sweet and defenceless. I wasn't in the most pristine of states given our earlier activities; my placket was still puffy and slick with moisture. But as he stood there examining me I felt a sudden gush of new warmth and I knew that I was creaming up for him all over again. I was glad then that it was dark, because my face was burning with humiliation.

Firmly, Michael cupped my pussy in his hand and squeezed. My juiciness was only too apparent. Still it did not seem to be enough to satisfy him; he spent some time adjusting my stance, spreading my bum cheeks with his hands, running his fingers up the deep cleft and over my buttocks and through the slippery petals of my sex. He stroked the tight iris of my anus until I whimpered, feeling myself yield. There was nothing I could hide from him and, when I heard the sound of his flies being opened, I knew that there was nothing I would not let him have.

I wanted him to fuck me.

I wanted his cock so much that when he put it to the wet lips of my sex and pushed bluntly into me I sobbed in relief. And Michael heard and understood perfectly: 'Yes. There it is. It's OK,' he murmured. 'You're all right now. You've got it.'

I had to bite my lip to hold back the tears of gratitude.

He fucked me very thoroughly, his hands on my hips, his groin slapping into my backside. He made no attempt to touch my clit. This wasn't about making me come, I understood: this was about him taking his pleasure of me and it was about me loving that. It was about restoring the balance of power between us to the place it had been at the start. Where he liked it.

When I heard the sound of a car engine coming towards us I quivered and almost tried to break position. Michael put one hand on the centre of my back and pushed me down firmly against the hot steel. I didn't fight, but sweat broke out all over my skin; inwardly I writhed. What if they recognise us? I howled inwardly. What if they're local to the Grange and they know exactly who we are and they see me being fucked by my boss, fucked from behind, fucked like a cheap slut in my shiny high heels on a public road?

Gradually the sweep of their headlights over the beetling

hedges pushed back the night. They were going to come up on us from behind, I realised. There was no chance they'd miss us behind the bulk of the 4x4. They were going to pin us in their headlights and see exactly what was going on: Deverick's hands biting into my bum as he rammed his meat rhythmically into my willing snatch. I whimpered and thrust back against him; he quickened his pace, his breath coming hard and shallow

They were coming. There they were. The night was split asunder by light and the roar of the motor was suddenly on top of us as they emerged round the bend. As the headlights swept over us I saw for an interminable moment my hands spread wide on the bonnet and my face reflected in our windscreen, eyes wide and mouth slack. The humiliation was too much to bear; I came, crying out. And as my sex clenched and my arse bucked Michael filled me to overflowing.

Then the car had swept past us. For a moment its brake lights glowed a frantic crimson and, in the midst of the pulsations of pleasure and shame, I wondered if it were about to stop and the passengers leap out for a longer look. Then it was gone around another bend, and we were alone again.

Without any hurry Michael withdrew, wiping his turgid prick on my buttocks before tidying himself away. I didn't move. Not until there was a soft flash of light and he leant back over me to show me the screen of his mobile phone and the close-up picture he'd just taken of my rear. It was a small screen but the definition was good; you couldn't miss the glisten on those plumped-up lips which made it clear this anonymous gash had just been well used. 'For personal use,' he said as he flipped my skirt back down over my bum.

Perhaps he meant to be reassuring. There wasn't really anything I could say to him. Dumbly I turned away, my heels wobbly on the granite chippings as I fumbled for the keypad of the electronic lock on the gate. I heard the engine growl as he slipped his car into gear and eased back onto the road, leaving me to open the gate and set off down the drive in nearly complete darkness. I welcomed it. I welcomed the silence. I wanted to be invisible.

Michael's calling card slipped wetly down the inside of my thighs as I walked home.

I didn't think about the possibility of bumping into Bull Peter or someone less friendly on my way. I didn't think anything coherent at all, not until I drew close to the glow of the outside light on my cottage. My door, draped in exuberant wisteria, looked humble and inviting. But when the slab just outside the threshold rocked under my feet I glanced down and saw that on the step lay a bunch of flowers. I picked it up and stared.

What a strange choice of blooms, was my first thought. No roses here; they'd clearly been gathered from round the estate, though even then I wasn't sure how some of them had been found. The showiest were big magenta rhododendron blossoms; they far outshone the purple geraniums and the asters, the yellow loosestrife and the tickseed and the drooping strands of periwinkle. There were foliage plants in the mix too – bindweed and bracken and some twigs of blackthorn bearing unripe sloes – all tied in a bunch by a rope of bramble.

Weird. But beautifully presented. There was a translucent scrap of pink birch bark in the centre which I fished out. *Betula albosinensis*, I thought absently. Ash would have got it from the Winter Copse beyond the pond. Inked onto the bark was the message 'Please forgive me'.

6: The Green Man

'Is Ash around?' I leant on the top of the gate as I called to the young man with the juggling clubs. He'd had his back to me as he threw and my voice startled him, but he caught the clubs neatly as he turned. In his headscarf and waistcoat and cut-off trousers he looked distinctly piratical.

'Ash?' His eyes were wide.

'Can I have a word with him?'

Golden fluff graced his jaw; he was rather cute, I thought. But there was an air of confusion as he considered my words, as if I'd failed to stick to the proper script and he was racking his brains for an improvisation. 'You want to see Ash?'

'Please.'

He regarded me blankly. 'OK. Come on in.'

I climbed the gate and followed him through the teepee village. Several other tree-huggers were about, not doing anything more active than lolling in the sunshine. They looked at me curiously. Pirate Pete led me to a fireplace surrounded by seating logs. There was a billycan of water hanging over the embers, and Ash was sitting on one of the stumps adjusting the can with the blade of a knife. His cool eyes lifted to study me as we approached.

'The girl came,' said my guide, and immediately walked away back towards the gate. I put my hands in my pockets self-consciously. Ash was as inscrutable as ever but his pale gaze made my skin prickle.

'They're not real, are they?' I said, indicating the other activists with a twitch of my head. None of them were within earshot of my words; real or not, it would have been rude.

He raised one eyebrow. 'Real enough to fool the bailiffs. Real enough to kick up a fuss and get this place in the news, if necessary. They've got names, fingerprints, personal histories, family backgrounds – even previous convictions for trespass, some of them. It nearly killed me.'

I blinked. 'What happens if they're arrested?'

'The police find holding cells adrift with dead leaves next morning and the detainees gone. Very embarrassing. And . . . the attention of certain people will be drawn to this place before Deverick is ready for it. Which is why he's staying back for the moment.'

'Right.' So, I told myself, one of them can summon the gods of Ancient Greece and the other can build hippie protesters out of dead twigs. I couldn't complain that the men in my life were dull.

'You got my flowers, then.' Ash's teeth grazed his lower lip.

'Uh-huh.'

'I'm sorry, you know. I acted like a complete tool.'

'I'm the one who came to apologise.' My face was burning all of a sudden, and Ash frowned. 'I had no right to jump you like that. I . . . I just assumed you'd be up for it.' I swallowed hard.

'No. I overreacted. You took me by surprise.' He winced at his own double entendre and we shared a rueful smile. 'Literally.'

I shifted my feet. 'Um, yeah.'

'I think,' said he gently, 'that given the circumstances we need to be a bit more careful.'

My shoulders sagged. Circumstances? He meant the situation with Deverick, did he? Or was he just saying he didn't fancy me? That hurt. 'OK,' I agreed, determined to show no weakness. 'No problem.' I took a deep breath. 'There was one other thing I wanted to talk about.'

He pointed at a log. 'Have a seat. How about a brew?'

There were flecks of wood ash floating in the billycan along with green leaves. 'Herb tea?'

'Just mint.'

'That's OK, I'm fine.' I sat down. 'You asked if I'd help you against Michael. I came to let you know that, yes, I'd be ready for that.'

Ash looked down at his hands as he turned the knife over and over between them, and did not answer for a moment. 'What made you change your mind?'

'Personal reasons.' I couldn't quite keep the bitterness out of my voice and he looked up at me keenly.

'Can I ask what?'

'No, you can't. But if you want to rain on his parade then I'd love to help. One condition, though.'

'And what's that?'

'I want to know what's going on. I don't like blundering about in the dark and I don't like being lied to. I want the real story. I want to see proof of what's at stake. I want to see what it is you're hiding in the wood.'

He gave me a searching look and answered quietly, 'You know there are serious problems with that, Avril. I told you before.'

'Hey, don't mess me about, not if you want my help. This is my employer you're asking me to betray – and I'll bet he's not the forgiving type either. You can get into the wood, can't you? Then logically you can get me in too.'

'Logically, yes.' He looked at the branches overhead. 'You're asking me to take an enormous leap of trust, you know.'

I snorted. 'You? What about me? You think I should get involved in some spat between freaky magic-wielding weirdos without even knowing what it is you're fighting over?'

Ash blinked. 'You have a point. And you're right, there are ways in. But I can't see you agreeing to them.'

'Try me.'

'Well, the defences are keyed to me, to my signature. It's possible to fool them for a while, with the right materials.'

'You mean like some sort of DNA key?'

He shook his head. 'Not DNA. Don't go trying to make magic into science. Its rules and correspondences are those of symbolism and significance and sympathy, not fact. Like affects like. The part is always connected to the whole. There are certain... body products... that are considered intimately connected to a person. You've heard of casting a charm using hair or nail clippings, haven't you?'

'I guess.'

'You can use someone's body signature against them – yet there's no complete DNA in hair or nails. Or in blood.' He tapped the point of his knife against the tip of his finger. 'Blood's the really obvious one, though there are others. I could get you into the wood by painting you all over with my blood.'

'Yuck,' I said with feeling.

'Believe me, I'm not exactly keen on the idea myself.'

'You said there were others?'

'I think you'd like those even less. Semen. Urine. Sweat. Saliva. Does it still sound appealing?'

He was trying to freak me out. I stared at him as the light slowly dawned. 'Is that why you were so worried I wasn't going to swallow? Is that it? You thought I might take your... that I'd go running off to Michael with it?'

Ash looked pained. 'It was a distinct possibility.'

I didn't know whether to laugh or be horrified. 'Christ, that is paranoid.'

'I have to be paranoid.'

My cool deserted me. 'And gross! Oh, yeuch!'

'Gross?' He leant in to push the stub of log further into the fire. 'Yes, we are. Gross matter: dust and slime. A little water, a little wind, the slow burning of chemical fires. That's all, from conception to dissolution, until you take spirit into account. Revile it if you want. Matter is the human condition, and it makes us incredibly vulnerable.'

'OK . . .' I looked into the embers, words failing me for the moment, as I tried to think my way past the tangle of words. 'OK. No blood. We don't do the blood thing. Well, I don't mind . . .' I hesitated. 'I mean, I don't have a problem with other stuff.'

Ash choked back a cough, his eyes flashing above his fist. 'Huh?'

I shrugged. 'You said saliva. I don't have a problem with that. You'd have to . . . What? Lick me?'

His look was very nearly a glare, but his words were soft and carefully considered. 'This isn't some sort of kinky game, Avril.'

'You're the one who brought up the possibility.'

'So I did.'

'Then yeah . . . I'm up for it.'

'Are you sure?'

'Absolutely.'

He looked very wary, but eventually he nodded. 'All right. Follow me.'

Pouring his mint tea into a mug he led me out of the encampment and over a rise into a natural hollow in the ground. All around us were oaks, but the centre of the dell was a clearing and the summer sun lit a carpet of dog's mercury.

'Go down into the centre and wait for me.'

'Where are you going?'

'To get you some of my clothes.' He looked me up and down. 'You need to take your own off, down to your knickers. We need a lot of bare skin for this. Take them off and wait.' I think he must've spotted the sudden doubt on my face, because he added, 'You have to trust me, remember. Like I have to trust you.' He handed me his mug. 'Take that.'

As he slipped away I descended into the hollow and slowly removed my trainers and socks. The leaves felt cool beneath my feet and I shifted into the brightest patch of sun before following suit with trousers and top, which I folded neatly and laid aside. I couldn't stop myself checking my narrow horizons, but there was no sign of anyone watching. A woodpecker rattled in a stag-headed oak. Standing there in sports top and knickers I shifted my shoulders in the sun, getting used to the lick of the breeze on my skin and relaxing just a little. What better way to spend a spare Sunday afternoon, I asked myself flippantly, than getting involved in a little perverse ritual magic?

This wasn't about prurient curiosity though. I knew that really. It wasn't even about taking sides. This was about vengeance on Michael. This was about getting my own back before the humiliation gnawed a hole in my self-confidence that I wouldn't be able to heal.

Ash took his time returning. I wandered around the hollow, careful where I put my bare feet. Without pockets I hardly knew what to do with my hands. God, I thought, as the quiet of the woodland settled upon my mind and my determination started to cool, how the hell had I got myself involved in a situation like this? Michael was using me against Ash and Ash was using me against Michael. Did I care so long as I could make my own decisions? I had to know what this was all about. I had to see for myself before I acted. That meant I had to trust Ash. The question was, did I? I scanned the walls of the hollow yet again. For all that he painted himself as the good guy, he wasn't above a certain ruthlessness. Wolves and wasps were hardly non-lethal weapons. He'd shown no remorse over the man who'd died.

And did Ash trust me? He clearly feared that I was working in Michael's interests, yet he was desperate enough for allies to risk showing me his most closely guarded treasure. Or maybe he was luring me into a position more advantageous for him.

This was a weird, weird situation. Was I getting in too deep?

'Don't turn around.' Ash spoke from behind me and up the slope. I half-turned anyway, automatically, before his words registered and I forced myself to swing back. My hands were clenched as I listened to him descend towards me, and my spine prickled. 'OK?' he asked as he got to within a couple of paces.

'Yeah.'

'Good.' He dropped a bundle on the ground nearby and I couldn't help taking a sideways glance at that. It was a heap of clothes, with at least two pairs of boots included. Was he barefoot himself then? I thought I recognised a khaki shirt he'd been wearing when I saw him by the fire too.

'Right, Avril. You need to take your top off.' His voice was soft.

'Are you starkers?'

'That's the way I usually work – bare to the air and earth.'

'Right. That's …' I didn't know what to say. My heart was racing.

'Believe me, I've taken precautions.' I heard an edge to his voice. 'We're being careful, remember? Now, please, take your top off. You can keep the pants on.'

With an effort of will I obeyed, dropping the Lycra sports top among the dog's mercury. It felt like I'd taken a huge leap into the unknown. My skin went to gooseflesh though the air wasn't cold.

'Where'd you put the tea?'

I pointed to where I'd propped the mug against a root. 'Is it magic then?'

I actually heard him smile. 'No. It's because my mouth's going to get a bit dry. No more questions, please. Don't talk. Try to empty your mind.'

I tried, but there's no way anyone can maintain an empty mind when a naked man steps up behind them. I tried to steel myself for his touch too, but that didn't stop me jumping when he put his hand on the nape of my neck. He waited until my shiver had passed. Then he bent and I felt first his breath warm on my skin and then the soft brush of his lips and then his tongue, hotter and wetter. I forced myself to hold still but in secret I squirmed. My sex felt a rush of heat, my nipples tightened and I could only hope Ash hadn't noticed.

Oh God, this was not playing safe.

Ash worked carefully, touching moisture to my skin and smoothing it over, patch by patch, then writing upon the new vellum with his fingertip letters or symbols that I could not decipher. He did my shoulders and arms first, to the tips of my fingers, which he sucked. The evaporating moisture chilled my skin slightly, raising exquisite shivers. I set my legs and looked into the distance, my head spinning. I could feel his every breath and it was extraordinarily intimate. He wet his hand and passed it over my hair, then worked down the length of my back, his mouth and his fingers warm and strong and gentle, and I felt my body responding to his touch in ways that had nothing to do with magic. Standing there all but nude in broad daylight, exposed to the wood, exposed to the man caressing my body – that was frightening, but the gentle ticklish sensation was nothing but pleasure. Who wouldn't respond to such a feast of sensation? I certainly did. I liked the fear and the trust and the vulnerability. And God knows I liked

Ash – meaning as Michael would say, that yes I wanted to fuck him – for all his mixed signals and his rejection.

Span by span he worked his way down to the base of my spine. My Sunday knickers were wine-coloured and on the skimpy side; carefully he tucked the cloth into the cleft of my arse and kissed his way over first one bum cheek and then the other, taking his time. I swear I felt his teeth and I had to bite my lip.

When he'd finished with my bum he moved round to my right leg, kneeling to anoint the long lines of my thigh and calf. I'd never realised how sensitive the backs of my knees were until then. He lifted my foot behind me to lick the sole and each individual toe, and I had to put my hand on him to keep my balance, leaning my thigh against his bare shoulder. He felt smooth and warm. When I dared to glance down I could see his leg and bare back and the muscles of his upper arm, and I wanted so badly to wrap my fingers in his red-gold dreads and turn to press him against my muff that I nearly cried out. It was wonderful, beautiful torture and it got worse as he turned his attention to the front of my thigh, working his way up till his lips brushed the edge of my panties. The microclimate in there was by this point like that preceding a tropical storm.

I tried to empty my mind but the inrushing tide of sensation filled it to overflowing. Put your hand in my panties, I prayed. Please. Please.

My prayers went, it seemed, unheard. He moved back round behind me and ministered to my other leg with exactly the same thoroughness while I stared desperately at the branches criss-crossed overhead. Then he rested his forehead against my hip. 'Avril . . . I'm sorry.' His voice was husky.

'Sorry?' I didn't know what he meant until he rose to his feet and his erect cock brushed my thigh on the way up. Oh, was he hard.

'It's . . . not supposed to happen like this.' He pulled a face as he took himself in hand. 'I mean, there's no way . . .' He looked tormented. I had to stifle a laugh; this pierced and tattooed eco-terrorist was so much more gentlemanly than Michael Deverick.

'It's OK,' I murmured. I was dizzy with excitement, but I tried to sound calm. 'It won't harm the magic, will it?'

'Um. Technically it'll help.'

'Then that's all right, isn't it?' I slipped my fingers around and past his, circling the hot shaft. The look of relief on his face was as sweet as honey. He put his arm round the small of my back and pulled me closer. There wasn't much room for my hands.

'Want some help?' I whispered.

He bit his lip. 'That's not . . .'

'OK.' I let my head rest against his collarbone as I watched. Very carefully he began to squeeze his cock, pressing it against my skin and rubbing it up and down against the silken skin of my belly. I let him get on with it, leaning into him, giving him the friction and the solidity he needed. But as he pumped I reached down and caressed the silky and nearly hairless balls I remembered so well, my fingers dancing across his skin until he groaned out loud.

Tell me now you don't want me, Ash.

It couldn't last long enough to satisfy me. Sliding his arm tighter around me and burying his face in my hair, Ash clenched to his climax and unloaded in wet gouts upon my skin. His stifled groan sent a quiver through my whole body. Then he pulled away, steadying himself by gripping my hips until he got his breath back.

'Avril . . .' There was an expression on his face like that of a man who's just looked over the edge of a precipice and seen the vista beneath his feet, glorious and utterly terrifying. For a moment he visibly struggled to refocus.

'You OK?' I couldn't keep the wicked grin off my face.

'Uh ... yeah. Now ... shut your eyes for me, Avril.'

I obeyed. As I held my breath he baptised me in kisses, his mouth feather-light on my eyelids, sensual across my nose, my cheekbones, my chin. He traced the whorls of my ears and ran his tongue around my lips. And all the while he did this, he gently caressed his jism into the skin of my stomach and flanks. I tried not to squirm as he smoothed his way from my hips to my armpits and wrote his secret alphabet upon my ticklish flesh. His mouth descended to my throat and I lifted my chin for him like a sacrificial lamb. His hand reached for my breasts.

I can't cope with this, I thought, I can't cope. His hand was writing poetry on the cleft and the swell of my tits. My nipples were standing out hard like acorns and his fingers brushed them with unintentional cruelty. I wanted to cry out but the cries were bottled up in my throat, choking me. I felt like if Ash didn't fuck me then I was going to die, right there in his arms. Then his hand was gone from my breasts and moving back down over my belly. My hips twitched involuntarily. He was pressed up against me, one arm taking my sagging weight, and I was on fire inside. I shut my eyes, water oozing out from under the lashes.

All done then. All but the last few inches. He slid one firm hand over my pubic mound and squeezed me through my soaking panties. I dissolved in fire and water, a liquid ripple of orgasm spilling through my body, and slumped against him.

When the world stopped burning and I opened my eyes he was holding me upright. 'Ah,' I said weakly. 'Have I gone and wrecked it all?'

'I think we'll manage.' His voice was dry. I could only imagine what he was thinking as I covered my burning face with my hands. As he released me I felt bereft. The pulse in my crotch was so strong it actually sent aftershocks through my clit.

'Oh,' I whimpered as my legs wobbled.

'You need to get dressed,' was his next instruction.

We both dressed, he in a new set of clothes and I in the ones he'd been wearing earlier. They weren't really skanky but they did smell of him; I suppose that was the point. The pheromone rush made my head spin. We were both a little self-conscious, I think, as we stood fully clothed once more; the desire we'd both given way to was at such odds to our expressed purpose. The clothes weren't too bad a fit, considering, but his boots were far too big for me. Even with two pairs of his socks on they slopped around on my feet. 'Do I have to?' I asked.

'I don't recommend going barefoot.' He looked me over one last time and nodded. 'You'd better hold my hand.'

I raised my eyebrows.

'Ah.' He actually looked embarrassed. 'Just in case. It's still easy to get lost.'

I couldn't help grinning.

Taking my hand he led me out of the hollow on the far side and we turned uphill. I felt like a little girl being led by her big brother, which tickled me.

Climbing the slope all the time, we went deeper into the wood. The canopy was closing over now that we were well into summer, the leaves turning a darker, more opaque green, and soon we were in deep shade. Underfoot it was damp, every rock surface slippery with moss, and the lack of light ensured that ferns and dead wood were the mainstay of the shrub layer. Ferns and mosses grew overhead too on the twisting oak branches and, in the sunnier patches, tufts of grey-green lichen hung like Hallowe'en cobwebs from the twigs. My oversized boots found it hard going on the broken ground and I was glad of Ash's firm supporting grip. We crossed many tiny gullies where streams hurried down the slope, clambered over fallen trunks and skirted great upthrust boulders which looked ready to slip from their mossy sockets at any moment. Once, from within an earthen burrow scraped beneath the roots of a fallen oak, we caught a sudden sharp reek of pig, but nothing stirred. As we stooped to follow the faint path under a hanging deadfall heavy enough to break every bone in my body, I was suddenly fiercely glad I hadn't come this way on my own. The threats here were unconcealed. I felt like I was here on sufferance.

'What's that?' I asked as we passed one of the bundles of twigs hanging from scarlet thread.

'Rowan.'

'Rowan doesn't work against Michael Deverick. Neither,' I added, 'does holy ground.'

Ash cast me a questioning look.

'I first met him in a churchyard.'

'Necromancy?' he enquired.

'My cousin's wedding.'

'Ah.'

'Necromancy would have been far more entertaining.'

'It has its moments.' Ash didn't give me a chance to follow that one up; he stopped dead and I nearly ran into him. I followed his fixed stare up the slope. The tangle of dead branches and twisted living trunks made it impossible to get a clear view of anything, but I was sure there was movement and a moment later the crunch of breaking twigs confirmed it.

'Wild boar?' I whispered. There are feral boar running loose all round the South of England and they're no joke. The smell from that lair had really worried me.

'No.' Ash stepped off the path, pulling me into the lee of a big rock. He put my back to the stone and stood before me, facing out but shielding me from the woodland beyond. The sensation of his body against mine was almost enough to distract me from whatever our peril was. His back was warm, his outstretched arm rigid, and I could only get a partial glimpse over his shoulder. I took hold of the back of his belt, mostly for security, but my fingers slipped down the inside of his waistband and nested against the small of his back where the skin was satin smooth, and I felt him shiver.

Then something came down off the path, moving ponderously, and passed by heading downhill. I couldn't get a proper look but I heard it: the stertorous breathing, the rumble of its guts, the branches snapping under its mass. It was grey and brown and green, the same colour as the woodland, shaggy with moss and bearing – high on one shoulder – a livid yellow cluster of fungi. And it was about as big as a rhino would be, if a rhino walked on two legs.

I don't know if it saw us. Slowly the noise faded as it disappeared downhill. Ash wiped the sweat off his upper lip.

'What the hell was that?' I breathed.

'A troll.'

I goggled. I hadn't let go of his belt and I had no plan to. 'What's going on?'

'I told you, this is Wildwood. The forest as it once was.' He twisted to face me, and with that movement my hand slid round his waistband to his stomach. The skin there had more heat than at the small of his back. He put his hand over mine and I couldn't tell if he was trying to keep my fingers out or to trap them there. He bit his lip. 'Careful, Avril.'

'Or what?' I said weakly, but I pulled my hand away.

For a moment he seemed to hold on to my fingers. Then he blinked and shook his head. 'Come on. We're nearly at the top.'

As the ground underfoot levelled off the trees changed:

instead of big trunks with wide-spread branches this was scrub oak and birch, their narrow branchless stems tightly packed together, one canopy indistinguishable from the next. The ground between the stems was wetter – in fact standing water in some places, black and evil smelling. Devon, I thought grimly as I put my boot up to the ankle in a pool and felt the cold water rush in over my toes, was a county without the good sense to put its bogs at the bottom of hills where they should be. The water wasn't doing the trees much good either; many were dead, and those gaps in the canopy were the only places where shafts of light found their way in. The ferns, the mosses, every sign of the verdant burgeoning life in the lower reaches of the wood had vanished.

Ash's grip tightened as he led me through the maze, choosing with care which trunks to step between. I clung to him and tried not to get impatient, uncomfortable though it was with my soggy feet and the stagnant tang of the mud and the buzz of insects in my ears. Or at least I thought they were insects until one whipped past my left cheek drawing a stinging razor line of blood and, as I turned, I caught a glimpse, just for a moment, of a face made up of shimmer and shadow: a face so horrible that I yelped in shock and grabbed Ash's wrist with my free hand.

'Ignore them,' he said grimly. But when he saw the scratch on my cheek he pulled me to him and licked it clean. I winced; though his tongue was gentle, the intimate gesture was far too primitive for comfort.

'That isn't healthy,' I protested.

'Healthy?' He laughed suddenly. 'No, you're right. Magic isn't healthy. Not in any way. It's categorically no good for you at all.'

'Why'd you bother then?' I asked as he hauled us off again, splashing and stumbling. 'If it does you no good?'

'Why bother with magic? At bottom it's about not being under anyone or anything's control – freedom of will. It's not about power as most people assume. Actually most people assume that it's about dressing up and getting your rocks off in a magic circle which, I admit, is something that may have influenced my own entry into the art.' He spared me a wry glance over his shoulder. 'But it's really about attaining freedom from coercion of any kind: other people, circumstances, the laws of nature and of physics. And when you've attained all that, when no one and nothing can bring you into submission, then you have true freedom. And then you realise that the coercion that comes from within, from your own pride and ego, your drives and instincts and beliefs and habits, are a thousand times more tyrannical than any outside agent, so you shed those. And then . . .' He stopped, frowning.

'Then?'

'Then you have perfect will. And you are capable of anything, except that you no longer need or desire to do it. In many ways there's no longer any "you". That's the paradox.' He shot me another glance. 'I've never known anyone get that far. But that's the theory. We're here, by the way.'

I followed the direction of his nod and realised that the darkness ahead was not the gloom of infinitely receding woodland but a wall of yew trees, their foliage so dark that it looked black. 'Yews shouldn't grow in boggy conditions,' I said, then felt stupid.

Ash squeezed my hand. 'Come on.'

He led me up to the wall. The yews in fact were rooted on a circular bank. We ducked beneath a branch and crawled into the space they enclosed. The first thing I noticed was that the ground inside was firm and mossy and the yews formed such a dense wall that they cut out all the daylight except for a circular patch over the centre of the clearing. My eyes went up to that, thirsty for a glimpse of the sky. Only then did I look about me for the thing we'd come all this way to see.

It was a tree. The moment my eyes fell upon it I recognised it, because every fibre in my body recoiled like I'd just received an electric shock. It was the stump of a huge oak, covered in green and black mosses, and though it still stood higher than my head there wasn't a leaf on it. Great fissures had rent the bole. The only things holding even the remnant of that trunk together as a whole were two metal bands that circled its girth, and they were green and eaten away with corrosion.

All around the stump fluttered velvety-black butterflies.

'That's it,' I stammered. The hair was crawling on my neck. This tree was unlike anything else I'd seen in my life. It seemed to radiate a palpable energy and I could feel it throbbing at my fingertips and catching at my pulse. It wasn't exactly unpleasant, but it was incredibly intrusive. I shut my eyes, then squealed and jumped back. Ash grabbed me before I could crash into a yew branch. 'You can see it with your eyes shut!' I cried.

'Oh, I know.'

You could see it *better* with your eyes shut. Eyes open, it looked like an impressive woodland relic. Eyes shut and it stood out like a great black tower, outlined by crawling red worms of fire which reached out to the yews all around and into the ground and towards us. And the biggest cleft in the trunk glowed with a ruddy light like a furnace. It sent all my smug everyday conceptions into a flat spin. 'Is it . . . evil?'

The question seemed to puzzle Ash. 'Evil? I don't think so. How does it make you feel?'

I decided to keep my eyes open, because that was far less disconcerting. For a moment I just stood, sensing that energy surging in my belly. 'Horny,' I admitted.

'Hah. You try living in the wood.'

'But not just horny the usual way.' I gulped. 'It's like ... like everything outside me suddenly matters. The trees, the rocks, the clouds up there. It all turns me on. They're filled with excitement. It's like I'm seeing them for the first time. It's like I could shag them all. The whole world.' I didn't dare look at Ash as I spoke.

'Oh yes.'

'What the hell is this thing?'

He was reluctant to answer. 'Is it what you were expecting?'

I shook my head.

'Go on: what did you picture while you were walking?'

'I don't know – a grave, I guess. Or, like, a sword in a stone. Something like that.'

Ash laughed, and I risked a glance at him. 'Not bad, Avril. Not bad at all, though the sword got thrown into Dozmary Pool up on Bodmin Moor.'

'So what is it?'

'This? This is Merlin.'

I scrunched up my face. 'Merlin? Like in King Arthur?'

'That's the one.'

The only picture I could associate with the words was of a cartoon wizard bumbling about with an owl. I think the stump was affecting my ability to think straight. 'He's a tree?'

'He was imprisoned in a tree – an oak – in the centre of one of the last patches of primary forest in Britain. Just too late to stop him doing something unspeakable and just in time to stop him doing something that would change the course of history.'

'I don't get it.' I couldn't remember what had happened to Merlin in the stories; he'd just faded out of the Arthur legend, as far as I could recall.

Ash took a deeper breath. 'You have to go back to the fifth century when it all happened. The Roman Legions had pulled out of Britain leaving it at the mercy of Saxon invaders, who were pushing westwards from their footholds in the east of the country. The British – partly Romanised, partly Christian-ised – were desperately struggling to hang on to their land and the civilisation they believed was their birthright. Arthur was a military commander who for some time managed to hold the whole sorry mess together, but he was only a diversion as far as Merlin was concerned, a holding pattern. Merlin had a plan. Merlin was going to make himself into an unstoppable weapon and he was going to wipe the Saxons off the face of the earth.'

'How?'

'He was a great magus and, unlike Arthur, no Christian. He worked a binding ritual. He travelled about the country and every time he found a source of power – a god, a gateway, a sacred item – then he would . . . consume it. He ate Cernunnos and Epona, Coventina and Andraste and Cocidius and Nodens of the Silver Hand. He ate twelve of the Thirteen Treasures of Britain, and nearly destroyed Arthur's fighting force, sending them searching after the last, the Cauldron of Annwn, though they found it too late. He ate the little deities of springs and mountains and trees, the water hags and the apple men, the sea serpents and the dragons and the sprig-gans, the merrows and the barghests, the trows and the ettins. Even the slivers of foreign gods brought in by soldiers and traders of the Empire – Isis and Mithras and Hercules and Serapis – adding all their power to his. He closed the gates of stone and of water to the underworld. It took him years, but he assumed all the power in the land into himself. He drained it dry of puissance and meaning. Well, the odd hob in a farm-yard barn slipped beneath his notice, and he never lifted the water horse from Loch Ness, and some of the fay realms were sealed from him in time, as news of his quest spread. But very few escaped. He emptied the land and left only legends and tattered fragments in his wake.'

'So what went wrong?'

'Ah. The Saxons caught wind of his plan, and they petitioned a sorceress called Nimue to stop him. She was a Briton, but she betrayed her people. She seduced Merlin, and she learnt his magic off him, and she imprisoned him in an oak by his own spells.' Ash waved a hand at the stump. 'This is the Green Man.'

I flashed on sweet-smelling shops filled with crystals and peculiar pottery. 'I thought that that was an old pagan god?'

'New Age wishful thinking, Avril. The Green Man's a Christian symbol. You see his effigy carved into the roof bosses of medieval churches: a man trapped in agony, branches bursting from his mouth and his flesh, a perpetual warning to those who'd dabble in devilish magics and give in to feminine wiles.'

'Oh, that's right, blame the woman.' What was Ash's problem with sex?

'Who said anything about blame?' He looked at me wonderingly and I felt a tinge of shame. 'I doubt either of us would be standing here if it weren't for Saxon bloodlines. And besides, whatever her motives, Nimue was right. No one man should have the sort of power Merlin had, under any circumstances and no matter what the cause. Can you imagine what sort of world he'd have wrought, given the time to do it?'

I stared into the depths of the rotting trunk. 'Poor bastard.'

'What?'

'Fifteen hundred years in that ... torture cell. Don't you feel sorry for him? He was only trying to save his people.'

Ash frowned. 'Sorry for him? No. Any part of Merlin that was human will be long dead by now. And he was only half-human to start with; they say his father was an incubus.'

'Was he?'

'A god, more likely. But believe me, whatever's left in that oak now is not human. And it is extremely dangerous.'

I eyed the two corroded bronze bands dubiously. 'Well, I hope you don't mind me saying, but it doesn't look very well contained.'

'Yes.' Ash shook his head. 'That's the long-term problem. The binding is weakening. It's not going to last forever. If I had the time or the energy I'd be panicking about that right now.'

'But what happens if it breaks? Will he get out?'

'Lots of things will, I imagine. All the gods and beasts and horrors he's got locked away inside, they'll all come out to play again. Remember that the land in Merlin's time was a source of terror. Every lake and marsh and forest was a potential threat whose inhabitants had to be propitiated with sacrifices made in gold and in blood. But no one knows how to do that any more – and your average teenaged mother, living in a hutch on a sink estate and breeding like a rabbit while doped up on soap operas and antidepressants, isn't going to have a clue what to do when Raw-Head-and-Bloody-Bones comes crawling out from under the bed to attack her offspring.'

'Hey,' I said pointedly, 'my sister was a teenaged mum.'

He blinked hard. 'No offence. I'm sure she's a wonderful human being. It's just that she wouldn't really cope with the return of the Old Ways. Shorthand is, if he gets out lots of people will die. That's just for starters. I can't even guess what will happen after that.'

'So you need to rebind Merlin.'

'Nice idea. I'll add it to my "To Do" list.'

I might have got mad at him except that I saw his shoulders sag and suddenly in those sharp hazel eyes I caught a glimpse of a bleakness that made me hurt in sympathy. 'Are you all right?'

'Yes. I'm fine.' He passed his hand over his face. 'I'm just tired, Avril. I feel . . . trapped, like Merlin there. The fact is, I don't know at the moment how to rebind him. I don't even know how to stop Deverick, which is the immediate problem. It was pure luck that I got here ahead of him.' He gestured around us. 'Nimue never intended anyone to know what she'd done. It was only by chance that a passing knight stumbled on Merlin's oak and heard his story. He could still speak then, apparently. Anyway, when Arthur died at Camlann there was a single knight – Bedwyr – who survived the battle. He threw the sword away. Then he chose to spend the rest of his days here guarding the wood and the wizard, the last link to his king. His children and descendants followed in the task, and somewhere along the line they put an enchantment about the estate so that if you knew what it was you were looking for you couldn't find it. Magi have searched for years for this spot, and no one's ever succeeded.'

'Until you.'

'I wasn't looking for it. I knew Deverick was searching for something in the West Country, but not what it was. I was just nosing about. And . . . I worked out what sort of area it was likely to be in. You see, Merlin's started to leak.'

'Leak . . . ?'

'That's why the fay are all over this place. I think the odd thing has slipped out occasionally over the centuries, but about sixty years ago the binding really weakened and things began to leak out much faster. The brood of Bastet were among the first: big cats not real enough to be caught but real enough to leave tracks and kill sheep. There've been lights in the sky since the 50s – not visitors from other earths but from this one; hinky-punks are what they used to call them. Morgawr shows up off the Cornish coast. Mowing devils infest the ripening wheat. Even some of the old gods, in a small way, are making a return to the nation's consciousness. We're becoming heathen again.' He laughed and shook his head. 'So much strangeness, and so much of it concentrated in the West Country. I put in a lot of legwork and, eventually, I stumbled across this place. I wasn't exactly welcomed, and in the circumstances you can see why. The sitting guardian was an old man by then, but he had a son in Canada and a younger daughter with two grandchildren in Nantes. The succession should have been assured.'

'It wasn't, I assume.' From nowhere a shiver worked its way up my back and I felt my nipples tighten in sympathy.

'John Kester died of a heart attack. Inside two months his son developed a brain tumour. The three in France were wiped out by a motor accident on the way to the airport, having received the diagnosis.'

I ran my tongue across my lips. 'You think Michael Deverick did it?'

'I think those sorts of accidents are relatively easy to arrange once you know your target. The line of Bedwyr was broken, leaving no heir. The estate was intended, in case of such an emergency, to pass into the hands of a trust, but what with multiple death duties...' He shrugged. 'There was considerable legal wrangling and large sums of money changed hands, I understand. But he got it in the end. And with the breaking of the family line the magical misdirection failed. I was the only one who knew. I had to do something to stop him.'

I looked at my feet. The suggestion that Michael had been directly responsible for several murders wasn't comfortable. 'What will he do if he gets hold of it, then?'

'Its power is tied to the earth and the natural cycles. If Deverick could bind Merlin to his will and command that power, then he'd be able to, oh, I don't know... find new oil caches underground, make changes to the weather, raise up new diseases. I'm no economist, but I know scarcity raises prices. Wipe out the coffee harvest in Ethiopia, say, and you push up profits elsewhere. He could do that. He could do pretty much anything he wanted. He could hold nations to ransom.'

'Christ.' I shifted uneasily in my too-big clothes. 'So what can I do?'

'Well. You can keep your eyes open for me. If Deverick's going to bind Merlin he'll need two things. He's got them already, I suspect. The first is a receptacle of some sort; he's not going to leave the source of his power in the middle of some wet woodland in the arse-end of England. He'll want to move Merlin. So he needs an object to carry him in. The second thing he must have is Merlin's grimoire.'

'That's a spell book, isn't it?'

'Yes. All the legends say that Nimue bound Merlin with his own spells. If that was the case then why couldn't he break himself free? No. She used his grimoire and the spells within as a focus, as the key that locks the chains. The binding can't be broken without it, so if Deverick's making a move then he must have the book – somewhere. I don't know where. It's not the sort of thing he'd trust to a bank vault, in fact I think he'd keep it by him nearly all the time. If I could get the book away from him –' his eyes glinted '– it would change everything.'

I shook my head. 'He'll have made a copy,' I pointed out. 'He'll have had it scanned and backed up electronically.'

'No. No, he won't. Magic is the occult art, Avril. It has to be hidden. Things gain their power by having intense private meaning, by being unique and personal. It's … It's like sex. What you do in private is wonderful; do it in front of twenty people and it becomes undignified and open to criticism; do it in front of a TV audience and you're a laughing stock. The very worst thing you can do with a real grimoire is turn it into a mass-market paperback with a pentacle on the cover – all the power is lost. Deverick won't have scanned or copied

Merlin's book; he won't even have had it translated. He'll have to work from the original.'

I bit my lip and rubbed a hand up and down my arm. The outwash of power was making a pulse throb in my inner thigh. 'What does it look like?'

'It'll be in Latin I'd imagine, given its age, and written on parchment not paper. It might be a scroll, or a scroll cut down to look like a book.'

'Well, I could look for it,' I said doubtfully. 'It's not easy to get into the house, if that's what you're thinking – that's builders only and they're there right till nightfall every day.'

'Well, don't try it after dark. Deverick's put a guardian on the Grange.'

'A guardian?'

'It looks like a big black dog . . . at least from a distance. Stay away.'

'Fine. I'll just keep my eyes open.' Maybe one of the builders would give me a tour of the Grange, I speculated.

'If you do see it, don't touch it. Deverick will have put wards on the book. It could be lethal.'

I bristled at his overprotectiveness. 'OK, OK. Do you want my help or not?'

Ash put his hands on my shoulders. 'I want it very much.' His words hung in the air for a moment as his gaze held mine. Then, reluctantly, he pulled away. 'Um. I think we should leave.'

'Yeah.' We were supposed to be being careful, after all. I didn't feel like being careful. There was a wet, squirming itch between my legs that was nearly unbearable. That was the advantage of being a man, I thought, as Ash led me by the hand back under the yew barrier and into the bog: once you'd come once or twice your mind could be free to concentrate on other things. I wasn't so easily satiated, myself. As we descended through the wood I wasn't thinking about Merlin or magi or the ancient powers of the landscape; all that was just too much to deal with at the moment. My mind was filled with other things that seemed far more important: the crook of an ancient oak limb, the green firework of an unfurling fern, the dance of golden dust motes in a shaft of light, the strength I could feel in Ash's arm even when it was relaxed. I felt charged with purpose, though I couldn't have named what that purpose was; perhaps being part of all this was sufficient. No longer did I feel like an interloper in the wood. I felt like my life was a part of its life, and all around me and through me the great green tide of nature tumbled and surged.

When the stag stepped out of a thicket and stood before us, head lifted proudly, I wasn't afraid despite its size. Its seven-tined antlers trailed scraps of velvet it was burnishing off in readiness for the rut, and its shaggy neck was as red as autumn bracken. Some trick of the light as it was sieved through the leaves made those antlers look golden. I slipped my hand from Ash's and stepped forwards towards the deer, fingers outstretched. It wasn't afraid. It dipped its nose, nostrils flaring as it sought my scent, then suddenly – and yet without a suggestion of haste – turned away and with a kick of its elegant legs was out of sight among a stand of saplings.

Ash caught me from behind. 'Careful,' he murmured, as if I were drunk. I could hardly complain; I did feel tipsy. It hadn't occurred to me that the stag might have been a threat.

Ash led me back to the hollow where I collected my small bundle of clothes and changed into my own trainers. Then he walked me home, steering me cautiously through the orchard and keeping a sharp lookout. I had rather more idea now of what he had to fear away from the shelter of the wood and told him, 'It's all right: Michael's not on site today. He got called away suddenly at the start of the week.' My words sounded sour even to me, but Ash visibly relaxed.

It didn't deter him from his mission of taking me back to my cottage. He didn't ask permission this time to enter, either, steering me right through to the bathroom. My blood leapt hopefully as he reached over and turned on the shower. 'You've got to wash, Avril.'

'Join me?' I suggested, easing off my shoes.

Ash smiled and shook his head. 'Come on.'

I stuck my lower lip out and backed up against the door frame, refusing to oblige. I didn't care if he was all spent up for the day; we could work something out. I wanted to feel his hands on me and his skin against mine; there was an ache like hunger in my belly. 'Make me,' I said with a quick grin.

With a sigh, Ash began to slip the shirt buttons down my breastbone. I didn't resist. I bit my lip and watched his face, fascinated, as he undressed me. He was acting like a responsible bloke looking after a very drunk female friend, all detached self-deprecating concern. I liked that, in a strange way. I liked the gentleness of his hands too, and the way he took his time. I liked the way he had to keep reminding himself to look away from my breasts as he slid the shirt off my shoulders and undid the webbing belt cinched at my waist. I liked the line of his lips and the fall of his hair against his cheek and the glint of the rings in the red gold of his eyebrow. I wanted so much to touch him. But I didn't dare, not after the mess I'd made of things last time.

Out of nowhere, tears welled up in my eyes. Christ, I am drunk, I thought in amazement.

The bathroom was starting to fill with steam.

Softly he let the trousers slip down from my hips and pool on my feet. There I was standing against the door frame, naked but for my wine-red knickers, yet it was the desire in my expression that was the most shamelessly naked thing about me. His fingertips brushed my hip and he caught his breath. As he lifted his eyes to mine I saw my longing mirrored there, its edge as keen and cruel as my own.

'Avril.' The word was inaudible; I saw only the movement of his lips.

Oh God – I was on the verge of begging, and I mustn't do that. 'I dream about you,' I told him, and something flickered in the depths of his eyes.

'Do you?'

'Do dreams matter?'

'They can do. Depends what you dream.'

'I dream we're in the wood. It's always the wood. Why's that?'

'"I have come to the borders of sleep",' he quoted softly, taking me by surprise. '"The unfathomable deep / Forest where all must lose / Their way, however straight / Or winding, soon or late; / They can not choose".'

I shivered. 'That's good. Who wrote it?'

'A poet . . . A friend of mine.'

'I like it, but it's a bit creepy. Like the wood.'

'Ah.'

'Do you feel that way too?'

'About the poem?'

'About the wood.'

'Ah. Yes, of course. It's too old for humans to be comfortable there.'

'There are places where we should be uncomfortable though,' I answered. 'Like the deep ocean. The forests. Under the stars. There are places we shouldn't feel safe. It's good for us.'

Ash nodded, seriously. His fingers curled around the curve of my bare shoulder. 'Are your dreams comfortable?' he asked.

I moistened my lips. 'I dream that we're together.'

He exhaled. 'Am I . . . fucking with you?' His words filled me with cream.

'Yes.'

'In the wood.'

'Yes.'

He nodded, slowly. 'Sounds like a good dream.'

'It is. It could almost be real.'

He looked at me silently, need balanced against doubt in his face.

'I wake up wet,' I whispered, touching his lips with my fingertips. He didn't flinch away. 'Nearly every night. Wanting you to finish what you've started. Wanting it to be real.'

He seemed to have stopped blinking. 'And what . . . What do we do? In your dreams?' We were so close, standing there in the bathroom doorway, that the softest murmur could be heard even over the hiss of the shower. I held his eyes with mine, light-headed with the unexpected power.

'Sometimes we run through the woods and you throw me down on the moss and take me from behind. Sometimes you put me up against a trunk and do me rough and hard. Sometimes you just lick my tits and I go crazy. I have,' I explained, and I was nearly trembling, 'very sensitive nipples, you see.'

He looked down. 'In your dream, this is?' His fingers brushed my right nipple. I felt the tiny shock through my whole breast, and the tip tightened.

'No,' I whispered. 'Really.' I bit my lip as his thumb circled the rosy halo and it responded eagerly. 'The first time you sucked my boobs . . . Ah . . .'

'I remember.'

'Christ. You nearly made me come there and then.'

Ash seemed almost hypnotised, though his hand kept moving. 'I didn't know –' he flicked the flushing nipple, watching it swell and harden '– you're that sensitive.' His eyes rose to meet mine. 'Soft or hard?'

'Ah. Oh.' My mouth had become disconnected from my brain

'Both. In turn. You know.' My eyes were pleading. 'Quite hard, near the end.'

His fingers closed slowly in a pinch. 'Like this?' he asked as lightning flashed behind my eyes and my clit spasmed. I made an inarticulate noise halfway between a yelp and a moan. 'Oh. I see.' He seemed quietly pleased by his first experiment and pulled on the nipple, distorting the swell of my breast.

My eyes rolled. 'Ah!' Without thinking I reached out to press my hand to his chest; he reacted instantly, letting go of my hot little stud and grabbing my wrists in both hands.

'Oh no,' he said, shoving both wrists to the small of my back. His body was suddenly pressed up against mine. Then, still gripping my crossed wrists in one hand, he cupped the breast he'd just abandoned and squeezed the soft flesh. My torment turned instantly to delight as he stooped to seize the nipple in his mouth. I arched my back, pushing up against his parted lips and sliding tongue, and my body writhed though I made no real attempt to pull out of my bondage. He ate at me hungrily, suckling one breast and then the other, and it was nothing like the gentle attention he'd paid with his mouth when he'd anointed me for going into the wood; it was slow but deliberately provocative, like a challenge. My nipples rose to meet that challenge, hard and plump as cherries even under the threatening nip of his teeth.

But it was all awkward work for a man of his height and he changed his mind suddenly, bending to catch my thighs in both hands and lift me bodily from the floor. I gasped, taken by surprise; it was easy to underestimate the strength behind Ash's long lines. Suddenly I was taller than him, looking down on his face levelled with my breasts. He jammed me back against the door frame, pinning me with his body, and I wrapped my thighs about his chest. My mons was mashed against his hard torso. His forearms were taking the weight of my thighs and the tips of his fingers stroked the gusset of my panties, making me quiver. He wasn't in any position to secure my hands now and he didn't try to shake me off as I buried my hands in his long hair and urged his mouth back to my wet, erect nipples.

It was the most tender, exquisite, terrible mauling he gave me; gentle one moment, wickedly stinging the next. He wasn't impatient like so many men; he seemed to revel in it. I watched his mouth tugging my tit, his eyes closed, his throat working in smooth swallows. I ran my hands over his face and he cast me a burning glance from those hazel eyes that took my breath away.

'Oh, you're beautiful,' he whispered, his mouth moving from my right to left breast. Somehow, when he said it I believed it.

He set my breasts on fire with those hot kisses and, as if my body was touchpaper, the flames ran through my shoulders and down my spine and set off an explosion in my sex. I came without bothering to restrain my screams, reckless with delight. Delight that my tits were getting eaten. Delight that at last Ash was making love to me.

As I gasped my way through the sweaty afterwash of orgasm he buried his face between my glossy, reddened orbs, his breath hot and harsh on my breastbone. Then he let me slide back down to earth, holding me against the door frame until he could be sure my feet were firmly on the floor. 'I dream too,' he whispered in my ear.

I drew back to stare at him, breathless and not sure what he meant. 'The same ... ?'

'The same dreams. It's the Wildwood, Avril; nothing but the wood at work in us. It's not just a place on the map, you know.'

I shook my head. I could feel him pressed up against me, feel the solid curve of his cock.

'Have a shower, Avril. Wash it off. Get some sleep.' Ash let me go.

'You're going to leave me like this?' I whimpered.

Ash bit his lip. 'Yes.'

How? I wanted to yell, but what I asked was 'Why?'

He touched my face, his eyes dark with desire. I held my breath. Then he blinked, and in that tiny movement he somehow withdrew from me, mastering himself. 'Avril, you need to choose which side you're on.'

My heart fell with a crash. 'I thought I had done.'

'It takes more than just words or dreams. Now, come on. In the shower.' Carefully he drew me to the bath and put me under the warm water, knickers and all. All the fight had gone out of me. I accepted the bar of soap he put into my hands. He watched to make sure that the water had touched every inch of my skin and soaked my hair before quietly turning away and, gathering up his fallen clothes, leaving.

7: Hunting with the Hounds

Michael didn't show up on site for weeks. We were working on the lawn below the house when he did. Some previous landowner had had a summerhouse built right around the trunk of a big walnut and the wooden structure had collapsed in on itself over the last few years. I'd spotted dieback in the tree's crown and I wanted to inspect the bole for signs of honey fungus, so the three of us were dismantling the rotted timber of the Edwardian pergola and throwing it into a skip. Tony looked up as he swung a beam onto his shoulder, grunted and indicated with a jerk of his head that I needed to take a look behind me.

Michael Deverick stood on the gravel path, hands in his trouser pockets, with the rueful air of someone who couldn't walk across the lawn without ruining his £300 shoes.

'Wants a word, you reckon?' said Tony.

'Tosser,' said Owen amiably under his breath. They had nothing personal against Deverick, who almost never interfered with our work, but Owen regarded anyone who wore a suit for anything but funerals and weddings as a waste of space.

'OK.' I shucked off my heavy leather gloves and dropped them on a clear patch of grass before strolling over, taking enough time to compose my features. Over the days I'd had time to shuffle through every emotion and attitude in the deck as far as Michael was concerned. I thought I was ready to face him again. That didn't prevent the sudden lurch in my belly as he turned that smile of his on me.

'Avril. Seeing you makes the journey down here worthwhile.'

I said nothing, but raised an eyebrow cynically. I was tanned a deep copper brown by the summer but right now I was gleaming with exertion and flecks of paint and smears of mildew were gummed to my skin. I put one hand on my hip and stood with my back straight, refusing to yield under his alarmingly intimate gaze. At least we were out of earshot of the others, so long as we kept our voices down.

'You must know what it's like to be at the beck and call of your work,' he added.

'I certainly do.'

'I didn't mean to be away so long. I've missed you. Believe me. I've had to resort with distressing frequency to your fine, fine photo.'

I couldn't match his gaze steadily, no matter how hard I tried. 'Right,' I muttered. I'd not demanded that he delete the damn thing as I figured there was no point. He was perfectly capable of either refusing point-blank or of acquiescing only to lie.

'It's extraordinary, you know. Nobody would believe me. To find, in the middle of bloody nowhere, such a treasure: the most perfect, beautiful arse on the planet.'

Every card in the deck, and the one I turned up right now was desire. I was hot and melting already. It was his gently teasing voice and the tilt of his lips and those goddamn eyes. I had no resistance. It was so unfair.

'You've no idea, Avril, how tempted I've been to boast about you. To let others see what I've seen.'

'I bet.'

He grinned. 'I've thought about taking you up to London for a board meeting. Just to see you walk the length of a long table on hands and knees, arse up, and get a standing ovation from every man in the room.'

'What do you want?' I growled.

'Ah.' His eyes widened. 'Where to start? I did want to discuss the state of the rhododendron shrubbery. Perhaps we should stroll down there for a look.'

I cast a despairing glance around. 'It rained last night,' I managed to say. 'Your suit will be ruined.'

'Well, there's always my office.'

My heart gave a bump. 'OK.' I looked over to Tony and Owen and waved. 'Just carry on,' I called. 'I'll be back in a minute.'

'I'm hoping to take a bit longer than that,' said Michael softly.

We entered the Grange by the front door because all the others were still boarded over. I noticed then for the first time how strong the door was, reinforced with sheet steel. This place was going to be security conscious. I looked around curiously because this was my first glimpse inside. The lobby wasn't even half-finished, with swathes of wiring hanging down from junction boxes and plank walkways angled across a tiled floor that was partly laid. From other rooms came the sound of power saws and radios and men talking. The place smelt of wet plaster and fresh wood. But right in the middle of the atrium, bolted into place under the soaring glass roof, was a plinth bearing a huge sculpture of twisted brass rods and polished stones. It was still wrapped in a shredded plastic shroud.

'What's that?' I asked, going over for a closer look.

'It's called *Love is the Law III*. Do you like it?'

'It's a cage,' I said flatly. Ash would want to know about this.

Michael moved to my side, smiling faintly. 'You think so? Who should I put in it then? You perhaps?' I shot him a warning look and he seemed amused. 'When the conference centre is opened I intend to throw a very select party, and they'll certainly expect some special entertainment. I might even invite Ash, if he's still alive.' He laughed out loud then at my expression. 'What do you take me for, Avril? You think I'm going to have him bumped off?'

'What *are* you going to do?'

He snorted. 'I can afford to be patient a little longer. It's going to be a cold winter, they're predicting. I think I'll block off the exits from Grange Wood. If I can't get in, it's only fair that he can't get out. I'll be interested to see how long Ash can hold out when he's reduced to eating squirrels.'

Given that Ash was one of the most contrary, bloody-minded, stubborn men I'd ever met, I suspected that he'd hold out until he was a frozen corpse. I didn't say that, only: 'You can't block the bridle path. It's a public right of way.'

'I'm in negotiations with the county council right now. The outcome is likely to be most advantageous for them.' He looked back up at the sculpture. 'Would you like to attend my party, Avril? I could put you in here and everyone who came in that door would be able to see you. A black leather outfit, I think – that would suit you best, and people like the traditional look. Lots of straps. High heels. Your hands tied together behind your back.' He laid a light hand on the small of my back. 'Your beautiful behind quite bare, of course; that would be the point. And your lovely tits out. A leather collar round your throat, I think. Would that please you?'

I couldn't answer. Michael lowered his lips to my ear and carried on in a low, pleasantly conversational tone.

'You'd be the first thing everyone saw as they entered. Your ankles, chained apart. Your long leather-clad legs. Your beautiful pert bum, the cheeks a little spread. Your bound wrists. They'd be able to walk right round the cage and look up at you, at your face, at your tits, at your arse. Up between your thighs, at your soft, sweet little pussy. And later in the evening . . . I think there'd have to be a chain attached to your collar, a long chain leading down through the floor of the cage . . . and I'd come and shorten it. About halfway at first, so that you had to bend over with your bum out and open and your pussy properly displayed. Then I'd shorten it all the way, until you were forced to kneel on the floor with your face pressed down and your hands up behind your back and your thighs apart, so everyone could see your open crack and your tight freckle and your juicy slit. I'd have to put bodyguards round you, wouldn't I? Or else people would put their hands through the bars and touch you. Touch your softness and your wetness. But maybe you'd like that. Would you prefer I gave the bodyguards the night off so that everyone can finger you?'

He touched the nape of my neck gently and I nearly went into convulsions. I don't think it would have made any difference if there had been builders in the room at the time, I'd have still melted helplessly under his words.

'Later on, I'd let you out of the cage. Then I'd take the end of the chain in my hand and lead you about the room. Every time I stopped to talk to someone you'd have to kneel at my feet with your thighs spread. You wouldn't be able to speak even if you dared, because in your mouth you'd be carrying a leather riding crop. Your hands would still be tied behind your back, you see. Every time someone got too excited by your beautiful body and they came up and grabbed your bum cheeks and tried to stick their pricks into your deep, willing pussy – because you'd be so turned on by now that you'd be ready for any prick at all, wouldn't you? – I'd have to take the riding crop and thrash them off you. And if you were naughty . . . if you tried to lure men to ride you by wiggling that bum around and spreading your thighs . . . then I might have to use that whip on you. On your beautiful arse. Until you squealed. And if you were very very bad and you enjoyed that, then I think I'd have to put you over my knee and spank your bum cheeks and finger your pussy in front of everyone until you came.'

My body – the strong body I had so much confidence in, so much trust – was betraying me utterly. My panties were awash for a man who wanted to degrade me in public. Swallowing, I mustered the remnants of my defiance and whispered, 'You go to the wrong kind of parties.'

'Oh, I prefer to host that kind of party. It's amazing the hold you have over people if you can give them exactly what they really want.'

'Cabinet ministers?' I sneered.

'I wasn't just referring to the guests, Avril.' I fell silent and he chuckled, his lips so close to my ear that I could hear the sound of his tongue against his teeth. 'You have an exhibitionist streak a mile wide, you know? You're fascinating. You crave respect, yet you want to be the most monumental slut.'

Is it my fault the two aren't compatible? I wanted to ask, but at that moment a builder came in through the front door with a wheelbarrow of dry mortar mix and Michael withdrew smoothly from my side.

'Shall we go upstairs?' He indicated a sweeping curve of wooden risers that seemed to emerge from the wall with no support of any other kind. 'Straight through at the top to my office.' It was obvious that he wanted to follow me up for the sake of the view of my backside. And it was too late to begrudge him that.

His office was a bit of a shock. I pushed through two layers of thick plastic sheeting, expecting to find a room which was still under construction like all the others. Instead, aside from the plastic covering the thick cream carpet pile and a certain disarray upon the furniture surfaces as if he were still unpacking, the room was finished. A huge desk dominated the far end, beneath an oriel window. Into one wall was set the biggest television screen I'd ever seen. There were quite a lot of electronic toys around in fact, but also lots of books, some of them stacked on sofas and armchairs.

'What do you think?' Michael came up behind me and put his hands on my shoulders, smoothing off the flecks of paint.

'You moved in already?'

'Almost. The important parts of the build were given priority and this ... is important.' He traced the edge of my top, sliding a finger beneath the fabric.

I shrugged off his hands and stepped away. This was my first, perhaps my only chance. My gaze swept the room. 'It's ... sort of old-fashioned.'

'Old-fashioned?'

The books I glanced at first were all on business theory. 'Well ... classical.' I indicated the niches down the walls. In each was a white statue, almost life-sized, on a plinth. 'You surprise me. I thought you'd be a chrome and gadgets sort of guy. Not ... Roman gods.'

'Greek.'

'Whatever.' I was deliberately taunting him, playing for time as I looked around. 'Dead ones, anyway.'

'Dead?' He'd folded his arms across his chest. 'These aren't dead, Avril. The Church of Rome did its best, but even it only managed to hold them quiet for a millennium. The gods are with us, Avril. Here.' He tapped his temple. 'Every god, in every one of us. We are the gods.'

That was weird enough to get my attention. Crossing the plastic floor he clasped my arms and turned me to face a niche.

'There.' The statue was of a young woman wearing a short dress, with a bow and a greyhound. 'That's you – Artemis. The goddess of the deep woods, rejecting the rule and the love of men. Protector of wild nature. Fiercely independent. Prickly.

Quick to anger. An object of worship from afar.' He pulled me sideways to the next niche; the statue it contained was of a much more voluptuous woman, quite naked. Her blank eyes stared straight into mine. 'This is you too – Aphrodite Porne. Goddess of primal, conscienceless, self-centred desire. The slut, burning to be filled.' He kissed the side of my neck and I instinctively moved to accommodate him. He bit my ear softly. 'The source and the object of all lust.'

I pulled slowly to the next niche along. It was Poseidon, bearded and wreathed in waves. 'What about him? Is he in me too?'

'Yes, if you know where to find him. Mysterious, sullen, vengeful. A rememberer of wrongs. Like our friend Ash.'

'Ash? How did you wrong him?' Given what I knew of both men, I guessed the obvious: 'Was it over a woman?'

'Not quite. All the gods are within us, Avril, in all their majesty and power. If you know how to invoke them properly you can do anything: call down the lightning, raise the seas, look into the future, speak to the dead, bend the wills of others...'

'Michael,' I had to ask, 'was it you who made Simon fall?'

'Simon?'

'At the wedding. The bloke on the fountain with me.'

He turned me to face him. 'What if it was me?'

'I...' I didn't know what to say. I'd never really believed that Michael was guilty of the sheer nastiness Ash accused him of. But his eyes were remorseless.

'What if it wasn't me – what if it was you?'

'Me?' It came out as a squeak. 'It wasn't me!'

'Why not? Because you couldn't or because you wouldn't?'

'Both.' I shook my head. 'It's just sick. You don't do that to people. Even if I knew how – which I don't.'

'Don't you?' Mischief glinted in his eyes. 'Yet every day you invoke the god of the gardens. I've seen you at work. I've felt his presence. I'm not the only one either; I'll bet your men feel him moving on them every damn day.'

'What are you talking about? The garden god? I don't even know who that is!'

Michael hooked his hand down the front of my jeans and pulled me up against him. At the same time he took my hand and pressed it firmly to his crotch and, through the fabric, I felt the thick cylinder of his erection stir. 'There. He's called Priapus. And you're calling him into manifestation right now.'

'Oh . . .' I couldn't help squeezing him through his trousers; my hand seemed to have a will of its own. I couldn't help measuring his length with my fingers from scrotal sac to solid tip. He was very very erect. Knotting his fingers under my shoulder straps he pulled my lips to his. Then without warning we were pressed up against each other, writhing, fumbling frantically at each other's clothing. I got his belt open and his fly down and his shirt pulled free; Michael got my top off over my head. We kissed like we were trying to eat one another alive. He scored my shoulder and sides with his nails and I dug my fingertips into his chest so hard I'd be leaving bruises. I bit his throat and nipped at his collarbone and he got his own back by grabbing my crotch so hard that I saw stars and cried out loud. Pushing me back across the room he pinned me against his desk and shoved me down on its wooden surface, clearing papers and clocks and pen trays with a sweep of his arm. The shock of collision with the mahogany top knocked the wind out of me for a second, and he took the chance to pull open my jeans, his hands working with savage efficiency, and yank them down, panties and all, to bare me. He couldn't get my trousers down past my boots, which were too big, so he left them there, manacling my ankles. I bent my legs at the knee, spreading them wide.

'Slut,' he whispered, bending forwards to capture a nipple between his teeth and worry my tit from side to side like a dog shaking a toy. I writhed and thrashed beneath him, stifling my own cries with the heels of my hands. Then I knotted my fingers in the curls at the back of his head and pulled on his scalp so hard that he was wrenched from his quarry and tears ran from his blazing blue eyes.

'Fuck me,' I moaned, half commanding, half pleading.

Michael put his hands to my wrists and broke my grasp with cruel pressure, forcing my hands to the desktop next to my head. As he leant in on me his hard crotch, barely restrained by his dishevelled clothes, ground against my open sex. I writhed against his bulge and he tutted. 'Fuck you?' he asked. 'You're saying you want me now?'

'Yes,' I whimpered.

'You've changed your tune, Avril. What happened to "I'm not your type"?'

'You are my type.'

'And what type's that?'

'Strong,' I confessed. 'Powerful. With a great big fucking hard cock.'

He hitched a half-grin. 'Flattery will get you everywhere, Avril. But . . . I find you a little too glib. I think I'll have to do something about that.' He ground his pelvis in a circular motion that made my pulse race. 'In the meantime . . .'

'Please!'

'Since you ask nicely.' Releasing me, he stood back so that he could extract his cock from his trousers, cradling it proudly in both hands. 'Is this what you want?' He pumped it lovingly, enjoying my frustration. His prick was dark with engorged blood and its blunt head gleamed wetly.

'Uh-huh.' I nodded, unable to trust my voice.

'I thought so.' He came down back over me to insert his

member, sliding it into my tight passage. I arched and gasped as he stretched me wide. 'You are a slut. Luckily, that's my type,' he whispered, sheathing it all the way with merciless, shuddering thrusts.

Then he fucked me, one elbow on the table, one hand on my knee holding me wide open. Unable to get a purchase with my legs I was nearly helpless, at his mercy for my own pleasure. I'd expected something quick and rough, and I wasn't wrong. What took me by surprise was how turned on I was by the discomfort of the hard desk and by the frustration of being unable to get my legs apart and round him. I writhed and jiggled like I'd never done before. As Michael quickened to his climax he ran the hand up from my knee to my crotch, his thumb stirring my clit to make sure I came. I was already teetering on the edge of that roller-coaster drop into orgasm, but I wasn't going to protest.

'Look at you,' he grunted. 'Legs wide open for the boss. Getting fucked by your boss. You're shameless. You shameless slut.' As I came down the plunge and went into roll after pulsing roll he thrust savagely, and then just as I was flattening out into exhaustion he whipped his cock out and came up the length of my body, ragged pennants of jism unfurling to splatter on my breasts and belly.

Over his groan I heard the sound of feet on the stairs.

'Christ!' My heart turned over and went crashing down into my stomach.

Michael's eyes flashed open. 'Shush.'

'Mr Deverick?' The voice was close, just outside the plastic barriers. A man's voice.

'Come on in.'

I felt a bolt of sheer panic go through me. I made one attempt to sit up but Michael put his hand on my breastbone and shoved me down flat on the table. His face was like a mask. 'Stay down.'

I heard the rustle of the plastic curtain. 'Mr Deverick . . .' Then: 'Jesus Christ . . .' I knew exactly what the builder could see: his employer stood between a pair of splayed knees. 'Sorry, mate, I'll come back later.'

'No. Stay.' Michael adjusted himself and pulled up his fly, his eyes never letting mine go. 'I've just finished.' He stepped away, leaving me totally exposed. 'Take a look if you like.'

'Fucking hell,' said the other man in awe.

It was my worst nightmare. The blackest fear I could think of. I put my forearm over my eyes in a pathetic attempt to hide. I tried to close my knees but Michael slapped them casually apart and I had no strength to resist; it was far too late. My breasts heaved as the air fled in and out of my lungs.

'Like her, Mr Dunster?' Michael walked smartly around the desk to my head.

'Fuck yes.' Dunster sounded more stunned than anything. I was glad I couldn't picture his face. I was glad it was no one I knew.

'She's beautiful, isn't she? She's a goddess, Mr Dunster, laid upon the sacrificial altar for you. Come a bit closer if you like.'

His feet squeaked on the plastic floor covering. He swore again under his breath, keeping it going like a mantra.

'You should worship her, Mr Dunster. Get your face down in there, why don't you, and pay her beauty homage?'

'Ah . . . Not where you've just dipped your wick.'

For a moment Michael's voice went very cold. 'I came on her tits, you'll find. Get on your knees. Taste her.'

I felt callused hands on my thighs and I cried out in protest. At once Michael clapped his hand to my throat, drawing my head back. His touch was gentle but firm. He laid my arm aside and suddenly I was looking into his face upside down over mine, his blue eyes like salvation. 'Shush,' he chided me tenderly.

Then he looked back down the length of my body. 'What are you waiting for? Make her come and I'll give you a fifty per cent bonus this month.'

Dunster's warm head pushed between the tops of my thighs and pressed against my slit. One arm circled my left thigh; I imagined that the other hand was going to his own crotch. I began to sob, the tears spilling out to run down to my ears, and Michael brushed the tears away with his thumbs and bent to brush his lips against mine, gently. 'It's OK,' he whispered.

Then Dunster's mouth found my wetness and my openness, his tongue delving the length of my split sex, and all the world went away. That world with all its fears and betrayals was too much for me to deal with. All that I knew was his mouth and Michael's, one on either end of my body, and Michael's hand sliding down to caress my breasts and throat. He'd never been so gentle with me. His lips were soft like the touch of petals. Dunster was serious, revelling in his task, his sucking mouth and lapping tongue dedicated. My body was still charged with desire from our frantic quickie and he found his job neither difficult nor unpleasant. His slurping was enthusiastic as he drank my juices. And I was nothing, less than no one, just lips and tits and cunt, no Avril attached to them any more.

Then I was all cunt.

I came, sobbing, three times, one after another like a cascade of fireworks. The last time Dunster was almost gobbling, and when he'd done he mashed his face, groaning, into my flesh and jerked off. I felt it splash up my leg.

'Tissue,' said Michael after a decent interval, opening a drawer and throwing him a pack. As Dunster fumbled about, Michael stroked the hair back from my forehead and kissed me again. His eyes were shining.

I didn't sit up. I felt so drained that I was sure I could simply cease breathing and die there. I closed my eyes.

'Well, um, Mr Deverick...'

'You wanted something when you came up here?'

For a few minutes they discussed the complications of customised soffits that were not up to the order specifications over the length of my supine body as if I were not there at all. I felt as if I'd ceased to exist. My breathing slowed until I must have looked as if I were asleep. I had nothing to fear about the future; the worst had already happened.

'I'll, er, keep this one under my hat, shall I?' Dunster still sounded dazed. 'Jesus.'

'It would probably be for the best.'

I heard him leave. I opened my eyes and looked up at the man who'd betrayed me. He was watching the plastic curtains with an intense expression. Then I heard it: a cry, a thump that became a long tumbling series of blows – the sound of a man falling headlong down a staircase. From the floor below came shouts of enquiry and alarm.

'A stroke,' said Michael quietly. 'Extensive damage to the speech areas of the brain. Even when he recovers he'll never speak or write an intelligible word again.' He slid his hands under my shoulders and sat me up on the desk. 'Your need for discretion,' he murmured into my ear, 'has cost me a foreman.'

I think that was the moment I first realised what Michael was doing to me. I should have been horrified and disgusted and frightened. And I did feel all those things, faintly. But overriding every other emotion at that moment was a great wave of relief.

Michael wasn't the only fleeting visitor to the estate. One warm August night I was just getting ready for bed when I heard something scraping and rattling outside my living-room window. Grasping a torch and a steel felling lever I went out to investigate. The torch, chosen in case it turned out to be Bull Peter again, wasn't necessary for the sake of illumination as there was a full moon that night. As I peered around the corner I saw it was a big deer rattling its antlers against my plastic water butt and, as it lifted its head, catching my scent, I saw the gleam of the moonlight on those tines and realised it was my stag from the wood, the one with the golden antlers.

I caught my breath. He stared at me, breathing hard. There were big dark patches on his flanks and I caught a rank whiff of his sweat. Then, still staring, he put out a foreleg and pawed deliberately at the empty bucket under the stopcock of the barrel, knocking it sideways.

'You want some water?' I whispered, not wanting to frighten him. The stag retreated a few paces. His ribs were heaving. 'OK then. Hold on.' Carefully I sidled along the wall to the bucket, watching him intently just as he watched me. Filling it from the butt, I swung it out into the open and backed off. The stag came forwards without hesitation, moving with all the unearthly grace of his species, and dipped his muzzle in the water, drinking greedily. Not for long though – all at once there came from over the other side of the house a sound of horns and the faint but insistent clamour of a pack of hounds. The stag's head swung up and a rasping bellow came from his throat. Springing away, he disappeared into the moonlit shimmer.

'Shit,' said I. Then, 'No you bloody don't!' and I ran back into the house, scrabbling through the junk on the kitchen table to get my phone. It's complete bollocks, the myth that every country person is in favour of blood sports, and stag hunting in particular turns my stomach. It used to be very big up on the Devon moors; more recently it had become illegal. But when I grabbed the phone two things made me hesitate: I'd never heard of hunting with hounds at night, and it had suddenly occurred to me that if there was a clandestine hunt taking place on the estate then my employer could well be its instigator.

As I stood there the belling of the hounds grew much louder, sweeping about the house, and with it came the thunder of hooves. Dark forms flickered past the windows. Stuffing my phone into my pocket I ran out of the house, not even stopping to shut the door. The noise and the figures of the rearmost riders were dwindling in the direction of the old orchard. I picked up my heels and ran after them.

I'd slowed to a jog by the time I got to the apple trees and caught up with them though, partly because of the distance run and partly through caution. I could see a crowd of riders dressed in tweeds and dark-green hunting jackets milling about in a cluster. They were brandishing, of all things, the phosphorescent glow sticks that you get at concerts and parties, and the sickly greenish light lit them with an eerie glow. Moving as quietly as I could I hurried from tree to tree, closing in until I could see what was happening. Then I crouched in the long grass behind an apple bole, my heart hammering.

The stag had come to halt and was standing at bay, pivoting in circles with his head down and antlers presented menacingly. All around him was a ring of hounds – great big ones with coarse white hair and reddish ears – who were snarling and yammering and looking for their chance, but every time one closed enough to snap at the stag's haunches he would whirl faster than I'd have thought possible and slash at it, sending the dog tumbling back into the pack. The men and women on horseback were cheering and urging their animals on.

I pulled out my phone with sweating hands, scanning the faces in the mob for Michael Deverick's. It was hard to get a good look at them, though the general impression was of exactly the sort of country set I would have expected. Then one of the men, a big, paunchy, florid-faced one in a black jacket and cream jodhpurs, rode at the hounds, flailing with his whip and shouting. The dogs scattered, moving off from the stag as he cantered in a circle around the beast, which took a moment to stand and draw breath. The crowd, like the animals, fell gradually silent. When the master of hounds had done his job he walked his horse away and dismounted.

Then another of the riders took centre stage, as she slipped down from her big bay and walked straight towards the stag. I stared at her, disbelieving. She'd been riding side-saddle and a split skirt draped her jodhpured legs. She was a tall blonde valkyrie of a woman, made taller by one of those weird little top hats with a veil you only ever see on riding displays. She approached the stag very calmly. He was obviously exhausted; he stood with legs splayed and trembling, his eyes rolling. But he didn't retreat from her or offer her any threat. He stood stock-still as she reached out a hand, laying it between his horns. Gently she stroked his forehead. He shuddered all over, steam rising from his wet flanks. Softly she murmured to him and ran her hands all over his head, stroking his cheeks and ears and muzzle until he had relaxed, resting his head against her, his great golden antlers almost grazing her face. Still murmuring in soothing tones, she turned her head and nodded at the circle. The master of hounds stepped forwards again drawing something from his boot, but the stag, if he noticed him at all, did not react. He didn't try to flee even when the man thrust the big knife through his neck and cut down, severing in a single stroke veins, arteries and windpipe.

My stomach spasmed. The blood was bright, bright red and it went all over the woman's legs and boots, steaming. She didn't recoil. She held the stag's head steady as his legs gave way and he folded to the floor. The dogs, as one, began to howl and the hunters joined in with horns and wild cheers.

I was beside myself with disgust and rage. I began to stab at the keys on my phone with numb fingers, no longer caring that these were exactly the sort of people that a country constabulary would recoil from arresting. Then, without warning, arms went round me from behind, a hand went over my mouth and I was hauled to my feet and spun around. I nearly slithered out of my skin with shock. Whoever it was put his back to the tree trunk, holding me to his chest, facing out into the dark. For a moment we struggled, silently. He wasn't trying to hurt me, but I was under no such restriction; I bit the hand clamped over my mouth and when he let go I jabbed my elbow into his ribs, hearing him gasp. His grip slackened enough for me to drop out of it, my T-shirt rucking up to my armpits. But he grabbed me again before I was out of arm's reach and slammed me back against him, and this time he had the sense to get his hand under my chin, pinning my head back again his shoulder. 'Avril!' a voice hissed in my ear.

It took the smell of wood smoke to tell me who it was. I'd seen little of Ash over the last few weeks; he seemed to have retreated deeper into the wood and was never at the camp when I called by. He did come around to my cottage every two or three evenings, usually very late when he felt safer leaving the wood, but he never stayed for more than a few minutes' conversation. I had no idea whether he was looking out for me or checking up on me. 'Shit!' I rasped. 'You've got to stop doing that!'

'Would you rather it was someone else?' His voice was tight with rage; I'd hurt him quite a bit I think. 'Put the phone away for fuck's sake!'

'No! Piss off!' I lifted it to my face, trying to make out the keys. 'They cut his throat, Ash!' I was trying to whisper, but it was coming out as a croak and only the horrible whooping of the hunters was masking my noise. 'They hunted him down and cut his throat.'

'I know.' His lips were so close to my ear that I felt his voice as a vibration. 'Avril. Avril, listen to me. It's not real. The stag is not a real stag. The hunters are not real people. You can't interfere.'

For a moment I set my shoulders, resisting him. My eyes were wide, but the apple trees blurred and slipped as they filled with tears of frustration. 'Not real?'

'It's Lughnasadh, Avril. This night the Summer King dies, like he does every year. He's not really a stag, and they're not really hunters. They're not even human, that's just the way they look tonight. It's their idea of a joke. It's just a glamour.'

'Not human?' It had suddenly dawned upon me that even when I could hear the voices of the hunters I couldn't make out any of the words.

'They're fay. And they don't tolerate humans interfering with their rites, Avril. This is really dangerous here. We shouldn't even be watching.' Ash let go of my throat and wrapped his hand around mine, mashing all the phone keys at once.

'Fay?' I only seemed capable of the dumbest questions. 'How do you know?' That was another, and I didn't wait for Ash to answer it. 'The stag . . . ?'

'Dies tonight. He'll reappear on May Day, having been reborn at midwinter.' As I went limp Ash's grip slackened very slightly, but he didn't withdraw his arms. 'Just leave them to it. There's nothing to be done.'

I fell quiet for a moment, then asked, 'What's that noise?' The voices had dropped to a murmur, accompanied by an indefinable snuffling.

'Ah... They're eating him. He's the first fruits of the harvest.'

'Oh Jesus.' I thought of lions I'd seen on wildlife programmes – their faces, as they lifted them from the belly of a felled wildebeest, painted red.

'Are you OK now?'

I didn't answer. I'd become acutely aware that my T-shirt was still rucked up exposing my tits, and Ash's forearm was tight beneath them. His body was hard against my back and both of us were still breathing raggedly. I had no idea how to define our relationship, or whether we could be said to have a relationship at all. All I knew as I stood pinned against him was that there was nothing in the least platonic about it. Our rough struggle had left my blood burning.

With a hiss of pain or annoyance Ash let go of my phone and turned his palm up so that he could examine the damage I'd done to him. The bloody imprint of my teeth was clearly visible on the heel of his hand. Without a word I reached out and took the injured hand and placed it onto my right breast. I heard his breath catch. For a moment he cupped the orb, weighing its softness. His skin was a little cooler than mine and my nipple tightened dramatically against his palm and, as he felt this, he groaned out loud. Then he took his hand away and turned me to shove my back against the tree.

'Avril, you...'

I dropped my phone, my heart beating wildly. He pressed into me hard, his hands heavy on my upper arms, his face hovering over mine until I could taste the promise of his kiss.

Then yet again that kiss was withheld, and I wanted to scream.

'Please,' I whispered, but in response Ash put his fingers over my mouth, very carefully this time. In this light it was impossible to read his distraught expression properly; it might have been rage or despair or desire, or all three. All I knew for sure was the hardness of his body as it pinned mine to the tree, so I parted my legs and he thrust one thigh between mine, pressing against my pubic mound. I couldn't speak with my lips held captive like that, so I pushed my tongue out and ran it across his fingers, feeling the calluses. Ash's eyes widened. He pushed harder against my pelvis, grinding his thigh from side to side, and I saw stars. I moaned against his hand.

My own hands were still free. I slid them down his torso to his groin where our legs meshed and my right found the bulge of his cock, ascertaining at once that beneath those baggy army trousers he wasn't wearing any underpants. I stroked him through the thick soft fabric and he clenched his teeth and retaliated, flexing the hard muscles of his thigh. I squirmed upon him and worked my mouth open and licked his fingers until he shook.

'Oh Christ,' he groaned. 'Give me a chance will you, Avril.'

No. No chance.

'I can't . . .' he said, but what he couldn't do was buried by what he could do, what he had to do, right now, with desire riding him like a demon. As my palm eagerly massaged the hidden length of his cock he bit my ear and surged against me.

I hadn't tried this in years, this frantic, furtive groping through layers of clothing that could not come off, not since I was a teenager. When it was no longer possible for him to deny that this was what was happening, that he was humping me on his leg and I was masturbating him through his trousers, then he let his hand fall from my mouth to my breast, capturing my nipple and rolling it cruelly. Cheek to cheek we panted, biting back our groans for fear of being overheard. He kissed my neck and licked at my throat. I felt like I was so open he'd be able to get his knee inside me, but as he started to come it was his hand he forced between his leg and my crotch, rubbing me off with his strong fingers as he went over the edge, so that I fell into the void after him.

It seemed to me as I came that in the gloom beyond his shoulder there were wicked red eyes leering at us and the glint of moonlight on needle teeth, but I was so surrendered to my pleasure that I paid them no mind.

When we came to we were alone. I mean, really alone. The sounds of the sacrificial rite behind me had gone. For a moment I rested against Ash's shoulder, my lips on his throat, feeling his pulse. He stroked the hair back behind my ears, wordless. When he released me and stumbled away into the night I turned to look, but there was no sign of any slaughter having taken place under the old orchard trees, not even a circle of trampled grass. Not even the remains of a dead stag. Where the body had lain was only a spill of early windfall apples, already rotting and perfuming the air with the reek of cider.

8: Running with the Fox

Michael rang from the motorway. 'I'll be with you in about an hour or so. Wear something nice, and a coat – we'll go to the coast.'

Even the sound of his voice made a shiver run down my spine and my nipples tighten. I stared out at the night pressing in on the window. I'd dreaded and raged against and fantasised about this call. I'd lain awake in the dark begging for it. Now my throat seemed filled with glue. 'I've got a better idea. Let's try something really unusual.'

'Such as?'

'How about you come over and spend the night?' There was no chance of Ash showing up this evening; I hadn't seen him since the Lughnasadh hunt, having pissed him off once too often, perhaps. Both men had marooned me, and only throwing myself into my work had kept me from going crazy with frustration. 'No tricks, no audience, no nasty surprises.' No one ending up in the hospital emergency ward, I might have added, but my mind refused to bring Mr Dunster into focus. 'Just sex, all night.'

'Sounds kinky. I'll try anything once.' But when he arrived on my doorstep an hour later there was a woman with him. At least, it looked like a woman at first.

'Who's this?' I demanded.

Michael leant casually against the door so that she could slip past me. She was short – only up to my shoulder – and slight, with long black hair that looked like it had just come

out of a swimming pool. 'This is . . . Jenny. You can call her that.'
He stalked into the hallway. 'I found her by the pond.'

'What are you playing at?' I was wearing only a light silk
dressing gown, which I wrapped around me self-consciously
as I followed them back into the house. 'Did you hear a single
bloody word I said?'

'Oh, I heard.' Michael stood in the middle of my living-room
floor. Jenny had climbed onto one end of the sofa and was
watching us from under hooded lids. She was wearing a dark-
green slip dress which seemed to be wringing wet even though
I was certain it wasn't raining out there. 'You are extremely
clear about the things you want. You'd like nice, fun, discreet
sex with someone you like, who'll treat you with respect and
never *ever* interfere with the rest of your life. Am I right?'

My jaw sagged. 'So why do you go out of your way to do
just the opposite?'

Michael gave an infuriating smirk. 'Do I?'

'You know you do.'

'And do you enjoy that bad sex with me?'

'I hate it.' My voice didn't carry much conviction.

'So much that you can't wait for the next time. So much that
you'd get on your hands and knees and beg for it if I told you
to. You're wet right now, and all I've done is walk into the
house.' He walked around me, hands in his pockets, and I
couldn't refute him. 'What does that tell you about what you
really want, Avril? What does that tell you about your rules?'

I didn't answer. I couldn't look him in the eye.

'The barriers are all in your mind, Avril. You don't need to
fear what's on the other side. All I'm doing is helping you break
out.'

'Right. They used to have a word for that.'

'Liberation?'

'Corruption.'

He laughed appreciatively. 'Look on the bright side: a few centuries back I'd have been getting you to kiss a goat's arse.'

No shit, I thought. And I've bet you've done it. 'I'd rather stick to my comfort zone,' I said through gritted teeth. 'It's comfortable. That's the point.'

'Wouldn't it be better if you felt at home anywhere in the world? If you could do anything, without guilt or fear?'

'That's your ambition. I've got no plans to be a magus.'

'Really?' He tilted his head. 'That's a pity, because I think you've got a certain potential.'

'Bet you say that to all the girls.'

He laughed. I didn't look at him. Jenny had my attention, and he noticed that. 'Ever fucked a woman?' he asked.

'That's not a woman.' She had a delicate face that ran down to incongruously pouty lips, but the bone structure was just wrong. And her eyes, as green as pondweed, had no pupils; they were completely green. As she lifted her head they reflected the light like the eyes of cats in the dark. I suppressed a shiver. 'That one's not human.'

'Close enough for our purposes. Just don't let her kiss your face. Have you ever been into girls, Avril?' He put his hand on the nape of my neck and drew his fingers all the way down my back.

'Not really.'

'Not ... "really"?' He clasped my bum cheek, squeezing gently. His touch seemed to draw the words from me.

'There was this sleepover once. Like a pyjama party ... without any pyjamas.' It had been on Emma's hen night, but I wasn't telling him that. I'd split up from Scott the week before it took place. 'We were really drunk; I don't remember much. Four of us. There was a lot of giggling.'

'That's ... a picture to savour. Well, tonight ... the three of us. I want to remember every detail. I want to see you go down on her, Avril. Then I want to see the two of you sucking my cock and licking my cum off each other's tits.'

'No way.'

'Is that jealousy speaking?'

I shook my head. 'She creeps me out.' Jenny smiled slowly, lips zipped together. 'Get her out of here. I don't want her in my house.'

Michael shrugged and stepped away. 'Your call. We can go. You always have a choice, Avril.'

I swallowed hard, flustered. When Michael glanced back over his shoulder there was a wicked glint in his eye.

'No?'

Bastard. He knew he had me. He knew that I was a junkie for the touch and the taste and the smell of him, for the way he looked at me, for the way he disturbed me. My mutinous glare meant so little compared to the weakness in my legs and the wetness between them. My whole body betrayed me. I couldn't keep up the defiance and its collapse must have been visible in my expression though I said nothing, could say nothing. Michael was suddenly standing before me. With complete assurance, eyes locked on mine, he reached through the slit in my robe, cupping my mons and delving between my legs. I went rigid. He withdrew without hurry, holding his hand up for inspection and raising an eyebrow.

'Hmm?' His fingertips were slippery with my moisture.

I shook my head, wide eyed. Jenny smirked.

'Taste it,' he ordered, showing his teeth. 'Taste it and tell me you're not ready for me.' He touched my lips. I licked my own sharp juices from his fingers, reluctantly at first, then thoroughly. My cheeks were aflame with shame. 'I think that's the answer I've been waiting for.' Still watching me with that appraising glint, Michael removed his jacket and hung it over the back of a chair. Then he sat down on the sofa, at the far end from Jenny, and patted his thigh. 'Come on,' he said softly.

Eyes downcast I came to him and sat in his lap. Every step was a surrender. I knew he could feel my trembling, the last vestiges of my inner struggle. He traced his fingers across the silk on my back and bum. His legs were hard slabs of muscle beneath mine. He kissed my cheek but when I turned my mouth to his, my lips already parted and yearning, he withheld his kiss, his smile lazily triumphant.

My dressing gown wouldn't stay together over my bare legs.

Without fuss and without force he took my wrists round to the small of my back and held them there, crossed over. He only used one of his hands to pin me, and I could have broken the grip easily, but the very fact that he had to put so little physical effort into mastering me was a glaring demonstration of my submission. The posture thrust my tits out. With his free hand Michael played with the open edge of my garment, the line where silk and skin met. Then he glanced over at Jenny. Uncoiling from her perch on the far arm, she came down the sofa towards us. I could see now that her slick, plastic-looking dress was made of pondweed, the kind that lies in sheets under the surface. With her nails she slit it down the front and discarded it, revealing a palely green body beneath, slight except for the swell of her rounded breasts. Her nipples were large and, like her nails, black; they seemed to stare at me. I looked away, unable to meet their unblinking gaze.

'You're mine,' said Michael in my ear. 'I'm going to let her play with you, because that's my pleasure, but you belong to me. Your body knows that already, doesn't it?'

I whimpered under my breath. I had no idea whether he was staking his claim or simply enjoying the game, but he was right about my body; it was wholehearted in its treacherous collaboration. As Michael drew back one side of my gown to expose my right breast my nipple stood proud to meet him, not so large or dark as Jenny's but hard anyway, a sweet brown nut.

'Well. Somebody's feeling ... perky.' He took it between thumb and finger, twisting it gently, enough to make me quiver. 'I get so carried away in admiring your arse, Avril, that I forget how much you love having your juicy little tits touched. You'd do almost anything to have me do this.' He pinched me softly and I cried out in pleasure and humiliation, causing him to smile. 'Oh, that's good, is it?'

'Yes,' I said in the smallest of voices.

'You want more?' He used his nails on my skin and I heaved against him. He kept playing as Jenny crawled up over me, and he traced the whorls of my ear with his tongue, his breath hot. His touch was nearly enough to distract me from her green, inhuman eyes. She made a low, musical, almost birdlike sound in her throat as she leant in to kiss me. Then Michael withdrew the tip of his tongue from my ear and turned to her. 'No,' he said in a voice like lead.

A sneer flickered over Jenny's face, but she lowered her head obediently to my breasts. She stroked one hand down my breastbone, easing the other panel of silk aside, tugging the knot of the belt loose so that I was bared all the way down to my pubic triangle. Then she returned her attention to my tits, stroking the sensitive inner surfaces until I shut my eyes, my skin singing. Her fingers were cold. Her mouth was too, inside and out, as it closed around my left nipple. I gasped out loud.

'Oh yes,' said Michael. 'You are particularly sensitive there, aren't you?' His own excitement was more than evident, pushing up against me through his trousers. 'Isn't she good?'

She was incredible. Her tongue was cold, and she used it to stir my nerve endings to tingling frenzy. She licked and she lapped and she suckled and she nibbled. I looked down at her only once and saw that there was sand in her hair, a fine drift of golden mica glittering in the natural parting lines. Then I had to shut my eyes again as the tide of sensation dragged me under and I gave way to the tormenting pleasure of her lips, arching my back to push more of my breasts into her delicious mouth. Michael abandoned that territory to his ally and slipped his hand between my thighs instead. I writhed and let my legs part, unresisting as he explored me thoroughly.

'Oh, Avril, your pot is quite full, isn't it? Full of your warm fuck honey. You are a wicked girl, getting so turned on. You know I'm a bad, bad man but you're sat in my lap wriggling like a whore and you're letting a strange girl suck your beautiful tits. You're in slut heaven, you wicked girl.'

From the other side Jenny's slim hand joined his between my thighs, slipping inside me. His hand was warm, hers was not; the contrast of sensations nearly turned me inside out. His imprisoned erection ground up against me. His other hand tightened on my wrists until the fingers bit into my flesh.

'You're so turned on you're about to come,' he whispered. 'I haven't even got my cock in you, and you're coming already.'

And I was.

'Yes,' he murmured as I writhed upon him, 'that's it. That's it.'

I came back downstairs in the middle of the night and stumbled into the kitchen for a glass of orange juice. I'd managed about an hour's sleep so far in the cramped confines of a bed most certainly not built for three and I was dehydrated and aching. When I did sleep my dreams had been so vivid that they'd woken me. I stood in the kitchen doorway sipping my drink and looking at our clothes, scattered where they'd been shed. My head felt like it was stuffed with memories and dream images too crowded together to take flight, stamping and clambering over one another and clamouring for release. I tried to ignore them; I knew it would be days before I could sort out my feelings. Michael had managed everything on his wish list and a few more. If I gave myself space the visual memory that pushed to the forefront now was of reaching up with my tongue to lick his dangling balls as he fucked Jenny, who was lying face down on me with her own face buried busily between my legs. The mental picture of his shaft sinking into her tight sex, inches from my nose, threatened to send my head into meltdown and I shook myself. It was too early to deal with any of this, and would have to wait for the morning. I needed to sleep on it.

I'd come so often that I'd lost count.

Michael had fallen asleep between the two of us, eventually. Jenny ... Well, I had no idea if things like her did sleep, but she'd certainly curled up into a ball and given the impression of it. She'd never uttered a word all evening, though she mewed like a cat when she reached orgasm. I ran my hand up my arm, shivering. She was cold as porcelain inside and out, that one, and had no sexual aroma at all. It was like fucking with a plastic toy. I wondered what would happen if you cut her: Was there any blood in those veins?

I was heading back to the stairs when I saw Michael's jacket on the back of a dining chair. That was when the notion first entered my head. Ash had said the grimoire would be kept close by him all the time and I was certain that if this was the case it wouldn't be in a hotel room or even the Grange; Michael simply wasn't here that often. He was always on the move. That left his car. I went and nudged the jacket, and felt through the fabric the hard cluster of a set of keys.

Despite the orange juice my mouth dried up again. I squinted up the stairs, alert for any movement or sound, but the tick of the landing clock was the only noise. I turned back to the jacket. A warning instinct prickled the hairs on the back of my neck:

if the grimoire was in the car, Michael was not going to have left it unguarded. Well, time spent with Ash had taught me at least one trick and I ran my hands across my skin and reached between my thighs, searching out the encrustations of Michael's semen. Only when I was certain my hands smelt of him did I reach into the pocket, holding my breath. The keys fizzed against my fingertips like a battery against the tongue. Gently I eased them out into the light. Then, my heart hammering in my throat, I stole out into the hall and slipped out quietly into the night.

My bedroom, converted from the roof space, thankfully didn't have a window overlooking the front of the house. I never would have dared to do what I did if there'd been a possibility of being overlooked. Stark naked, I pointed the vehicle's remote key at the big black 4x4 and saw the indicators flash once as it unlocked. I went into the boot first, careful not to touch the bodywork with anything but my anointed hands. The courtesy light cast a weak glow. There was a laptop in a zipped bag, a set of clothing hanging in a plastic cover from the high roof and a small travelling bag, the sort made of toughened security plastic, which was locked. I nearly panicked then. I had to force myself to go through the keys one at a time until I found the one that fitted. Looking over my shoulder every few seconds, I rummaged carefully through the contents. I was disappointed; it contained nothing but toiletries, more clothes and a few official-looking letters and documents. And, like a toy, a tiny wire model of the art installation in the foyer of the Grange, exquisite in its detail.

I could have given up then. I wanted to. It would have been so much easier just to sneak back to bed and lie alongside him. I was getting cold. But I moved the bag aside and went into the storage compartment under the carpet.

There it was, next to the tool set: a flattish cardboard box, dark blue and bearing no mark. A shirt box, maybe. When I eased off the lid I found a leather-bound book inside. All the breath came out of me in a moan.

This was it; I'd done just what Ash had asked. I could tell him where the grimoire was now, and leave the rest up to him. Or, I thought, I could take it. My stomach tightened. I looked out towards the wood, but there was no moon up and I could see nothing at all beyond the car's dim glow. I could take the book and run to Ash, right now; he could hide it in the wood and Michael would never get it back.

No, I told myself. I couldn't go to there naked and stinking of sex with Michael – the Wildwood would kill me. That was what I told myself, knowing full well that it was Ash I didn't want to face like this.

I could take the book and hide it, though the risk was terrible.

When in doubt, act. Thinking opens the way for fear and doubt. Thinking leads only to paralysis. The world doesn't belong to those who agonise over every decision and consequence; it belongs to men like Michael Deverick.

I took the book and left the box as one last layer of camouflage. I didn't open the volume; a look at the thick uneven page edges and the hand-stitched binding told me this was no photo album or keepsake, even if the faint smell of mustiness hadn't betrayed its age. I replaced everything as well as I could, locked the car and turned back to the house. Going indoors was nerve-racking; in my mind's eye I was already picturing Michael waiting for me, his face black with fury. But the living room was as I'd left it. I looked wildly around at the cupboards, then scooted behind the sofa and stuffed the book into the washing machine. There was a load of dirty clothes just sitting there in the drum and I buried the grimoire under them.

It was as I slipped the keys back into his jacket that I heard the creak of wood and looked up to see Jenny leaning over the banister, watching me. My brain seemed to freeze up; I stood like a moonstruck calf as she descended the last few stairs, her lips parting in a terrible grin. In the hours we'd spent together I'd never once seen her teeth, but I saw them now and it suddenly made sense of the strange shape of her skull because they were teeth like an attack dog's, only as green as pond scum.

They don't like artificial light, I thought dimly, wondering where the torch was, but then I realised that we were already standing under a light bulb. Silently, as graceful as a pike in deep water, she crossed the carpet to where I stood. There was no suggestion of violence in her body language, only desire, and I was so dazed I didn't know how to react. She was taller than me now; she could look me straight in the eye. She reached out her hands and clasped my numb face and brought her lips to mine in a lingering kiss. I tried to resist, but not swiftly or vehemently enough, and her cold tongue pushed between my lips. Then she hunched, her throat bulging, and began to vomit water into my mouth – cold silty water that went down my throat and back up to spurt out of my nostrils, into my stomach, down my windpipe. I tried to pull away but her grip on my head was implacable. I grabbed at her wrists but they were inhumanly strong. I clawed and punched wildly at her head, but she took no notice, and when I dug my thumbs in her eyes they yielded like frogspawn, only to fill the sockets again as my hands slackened.

Drowning is agony. I know, because that was what was happening to me; I was drowning, and the panic was over-whelming. I was partially aware that we were stumbling about the room crashing into the furniture, but the bruising I was getting from that was as nothing to the pain in my chest where it felt like liquid concrete was being forced into my lungs, tearing the fragile tissues. My vision began to cloud over, red and black. My flailing hands grew weaker.

Then suddenly Jenny released me, recoiling. As I fell to the floor I caught a blurry, lopsided glimpse of Michael standing there brandishing something white in his hand. It was the plastic canister of table salt from my kitchen, though I didn't work that out till much later. 'Avaunt!' he roared.

Jenny, clutching at her shoulder, hissed through her long green teeth. Michael flung his hand out, a pale slosh of salt struck her full on and she dissolved instantly into a sheet of water, which hung for a moment before splashing to the floor. That was all I saw before I began heaving out the fluid from my lungs and stomach. It was so painful I was convinced I had to be regurgitating blood, but it soaked into the carpet like Jenny herself had, a clear liquid rendered pale brown with silt. A few stranded invertebrates wriggled their death throes on the rug: water fleas, a tadpole or two, a small black beetle. When I saw that I threw up again, and kept heaving till my stomach was empty. I was only dimly aware of Michael putting his arms around me and holding me through the spasms and the shuddering.

When I'd fallen quiet with exhaustion he helped me to my feet and guided me into the bathroom, where he wrapped me in a towel and washed my face gently with a warm cloth. He fetched me a cup of tea to sip too, and that helped take away the lingering taint of the murky pond water. Then when I could hold my head up properly once more he picked me up bodily in his arms and carried me back upstairs to bed. Lying alongside me he tenderly stroked me, easing my muscles into relaxation and reminding my body that it could feel more than pain and revulsion, until in the end we made love, very gently, holding one another close as we slipped into orgasm and sleep.

I woke when Michael, smelling of toothpaste, leant over me to kiss my forehead. For a few moments I was too groggy to remember what had happened and I just blinked sleepily at him.

'Got to go,' he whispered. He was sitting on the edge of the bed, fully dressed. A grey pre-dawn steeliness picked out the pattern on the bedroom curtains in black. 'I've got a flight to catch from Bristol Airport.'

The sudden recollection of what I'd done made me pull the edge of the duvet over my mouth and nose. As if in recognition he patted his jacket pocket absently and I heard the chink of his keys.

'It's a pity really,' he said, almost to himself. 'Still. See you later, Avril.'

As he let himself out of the front door I shook off the paralysis that had seized me and bounded downstairs. The grimoire was still there where I'd left it in the washing machine. I stared at it, listening to the sound of Michael's car engine fading into the distance. It was my moment of revenge and I should have felt triumphant, but in actuality I felt terrible.

A faint smell of charring warned me as I reached in for the book. Extracting a dirty T-shirt I stared at the holes in the fabric, pale-edged as if eaten away by acid. Investigation showed that none of my other clothes had fared much better, and some – the ones immediately in contact with the leather covers – were hardly more than rags. In the end I used a clean towel to bundle up the grimoire, taking care not to touch it, and slipped it into a little rucksack. I was about to pull my clothes on when I realised I still stank like a sweet chestnut in full flower, so I dived into the bathroom. I think I broke all records for speed-showering, even allowing for frantic scrubbing and the washing of my hair – and for the ache in my muscles. Dressed at last, I shrugged into a coat and, seizing the daypack holding the book, locked up and then legged it at top speed across the estate towards Grange Wood.

Dawn was breaking and the trees were grey shadows in the pale haze as I ran through the wet grass, my trainers soaking up the dew. The bag clutched to my chest felt heavy. I tried to ignore the even more uncomfortable weight within my breast. I'd betrayed Michael and it was what the bastard deserved, wasn't it? He'd risked my life, hadn't he, just for a threesome? But still I felt nauseous. I got to the Wood Gate and threw myself over the beams, shouting, 'Ash! Ash!' with the last of my breath.

All over the wood the rooks rose in a great racket; I could only assume it was one of Ash's alarms. But in the camp nothing stirred. The little encampment had never looked so much like an assortment of litter. I stumbled among the bivouacs and the benders, kicking each structure and calling out between gasps. Then from under a canvas lean-to Ash emerged on hands and knees, face and hair rumpled with sleep. He was wearing the jumper I'd lent him the day of the bath disaster; the soft white wool suited him better than it had me and instead of hanging like a sack it outlined his chest and shoulders. At the sight my heart did a little flip

'Avril?' He rubbed his face. 'I was dreaming. I dreamt we were –'

'I've got it!' I cried, rushing up to him. The rooks were going crazy overhead.

'Got what?'

'The book. I stole it.'

His hazel eyes snapped into focus. 'The book?'

I pulled open the zip, thrusting the bag at him. 'There! There it is. Take it.'

He stared into the depths, uncomprehending. Then he reached in to touch the contents. Just as I blurted, 'Careful!'

he snatched his hand out again, recoiling as if he'd been bitten.

'Jesus,' he whispered. 'You stole it?'

'That's what you wanted!'

'Not here.' Horror was pulling his face tighter and tighter. 'You can't bring it in here.' Grabbing my shoulder he whirled me round and started hustling me bodily back towards the gate. 'Not inside the wood, Avril! It's the key, for Christ's sake. If he gets hold of it he can use it to break free.' His words were nearly drowned under the cawing of the rooks. Only when we got back to the gate and Ash snatched the bag from my grasp and hurled it out onto the meadow beyond did the cawing begin to diminish. We both scrambled over, following the fallen rucksack.

'You didn't tell me!' I complained, but Ash wasn't listening. He approached the rucksack as gingerly as if it contained a viper and pulled one corner of the towel until the book edged into view. The grass around it began to blacken and visibly wither. 'Bloody hell,' I muttered, retreating somewhat. I was surprised it hadn't set fire to my dirty laundry. 'Is it radioactive?'

'Not as such.' Ash seemed to have regained some self-possession. He produced his clasp knife, squatted down and stabbed the blade hilt-deep into the earth. Then he used the tip to gently open the book and get a look at the pages within. 'You didn't touch it, did you?'

'I used the towel.' From what I could see it was brown hand-writing on a brown page, very closely written. 'That is the right one, is it?'

'Oh yes.' He let the cover drop and then sat back, swearing under his breath.

'What are you going to do with it? You're going to burn it, aren't you?'

He blinked. 'It's trapped to hurt if you *touch* it, Avril. What do you think's going to happen if I throw it on a fire?'

'Then what the hell are you going to do?'

He chewed his lip. 'I need to get the wards off for a start. I need somewhere quiet and safe to work.'

'Well,' I pointed out, 'when Michael gets to the airport he's going to notice the book's missing from the car. That's only going to be a couple of hours, tops.'

Ash's eyes were particularly green today, I noticed as he looked up at me. 'Dismantling the wards is going to take a bit longer than that.'

I squirmed, frustrated. 'I've just committed career-suicide for you, Ash. I didn't plan on it being the other sort too! You've got somewhere to take it, haven't you? You've got a plan?'

'Avril . . . I wasn't expecting you to . . . just pinch the thing.'

'Shit.' I felt suddenly clammy.

'Deverick's going to come back for it.' He spoke quietly, as if ticking off a simple mental list. 'It can't go into the wood. We're not safe out here. I'm going to have to take it and go, Avril. You should . . . run. Get away. A long way off.'

'Like I'm going to be safe on my own?' I didn't mean it to come out sounding as panicky as it did.

Ash was keeping his expression closed but his breath was coming harder and faster than normal. 'Fair point.'

I stomped in a circle, stuffing my brains back into order. 'Have you got a phone on you?'

His eyes flicked to the trees, where the rooks were keeping up an ominous creaking. 'Back at the camp.'

'I've got an idea. I have a friend called Miranda, in London. She works for a publisher attached to the University . . .'

Fifteen minutes later I gave him his phone back. 'It's sorted,' I said, feeling dizzy. 'We get the book to her and she'll scan the lot. She can get pages posted to every academic institution on the planet with a medieval studies programme. Nobody's going to take it seriously as a grimoire, but she reckons postgraduates would rather do anything than get on with their everyday research. They'll start translating. And it turns out she runs this online magazine site which is where the Medieval Latin geeks hang out for fun, and she can put it up there. The book'll be public domain in a couple of days. That'll do it, won't it?'

Ash, who'd been pacing up and down, looked at me as if slightly dazed. 'Yes. It should do. It'll suck the book dry.'

'Thank God for that.'

'You trust this friend of yours?'

'Oh yes.' There was something nagging faintly at the back of my head but I pushed it away. 'She's great. She says to meet at her place.'

'Then we should go now.'

'My car?'

He gestured wryly. 'I'm at your mercy.'

Ash carried the rucksack as we jogged back through the grounds, and he kept a careful half-dozen paces behind me. I didn't think he entirely trusted me even then, and I didn't blame him: it could so easily have been a ruse of Deverick's to lure him out into the open. When we'd piled our stuff into my car he sat with the bag between his knees and the passenger window wide open, his long fingers trailing in the slipstream as if he were Braille-reading the air. 'Take a left,' was his suggestion as we exited the estate. 'The roads should be clearer that way.'

We didn't talk much as we travelled. Ash wasn't exactly the chatty sort and applied himself to following our route on my road map, while I had to concentrate on driving the narrow steep-sided roads in relative safety. Once Ash snapped, 'Brake!' and I slewed to a crawl just before a sporty Honda came zipping over the horizon and thrust past us, scraping its paintwork on the embankment. The near-miss left me shaken. There was no way that Ash could have seen that car was coming, but I felt it was a bit foolish to question his instincts at this stage.

After that we got onto a decent A-road and were able to head east at a proper speed. It didn't last even an hour. Without warning the car engine cut out and I had to coast onto the verge, where I sat and cursed and twisted the ignition key fruitlessly. 'It's just been serviced!' I complained.

'Not the garage's fault, unfortunately.' Ash opened his door and peered back down the road behind us. 'It's Deverick. He's had access to your car, presumably.'

I made a gurgle of incomprehension.

'He's noticed the book's missing.' Clutching bag and road map, Ash sprang up the verge to look over a field gate. 'Come on!' he urged as I climbed out. 'We need to get off the road right now.'

I followed him over the gate and we yomped through a pasture, watched by perplexed cows. Through a muddy cattle-wade, under two strands of barbed wire, and across a wasteland of stubble beyond, I gritted my teeth and kept up with his long stride. We forced a hedge to get to the road on the other side, yet somehow despite our being dishevelled and mud-splattered and panting, the very first car Ash put his thumb out to stopped for us. The mumsy driver – and as far as I know lone middle-aged women *never* stop for hitchers – took us thirty miles out of her way to drop us off at the nearest railway station, chatting away to Ash all the while as if he were a ten-year-old on his first camping trip. I'm not sure she even remembered that I'd climbed into the back seat. Before she drove off she called to him, 'Have fun, dear.'

Ash studiously failed to catch my eye.

It wasn't much of a station; it didn't even have a manned

office. Ash bought us tickets from a machine, using a platinum credit card. 'I thought you were on benefits?' I asked suspiciously.

'Computers are easy to fool with magic,' he said. 'More so even than people.'

Electronic boards flashed up a warning of an express coming straight through. 'The problem is that trains to London won't stop here,' I said. 'This place isn't big enough.'

'Wait and see.' He was right; the inter-city express, far too long for our platform, came in braking hard and stopped alongside. 'Faulty signal ahead,' Ash muttered. He went up to the carriage door and stabbed a finger at the lock, which was glowing an unco-operative red. To my amazement it switched instantly to green and the door slid open. We stalked down the centre aisle of the carriage to an empty table and chairs.

The journey to London was uneventful. I had to reassess the inherent glamour of being a magus when Ash spent an hour of it locked in the toilet with the grimoire, ankle-deep in wet toilet paper, and I stood at his request on watch outside. He emerged looking green but satisfied, having removed enough wards from the book to at least make it possible to handle. We'd lost our seats by the time this was done, but found another vacant pair. Ash took the window seat and I, exhausted by a hectic night and our flight from the estate, sat back in mine and fell immediately asleep.

I awoke to find that in my sleep I'd snuggled against Ash's shoulder and had my face pressed to his coat. Worse, my hand was resting on his right thigh, high up near his hip. For a moment I was too embarrassed to move. I couldn't see his face from my angle. I couldn't tell if he knew I'd woken. He didn't stir. Maybe, I thought, he was asleep too. I could feel the warmth of his thigh through the heavy cotton of his trousers, and it occurred to me that if the fabric hadn't been there I would be resting my hand on that intricate tribal tattoo. I wanted very much to touch that jagged black outline with my fingers, explore the soft skin that belied the sharp ink angles. My mouth went dry. I wanted to trace every thornlike curve with the tip of my tongue. I wanted to lick along the division between creamy skin and black ink and find out if I could taste the difference. I wanted to sink my face into the heat of his crotch and feel him stir and swell and rise against my lips. Desire was suddenly so hungry in me that it hurt. My heart began to beat hard.

Oh God, he knew. It didn't show much under those baggy pants, but he was half-hard, fat and strokeable like a curled-up cat. Was it my wicked thoughts that had stirred him, I wondered, or just the fact that I was pressed against him? Or perhaps he'd dozed off too, and his cock was merely swollen with sleep?

'Avril,' he said softly, 'we're nearly there. Time to wake up.'

'Mmm?' I sat back, faking more sleepiness and confusion than I really felt and dabbing at his coat sleeve. 'Oh God, did I dribble on you? Sorry.'

'I'll live,' said he with a smile. 'What were you dreaming about?'

I could only hope the flush in my cheeks looked innocent. 'What?'

'You were whimpering in your sleep.'

'Ah.' I blinked. The memory had faded quickly and I had to struggle to recapture it. 'It was just the one about the dragons.'

'Dragons?'

'Yes. There's a red one and a white one, fighting. I've had it a few times recently.' I wasn't going to let slip how much the dream turned me on. Every time.

'Red and white? Underground?'

'How did you know?'

'It's not your dream.' When I frowned at him he dropped his voice, explaining, 'It's Merlin's. When he was a boy he was about to be sacrificed in order to save a tower that kept falling down during construction. He had a vision just in time that revealed the cause: two dragons fighting beneath the earth.' He shrugged. 'It was a foreshadowing of the fall of Britain, I think – the battles between the British and the Saxons.'

'Right.'

'It's the book.' He tapped his fingers on the knapsack. 'It gets to you.'

I could think of another, rather more personal interpretation. Neither version really explained why the first time I'd had the dream was, as far as I could remember, in my mother's spare bedroom the night before coming to the West Country.

We disembarked in the echoing clamour of Paddington Station shortly before noon. 'We need to throw Deverick off the trail,' said Ash.

'You think he'll be following us?'

'I know he'll be trying to.' So we headed across London by foot and by Underground, taking trains at random, switching from Circle Line to District to Northern and back, criss-crossing over our tracks, climbing to street level to shift between stations, never keeping still. We ate on the move, and Ash took the paper envelopes of our tortilla wraps and the empty cardboard coffee cups and, folding them neatly, stowed them away in the pockets of the knapsack. We didn't talk much: a public Tube train isn't exactly the place to discuss the in and outs of magic.

I found the novelty of the big city stimulating at first with so many new faces and places to look at. Don't get me wrong, I'm not a total country mouse. I'd been to London before for the shopping and the sightseeing. But it was a bit of a shock to find out how much I had grown accustomed to quiet and space and solitude out in the country, and just how insecure I felt under those beetling buildings, how disorientated by the flash of a million different objects displayed in the shop windows and how much the constant press of the crowds jangled on my nerves after a while. I started to feel agitated. I couldn't handle the traffic either; Ash had to take me by the arm when we crossed the roads because my brain seemed incapable of assessing the gaps between so many moving vehicles. I felt useless and that made me angry, and the more angry I felt the less I could tolerate the stink of fumes and the babble of unfamiliar accents and languages. When we came out of yet another Tube station onto the street and I got jammed by the flow of pedestrians against the stall of an *Evening Standard* vendor, I lost sight of Ash temporarily and for a moment I felt a surge of real panic. I was carrying the rucksack at this point and I clutched it to my chest. 'Shit!' I hissed through my teeth.

'Are you quite all right, my dear?' An elderly couple had stopped, and the silver-haired man spoke with old-fashioned enunciation.

'I'm . . . OK.' The woman had eyes milky with cataracts, but that didn't stop her staring at me with a strange intensity.

'Are you sure?'

Then Ash was back again and his hand was on my shoulder. But he only had eyes for the couple. Nothing was said, but for a long moment they glared at each other. Then the elderly man inclined his head and Ash bowed his too, the politeness between them cold and as keen as a razor blade.

'Ashton,' said the woman before they retreated into the maw of the Underground.

'Who were they?' I asked. Ash's grip was uncomfortably tight on my upper arm.

'Some of the people whose attention Deverick doesn't want to draw.'

'Well . . . Could they help us?'

His lips narrowed. 'Only in the very resort. My enemy's enemy is *not* always my friend. And there are worse people out there even than Deverick.' Finally he turned his attention back to me. 'Are you all right? What happened?'

'Just too many people,' I protested, shaking my head. 'It feels like they're climbing about inside my skull and giving me a kicking.' I flinched as someone's suitcase banged against my calves; the man swept on without apology. Looking thoughtful, Ash took the rucksack from me.

'Let's head across the park,' he suggested. 'There's more room to breathe, and we can pick up the Piccadilly Line. We're nearly done.'

'I'm sorry.'

'Well, how many of them would cope with being dumped in a wood on their own?' he asked with a glance around at the press of people.

'Ah. But you're used to London, aren't you?' I was certain of that; he'd not bothered to consult any map as he'd led us on our winding dance.

'I used to live here a few years back. It's changed even while I've been away, mind you.' He was no more forthcoming than that and I felt a twinge of disappointment. Ash kept himself a guarded secret. I knew next to nothing about him, after all these weeks: rather less about him than about Michael, in fact.

We crossed a busy street and headed into the public park, and I felt better almost at once. It was a beautiful breezy golden afternoon, once you were out from under the shadow of those vast buildings whose neo-classical lines reminded me uncomfortably of Michael's office. The grass was close cut and worn in places and there was litter caught among the regimented flowering shrubs, so it didn't approach the half-tamed exuberance of the Kester Estate, but there were majestic trees here too. I felt my shoulders lose their tension as we got away from other human beings and I smiled as I admired the mottled, bulging bole of a vast plane tree. We crossed under an avenue of horse chestnuts – always among the earliest in leaf, they're the first to turn in autumn too and their bronzed leaves were tumbling already. I grinned cheekily at Ash. 'Catch a falling leaf to make a wish...Is that real magic?'

He hitched the bag onto his shoulder. 'It could be, in the right circumstances. Go on and try.'

Snorting, I rose to the challenge and set off in pursuit of a leaf. It was a bit childish, but I figured that if I could get scared like a kid by the big city then I could enjoy it like one too. It wasn't as if I had much dignity to retain in front of Ash. I'm pretty athletic but the chestnut leaves seemed determined to dodge my grasp and I darted about in vain for a minute or so, snatching at thin air while Ash watched. When I finally caught one I whooped and brandished it in triumph.

'Don't speak your wish aloud,' Ash warned with that crooked smile of his. 'It's got to be kept secret if you want it to come true.'

Grinning down at the fat fingers of the big leaf, now crinkled and ragged, I decided what to wish for and took a deep breath, shutting my eyes.

I wish...

It was a silly superstition, but I put my whole heart into that petition.

When I opened my eyes again he was close enough for me to smell the bonfire tang of smoke on his clothes, and he reached out for me and cupped my face in his hand and kissed me, long and soft and a little tentative, his lips begging my forgiveness even as they stole my breath away. And all of a sudden my breast was full of autumn leaves whirling about in a wild dance, and my pulse was hot under his palm, and there was no doubt and no shame and no hurt any more because his tongue was on mine and his breath was mine and my blood was thundering to the beat of his own pulse.

After a while we broke the kiss just so that we could look one another in the eyes and see the delight shining there.

'How did you guess?' I whispered.

'Magic.'

Then Ash kissed me again, drawing me up against him, and this time there was nothing tentative about it. I slid my arms about his neck. I was starving, and he filled my mouth with kisses that only increased my hunger. His hand was up under my T-shirt on the small of my back, skin on skin, holding me close. Our bodies burnt where they touched. My nails raked the nape of his neck. He kissed my throat and, as my head tipped back, I opened my eyes upon a deep cerulean sky filled with whirling golden leaves and I felt as if the whole world had been picked up by the wind and was dancing around us. But he couldn't leave my mouth alone for long and he returned to it hungrier than ever. His hands clasped my bum cheeks and squeezed voluptuously, pulling me up even tighter against the delicious bulge burgeoning in his pants.

'Do I have to catch another leaf?' I moaned into his mouth, writhing my hips to make the most of the embracing pressure behind and the jutting hardness before. 'I want this as well.'

His chuckling gasp tasted of sunlight on unfurling beech buds. God, he didn't laugh often enough. 'This you get for free. I've been wishing too, Avril.'

'Really?'

'Every day. Ever since the night I found you running about the lawn stark naked like a dryad.' He laughed, shaking his head. 'You beautiful crazy tree-nympho, with that stupid bloody climbing harness round your bum and your breasts all scratched and moss stains on your thighs . . . Oh, I've wanted you so much.'

Then what were you waiting for? Why did you keep pushing me away? I longed to ask, but I knew what the answer was: he'd been waiting for me to prove that he could trust me. 'You took your time,' I chided.

'Now that I'm good at,' he answered, and I didn't miss the promise in his words. Our mouths melted together, tongues fusing. And then, somehow, yet again he managed to pull away. 'I've got my limits, though. We . . . really should stop now,' he warned, breathless. 'Or else I'm going to have to have you right here . . . and that might draw some attention.'

God, I wanted him to fuck me right then and there. I wanted him to put me up against a tree trunk and shaft me senseless. I wanted him to throw me to the park turf where so many couples had lain and touched each other into a frenzy, and fuck me with my ankles over his shoulders. His erection was a knotted fist pushing into my belly. I could feel myself melting against his hardness, grown so hot and soft and slippery that he could have plunged his hands into me and moulded me like warm wax to any shape he pleased. 'You're right,' I acknowledged, biting his lip and running my hands down his hips, my thumb skimming his imprisoned cock.

Ash gasped out loud and lunged to catch my ear lobe in his teeth. 'Stop,' he growled. Bright little points of pain danced sparkling down my neck, stinging my nipples with their electric tingle. 'Jesus. Please. Just stop.'

I pushed him away. Our eyes locked. 'Promise you're going to fuck me,' I said, and I don't know if I was demanding or begging. 'This time. Promise.'

'Oh.' His eyes were like green stars and he was shaking with the effort of reining in the overwhelming imperative of his flesh. 'I promise. Trust me.'

'All the way.'

'I promise.' He stooped to kiss my lips one last time. Then he touched them softly, tracing their full lines with his fingertips, as if sealing his kiss inside me. I felt my spine turn to shimmering mercury. He held me tight for another moment longer, his hard cock an oath sworn in stone. 'Come on,' he whispered.

It was a good job he had that long coat of his to spare his blushes as we walked on. My own legs seemed to have lost all co-ordination. He held my hand tight, his fingers interlaced with mine, and luckily he knew where he was going because I wasn't paying attention to anything but the brush of his body against mine. He could have walked me off the edge of a cliff and I wouldn't have noticed. I hardly registered the renewed press of the crowd as we descended into the bowels of the earth again, sharing a single step as we rode the escalator, and the warm foetid breeze of the tunnels billowed up to meet us. I didn't mind the scurry down the tiled corridors or the wait on the platform. I was too happy to care.

Our train turned out to be the most crowded yet; perhaps it was the beginning of the commuter rush home. There were no seats available so Ash took one of the overhead straps and pulled me snug up against him with the other arm, slipping his hand beneath my coat. The rucksack was my charge, nestling between us. He was my only support as the train lurched into motion, and I leant hard into his chest and thigh. His grip was unmistakably possessive, but despite all temptation we weren't touching each other up; my mound was pressed against his hip and Ash's splayed fingers were equally firm but unmoving on the highest curve of my bum. We didn't even kiss, though his face was inclined to mine, his expression grave. A pulse beat, slow and hypnotic, in my groin. It was the strangest, strangest thing I felt then. I was aroused – horny beyond words, slippery with readiness, weak at the knees – and yet, for all my aching pussy and my fluttering breath, an extraordinary sense of peace was what filled me. No impatience. No anxiety. No greed. He could have held me there forever and I would have been content to stay that way. I felt as if he were already inside me and there was no more to fear. I felt as if I were already his. I felt surrendered.

I've no idea how long that journey lasted. I was in another place altogether, a place I'd only previously visited in passing.

'This is our stop, isn't it?'

I shook myself out of my trance. I'd forgotten I was supposed to be the one guiding the way to Miranda's flat. Squeezing out of the carriage we made our way upstairs and onto the street. I was familiar with the route and it wasn't hard to find her apartment block, a tall red-brick Victorian building. As I stood in the porch searching the list of names over the electronic lock Ash moved up to embrace me from behind, sliding his hands over my torso and cupping my breasts. If Miranda had responded to the buzz I don't think I'd have been able to speak coherently. But the doorbell went unanswered.

'She's not back,' I pointed out after Ash had run his tongue up my neck and circled the sensitive rim of my ear. My voice came out husky. 'She's probably still at work.'

'We're a bit early,' he murmured, his fingers closing deferentially on my proud nipples. 'We can wait for her. I'll try and think of some way to pass the time.'

The words made me shiver with delight. 'Where? I know where she keeps her spare key, inside, but I don't know the combination for this door.'

'Hm.' Ash reached out over my shoulder and hit one of the other intercom buttons, seemingly at random.

A female voice answered: 'Hello?'

'It's Serge,' said Ash, leaning in to the speaker. 'Can you buzz me in?'

'Oh right – come in.'

The door buzzed and he pushed it wide. 'Serge?' I mouthed at him.

He shrugged. 'The first name that came into my head.' Then he pulled me inside. Miranda's apartment block had been converted from a railway hotel, as I remembered, and still boasted elaborate glazed tiles in deep greens and blues and an openwork wrought-iron lift in the centre of the lobby, cables and pulleys exposed for all the world to see. Miranda had claimed that the rats and the leaks in the guttering were original features too but I'd had to take her word for that.

'Fourth floor up,' I said, pushing the button for the lift. As we waited for it to descend he took me in his arms and we kissed again, slow and dirty. Ash slipped his fingers experimentally down the loose front of my trousers and tickled the skin below my belly button, making me giggle and squirm. His fingers brushed the front panel of my knickers, finding heat and the rough lace of my pubic fleece underlying the smooth triangle of cotton. 'Oh,' I said appreciatively.

His eyes were wicked.

The inner and outer lift doors folded open and then closed again with a great clashing of metal and, as we started our ascent, Ash pushed me back, took my wrists and spread them wide against the wall of the elevator cage. I furled my fingers around the metal bars and bit my lip. He liked that, my arms held out, leaving my body vulnerable. He sank to his knees before me, opening my coat wide, and sucked my nipples through my T-shirt and the bra beneath, wetting the cotton so that if they weren't prominent enough before they now stood out like boiled sweets. There wasn't much time; the lift was slow but we would get to our floor soon enough – and we were visible on every floor as we passed. Ash pulled up the front of my shirt to tongue my flat belly and my navel and, while his mouth was at that, his hands were busy too on my belt and fly. Those combat trousers were really baggy; when he got the zip down they hung loose enough to expose the whole of the front of my panties, which were a hot pink today. He slipped a finger beneath the fabric to stroke me.

'Ash!' I hissed, scandalised but grinning from ear to ear. My expression changed when without warning he bent still lower and gently, but with great precision, bit my pubic mound. Sensation flashed through my body like an electric shock and I jerked wildly against the bars. As the lift rattled to a halt he did it again, teeth on damp, fragrant cotton, and this time I did come; a magnesium flare of an orgasm that was there and gone in an instant. I cried out too, mostly in shock. 'Oh my God,' I whispered as I recovered.

Smiling that smug bloody smirk that men get when they've brought you off, Ash opened the doors and ushered me out into the corridor. I was glad the building seemed deserted. I had to zip my trousers up before I led the way, my legs unsteady enough to make me weave a little. The kissing didn't speed our progress up either. Miranda's door, surrounded by plants in Chinese pots, was locked of course but after we thumped up against it in a clinch I knocked loudly, just in case she'd been in the bath or something and not heard the buzzer.

'Miranda!'

No sound came from within. Ash took my hand and ran my open palm firmly over his trouser crotch, making clear the state of play there. I nearly gave up on the idea of getting into the flat at all, I was so distracted. 'Oh, that's *nice.*'

'Nice?' He cocked an eyebrow, clearly pained by my faint praise.

'Nice and hard.' I squeezed his shaft through the fabric.

'Ah.'

'Your come tastes good too,' I murmured. 'As I remember.'

'I'm pleased you like it.' He was having some difficulty speaking.

I grinned, taking it slowly. 'I'd like a great big chocolate cake for my birthday, covered in your cream.'

'Really.'

'I'd like to take a wedge and smear it down my tits and down between my legs and I'd like to lick chocolate icing and your jizz off my fingers.'

'Ah. Who gets to lick the cake off?'

'You. I'd make you get down and eat it out of my pussy.' I was torturing him now, barely moving my hand.

'Make me? So you're into that?'

'For my birthday I'd tie you up in red ribbons and make you eat me out.' I pouted thoughtfully. 'If it was your birthday you could do it to me.'

Ash's face was a picture. 'Where's the key, Avril? Or am I going to have to fuck you right here in the corridor?'

I retrieved the key from its hiding place under a pot and we bundled through the door. Miranda's flat was as I remembered it: a corner apartment, open plan, the kitchen area in the far corner. It smelt like a branch of Lush. A framed poster of Botticelli's *Birth of Venus* dominated the wall over her bedhead, which was the only one that wasn't put to shelving. The whole place was mounded with stacks of books and papers – books on every horizontal surface, and clothes dumped on top of the books. It was impossible to tell if the laundry was discarded or merely stored there. The one thing Miranda really needed more of in her life was wardrobe space.

'Looks like she's tidied up,' I said weakly.

Ash shucked off his coat. 'What's that door?' he asked, nodding at the only other one in the flat.

'Bathroom.' Then I called, for the third and last time, 'Miranda!' getting exactly the same response as on previous occasions.

Ash was nothing if not cautious. Reluctantly he released me to go over and check and I took the opportunity to double-lock the flat door and dump my outer layers, stowing the rucksack under a dining chair. 'She's fairly laid-back, your friend?' he asked as he returned.

'Oh, yeah.'

'Then she won't mind us using her bed.' Ash picked me up bodily and dropped me on the duvet, among heaps of Miranda's underwear and rumpled dresses. My squeal was only a token protest and was cut off anyway as he moved down on top of me and captured my lips. We wrestled the clothing off one another as we kissed. I was more successful than him as I didn't have the bed to contend with, and managed to get him bare from the waist up. I raked my nails down his ribs, mesmerised by the pink tracks I could leave on his ivory skin. Ash shuddered rewardingly. He pulled up my top and sports bra to my armpits and sucked my puckered nipples until they pointed stiffly at the ceiling. He licked down my flat belly to my navel and gave it what was indisputably oral sex, while my trapped pelvis heaved frantically beneath his heavy body. Then he sat back up between my feet, picked up one of my ankles and, holding it high, stripped the laces out of my trainer. Yanking off shoe and sock in one motion he pressed his mouth to my instep and kissed it, letting me feel teeth as well as lips there.

I cried out, shocked by a gesture that felt, weirdly, more intimate and daring than anything he could have done to my pussy. Ash bared the other foot and licked from instep to big toe, making me squirm wildly. Then with swift impatient movements he pulled down my trousers and threw them aside. For a moment he looked down with predatory satisfaction at my legs and the pink thong that was so inadequately concealing my swollen sex, then he lowered himself to the bed, lifting my legs over his shoulders, and kissed his way up my silky inner thighs to my muff. I was entirely overwhelmed: by the sight of him breasting between my thighs as if I were a sea he were swimming through; by the way he brushed his nose and lips to the gusset of my panties, revelling in my scent; by the burning charge his touch sent through me.

My poor knickers. After what I'd put them through they were already drenched, barely containing their sticky-slippery contents. Ash ate me through the cotton, all heat and teeth and friction, driving me wild with his determination not to rip off the little triangle of fabric and press home between my lips. Sometimes his tongue would delve behind the elastic and tease my slit, but then he'd pull out at once as if I were some precious virgin who had made him promise that the clothes had to stay on. He reduced me to squirming, gasping, writhing desperation. My panties were soaked in equal measure with his saliva and my eagerness. I put my hands on his head and tried to hump up against his mouth but he chuckled dirtily into my pussy and drew away, kneeling up on the bed. His boots were making a hell of a mess on the duvet but I was incapable of worrying about Miranda's laundry right now.

'Thought this was what you said you wanted?' he murmured, opening his flies and easing out his tumescent cock from its red-gold nest. He cupped his balls with one hand.

'Yes,' I moaned, stretching out my hand. He let my fingers brush his length briefly. After all these years I'm still amazed that any part of the body so soft can get so bloody hard. He was hard like rock – and all for me. I anointed the tips of my fingers with the dewy moisture that oozed from his cock's slitted opening and then brought them to my own mouth to lick the salty-sweet lubricant, frantic with want. I think something inside him broke then. Something icy and obdurate and frightened to let go. I saw the look in his eyes.

He said nothing as he came down over me. He didn't bother

to remove my wet knickers; he just eased the gusset aside with his fingers and entered me as I spread my thighs to welcome him. Both of us were still partly clothed and it underlined the urgency of our rutting. We kissed again but I broke to groan from the pleasure of feeling him move on and within me. His cock was so hard and so, so good. Like waves we heaved together, deep-ocean waves that have the power to level islands, but roll slow and strong, their violence hidden across hundreds of miles until they approach the shallows and curl to white-topped foaming breakers. I ran my hands across his skin and gripped his thighs with mine and felt his lips on my jaw. I heard the breath catching in his throat. His fingers bit into my shoulders like he'd never let go. 'Avril,' he groaned under his breath.

It was good. It was better than good. How much in life can you be really sure of? We make our best guess, but even our own hearts deceive us. It's so hard to know what path to take, what battle lines to draw, to know what is wanted from what is good, to know inspiration from impulse, to know risk from self-destruction. As I fucked with Ash, as we explored and ransacked and possessed each other, I was sure. Absolute conviction held in my every fibre that here, with the magician with the copper hair and troubled eyes coloured like the woods, whose voice was hoarse in my ear and whose gentle hands were grown fierce on my skin, the man who filled me and pressed me down and lifted me higher with every stroke, above everything else in the world, it was truly *right*.

9: Snared

I woke hours later. Ash had spooned up behind me as we'd dozed off and I could feel his warm skin against my back and see his arm draped over me, his hand resting on the duvet by my breasts. I lay for a moment, wondering if that arm was protective or possessive or simply cosy.

Like everything else he did Ash's fucking had been careful, committed and so intense it was almost unsettling. He wasn't a man you went with for a bit of a laugh. In his own way, I thought, he was as just as emotionally dangerous as Michael – the two of them had a lot in common. Now, I added ruefully to myself, more than ever.

I slipped from under his arm and sat up on the edge of Miranda's bed. I expected Ash to stir but he rolled face down in the pillows, his breathing deep and even. Night had fallen and I guess the unaccustomed luxuries of a soft mattress and a warm room were too much for him. The glow of the bedside lamp picked out the shape of his muscles, the gloss of his skin and a strange scar on his back: a puckered sunken scar, perfectly round and about the size of a penny, close to his spine in the region of his right kidney. I wondered briefly what it was. My fingertip hovered over it. I didn't want to leave; I wanted to lick my way down his spine and sink my teeth into his biteable arse, but I was busting for the toilet. Reluctantly I scurried for the door.

A few minutes later, safely enthroned in the bathroom, I took the time to look about me. The room wasn't cold but it was a bit stark, tiled to the ceiling on all four walls in white, with white and chrome fittings. I'd have like to have drawn a bath and sunk into its soothing waters; I'd seen more action with more partners in the past 24 hours than I could usually claim in months, and my muscles were starting to protest. Sadly, Miranda did not possess a bath, but instead the whole of one end of the room was glassed off to make a magnificent shower cubicle. My casual interest gradually sharpened. It would be nice to get back into the bed scrubbed and fresh and smelling of perfumed soap. I love dirty, but I love clean too. First one then the other, turn and turn about.

Flushing the cistern I went over and experimented with the taps until I had a good strong cascade of warm water. Miranda had a fine stock of shower gels and soaps, and I happily let the water strip the salt and the ache from my skin as I lathered up with a bar smelling of coconut and ginger. I was busy shampooing when the door opened and Ash, muzzy with sleep, ambled in and lifted the toilet seat.

I stopped what I was doing to watch. I like to watch my men piss – it feels voyeuristic and transgressive and dirty on my side, and there is something irreducibly masculine about the way they do it. I admit I envy them the ability to take a leak standing up. It has so much more grace and dignity than being obliged to sit, I thought, feasting my eyes on the muscled lines of Ash's bum and legs, and, of course, they get to handle their cocks while they're at it. Lucky bastards. He pissed with force, a strong golden jet. I think Ash felt the weight of my gaze because midstream he cast me a sideways glance and a sleepy, knowing smile. My stomach made a funny little squirming dance at that look.

After pressing the flush Ash came over to the shower cubicle and slipped inside with me. I was just rinsing off, and he traced the wet ringlets of my hair. Then I pulled him under the shower jet and helped the water caress him. He stretched and eased his muscles and ducked his head under the spray to soak his dreadlocks. I loved the way he scrunched his face up as he lifted it to the shower's fierce caress, and the way the water flicked from the ends of his hair when he shook his head. He reached for the bottle of shower gel but I got there before him, squeezed it onto a big violet shower scrunchie and then used the nylon blossom to lather up his chest and shoulders. He submitted with a grin, not interfering or distracting me, just resting his fingertips on my waist. Stepping round behind him I scrubbed him with firmer strokes, revelling in his muscular back and his hard arse. I slapped his bum just to see the suds and water go flying. I raked my nails through the hairs on his thigh. His body was a great big toy for me to play with and he did not resist. When I slipped a soapy hand between his cheeks and right underneath he shuddered but spread for me. I was gentler there, respecting the more sensitive skin, cupping his scrotum in my slippery hand and rolling the balls tenderly in their sac. I was very thorough; these things are important.

Then I knelt behind him and scrubbed down the long lines of his legs, pressing my fingers hard into the muscle. His calves were like rock. Soap made up for the roughness of his hair, making everything slick and frictionless. Ash grunted and purred. I found out how much he was enjoying the attention when he turned to look down on me and his semi-hard erection bobbed in my face. Grinning, I ignored it and took up his feet one by one, resting each against my thigh as I poured on the shower gel and massaged his soles and his insteps and up between each toe. He had to stretch out his arms to the walls while balanced on one leg, supporting himself with fingertip pressure. The smile on his lips was touched with surprise. If he was ticklish he didn't let it show, but that's what you'd expect from Ash.

When I was sure he was completely clean I stood and lathered up his torso again, just for luck, paying special attention to his nipples and the tattoo on his hip. 'This drives me crazy,' I said as my fingers stroked the inked curves. 'Is it magic?'

He shrugged. 'Not in that way.' Great white creamy blobs of foam were running down his abdomen and thighs. He looked perfect. I'd saved his crotch for last, a treat for myself. I had the most indecent grin on as I squirted the shower gel over his jutting cock, admiring the aesthetics of the pearlescent goo on his flushed member. Ash groaned with anticipation. Then I put the bottle aside in order to lavish both hands and all my attention on soaping him up, mixing turgid cock and soft balls and the coarse coppery thatch of his hair in one glorious slippery, sudsy melange that my hands couldn't get enough of. Ash bit his lip. Strange things were happening to his breath, and in very short order there was nothing halfway about his erection.

'Avril,' he groaned, his hands suddenly closing over mine, stilling them on his hard-on.

No? I asked with my eyes.

Easing my hands from him, he pulled me full against him, and for a moment our bodies met in a wonderful slippery kiss, as if we were melting together. Warm steam billowed about us. Then he turned me in his arms so that my back was to his chest, and reached for the bottle of gel. Evidently it was my turn. I could have protested that I was already clean but I didn't think he'd listen, and besides there were bits of me that were feeling very dirty indeed.

With a firm clasp of his hand Ash squirted the creamy liquid over both my breasts and dribbled it down the line of my cleavage before discarding the bottle altogether. He didn't bother with the shower scrunchie; he used his hands. He'd worked out exactly how sensitive my nipples could be and he used the knowledge ruthlessly, rolling and rubbing the innocent pink tips until I was squirming against him, helpless and undignified, my bum grinding against his braced thighs. He ran his hand down my belly and caressed soap into the delta of my sex, his fingers soaping my folds. Then he rolled me, gently but firmly, to face the wall. I put my hands on the sweating tiles.

For a moment he released me in order to find a bar of soap. I whimpered with loss, only slightly mollified as he ran his slick hands down my back and over my bum cheeks. Then he delved between my legs, soap and hands equally hard and slippery, and I forgot I'd been disappointed as he worked me into a lather of pleasure. I pressed my forehead to the cool tiles, eyes shut, transported by the alien, frictionless pressure. He rubbed the soap bar over my clit and pressed it to my cunt and in my reckless trance I wished he could shove the whole thing inside me. I thrust my arse cheeks out, begging him for more. He stroked up and down the interior of my crack, tracing rings around the secret star of my anus. I squirmed. He slid one finger, lubricated by that alchemical mixture of sex juices and soap, in through the tight ring of muscle. I gasped against the tiles.

'Relax,' he whispered in my ear, circling that finger joint, easing me open. His other hand, losing the soap bar, slid in around the front of my pussy to make sure I did just that, taking masterful possession of my clit. When he slipped a second finger in to join the first invader I felt as if my whole body were yielding to him. My muscles fluttered, my cheeks opened. I was seconds from orgasm.

All that changed when his fingers eased out and he nudged the head of his cock to my bum hole instead. The spasm of fear was instinctive and instantaneous; my eyes snapped open wide. 'No!'

'Yes,' he murmured. 'Just relax.' I could feel his length, hot and so slippery, between my cool cheeks. The pressure wasn't unbearable, but it wasn't withdrawn either

'I've not . . . I've not done that before.'

His breath was hot on my ear. 'Then give it to me as your first, Avril.' He kissed my burning cheek. 'Give it up to me.'

My whole body seemed to have turned to jelly. I did want to give it to him; I wanted to give him anything he wanted. I wanted to surrender my soul. 'I'm not sure I can,' I confessed.

'Yes. Yes, you can.' His fingers stirred my clit, soothing, inflaming. 'Just relax and let me do it all.' He pressed against his target and I groaned, partly in fear, partly in discomfort, rising up on my toes. The fingers that had been playing with my bum slid round and fastened onto one nipple and I felt the little electric jolt chase all the way down to my clit.

The noises in my throat were suddenly less protesting, more helpless. 'Oh God!'

Ash was patient, and he was very well lubricated. Fraction by fraction he ratcheted his cock head up into my arse, sliding in through the sphincter which could clench and flutter but never fully lock against him. Slow, rolling waves of sensation radiated from my bum up and down my body. My spine seemed to be one crackling length of exposed nerves. I felt hot; I felt cold. My legs were trembling wildly. My tits screamed for comfort and I stabbed my nipples against the cool tiles until Ash pinched them and then I nearly wept with relief.

Michael would have talked me through this. Michael would have said, 'I want to fuck your ass. I want to fuck your beautiful big ass, you naughty girl, and you want me to do it, don't you? You want to give me your butt crack and let me stick my big prick in it and come in your dirty, wicked, tight little asshole.'

Ash said nothing. There was just his harsh breathing on my ear and his hands on my tits and my sex and his cock boring into me, filling my world. There was just my softness giving way before his hardness. Then suddenly the discomfort melted to a sensation of fullness and I knew that it was done, he was in, and there was a wet sensation running down my crack and my thighs that I couldn't tell whether it was sweat or blood or soap or just my imagination.

'OK?' he whispered, his lips trembling over my skin, his tongue etching his name on my soul.

What the hell choice did I have? I'd yielded to him and he'd taken it all. He had conquered territory I'd never given up to any other man and now he was going to lay claim to it. He began to move, sliding his cock in and out. I felt every inch. I think he was quite careful, but the sensation was extraordinary and my body very nearly could not cope. It was dirty and it was divine; it was like taking a shit on the high altar of St Paul's Cathedral while the entire choir sang the 'Hallelujah Chorus'; it was like fucking God.

I came on his hands and on his cock. My lips were pressed to the tiles, which spat back my cries down my throat as everything exploded. After that all my clenched muscles relaxed – except for my arse whose tight ring was spasming like a hand about his shaft, completely out of my control, gripping and relaxing in a pulsing dance. He took his cue from that, thrusting firmer and deeper. I felt his balls slapping my pussy and I felt him quicken and shudder and I heard his groan as he filled my virgin hole with his cream. Suddenly I was slippery inside as well as out. Ash's arms locked around me and he groaned into my wet hair and my throat, over and over.

'Good?' he asked, still holding me, when his crisis had passed.

'Good,' I whispered, twisting to lick the sweat from his jaw.

After all that, we needed to get washed yet again.

When I emerged from the bathroom there was a certain hitch to my gait, courtesy of a novel sensitivity in the tender membranes of my anal bud. I borrowed a pair of knickers from Miranda's drawer, figuring she could spare them and that my need was great. They were white lace with blue flowers, rather expensive looking, but I couldn't find anything plainer; the rest of my clothes seemed very dowdy in contrast as I pulled them on. Aching for a coffee, I filled the kettle at the sink. The wet street below the window was a confusion of headlamps and neon, blurred by rain.

'What's the time?' Ash asked as he came out, towelling himself. There was a slight frown knotted between his brows.

'Gone eleven,' I said, after looking around in vain for a clock and finally retrieving my watch from under the bed.

'That's late. She should be home by now, surely.'

'Maybe she's ...' He had a point; Miranda had promised to meet us straight from the office. 'Well, she works London hours. She might have had a deadline or something.'

Ash didn't answer, but he pulled his clothes on with swift movements that suggested eloquently that he was not re-assured. He got the rucksack out from under the chair too, to check that the contents were safe. I went to open the door, picturing quite irrationally Miranda coming up the corridor outside. Looking out, I stared, not really understanding. Then I pulled back in, checking the interior walls of the room.

'Ash!'

He looked up. 'What?'

'This door ... Ash. Which is the way out?'

Stuffing the book back into the bag, he strode over to join me. I waited for his verdict, still trying to orientate myself. There was no corridor on the other side of the door, just a bare, unfurnished room. The floorboards were rough, the walls stained to an indeterminate grey by years of dirt. There was a lone door in the wall opposite. The only feature was a single broken chair with no seat.

Ash too looked around Miranda's flat to see if we had somehow managed to mislay the outer door. 'Shit,' he said grimly. Then he crossed back over to the bathroom door and flung it open. No white tiles winked beyond the lintel, only another grey box room and a broken chair, at exactly the same angle as the first.

How do you get lost in a single room?

Striding back, Ash brushed past me into the strange room where the corridor should have been. I followed, uneasily. 'What's happening?'

Deliberately, he laid the chair over on its back and then pulled open the furthest door. It revealed a third grey room beyond, another identical door and another seatless chair – this one laid flat upon its back. It was like one of those infinite vistas you get by tilting two mirrors together. I felt dizzy. 'Ash?'

'Get back into the flat,' he said. I obeyed willingly, hurrying to the kitchen. Grasping the frame of the sash window over the sink, I tried to raise it but the wood resisted. I struggled for a minute, cursing under my breath. The sodium-lit vista outside twinkled mockingly in the rain. Then Ash reached in past me, grabbed the frame and heaved. Nothing budged. 'Step back.'

I retreated to the fridge. Ash picked up a saucepan and slammed it against the bottom pane, which smashed. I put my hands over my mouth. Two inches behind the glass on which was painted that glittering night street was a wall of grimy brick. Ash struck that with the pan and the handle snapped off in his hand.

On the largest shard of glass still in the frame the raindrops crawled down and a bus passed slowly in the street below.

'Ash! What's going on?'

Slinging the handle into the sink he looked me in the face for the first time. He was really pale, and there was a cold, glittery look in his eye that I knew and did not like. 'We're trapped,' he said flatly. 'This is a trap.'

'You mean ... Michael's caught up with us?'

'Caught up?' He glanced around our cluttered bolt hole. 'No. This is the sort of thing you do on your own territory. Deverick got here before us. Long before us.'

My stomach churned. I hated the way he was looking at me. 'How?'

'You tell me.' His voice was quiet, under iron control. 'This was your plan.'

'Me?' The look he had on made me recoil. 'Hey, I had nothing ... This isn't –'

'Does your friend Miranda even exist?'

'Miranda?' Suddenly the thing that had been nagging at the back of my mind all along stood out proud. 'Oh God.' I wanted to slap myself. 'Miranda knew him. Through her brother. She knew Deverick. Oh God, Ash ...'

'Really?'

'I'd forgotten. She mentioned it at the wedding. But she's never spoken about him since and I didn't think ...'

'I bet you didn't.'

'You believe me, don't you?'

'Believe what? That you didn't sell me out; that you're just plain stupid?' He might have noticed the rage kindle in my eyes but he marched on regardless. 'Yeah, I'd love to believe that, Avril. We both know what he's like. Women will do anything he wants. Miranda or you – what's the difference? And either you or I was dumb enough to trust that there was one female who wouldn't just open her legs to that man and let him take control.'

I whirled away across the room. There was nowhere for me to go but that couldn't keep me still. 'I did not betray you!'

'You were sleeping with him, weren't you?'

I felt like my stomach and my mouth were full of blood. 'You knew that,' I snarled. 'You never asked me how I got hold of the book and anyone else would have. You already knew, and you'd been using that – been using me – to get close to him.'

His eyes were blazing; everything else was cold as ice. 'Oh, don't worry, I'm paying for that. I thought you'd seen through him. I thought that since you knew what this was really all about you'd made the decent choice. I thought that maybe just one other bloody person in the world was capable of doing something that wasn't about how much money they could make or who they could fuck or what was in it for them!'

I felt like he'd knocked all the air out of my chest.

Ash spread his hands. 'All my fault,' he snarled. 'I'm the idiot here.'

My voice, when I found it, was gravelly with shock. 'You shit. You want to know something, Ash? You aren't the good guy you think you are. You are *exactly* like Michael fucking Deverick, down to the dregs. You both think that you're better than everyone else on the fucking planet and that gives you the right to tell us what to do. You're bloody identical.'

Ash looked like I'd slapped him. He took a step forwards, mouth open.

'No,' I said, holding up a hand. 'Sorry, there is a difference between you. *He's* got a sense of humour.'

Ash's mouth twisted as if he couldn't believe what he'd heard.

'Knock, knock,' said Michael acidly from the doorway. We both turned in horror.

All along I'd managed on instinct, refusing to analyse my decisions. I'd trusted to action and relegated the consequences to the back of my mind, refusing to show them the light of day. Now the consequences had caught up with me. Now the repercussions stood casually against the door frame in a black coat, his eyes glinting, and he was holding a gun. Behind him I could see the pattern of the corridor wallpaper. 'Actually,' he said, 'I haven't got a punchline for that one, but the compliment is noted, Avril.'

Ash retreated slowly behind the bed, and the gun's muzzle lifted to cover him. It was an old-fashioned-looking weapon, I thought from some disassociated corner of my mind, with a rounder barrel than the ones you saw on television.

'The real joke,' continued Michael, 'is that it is entirely your fault, Ash, that I was able to track you here. You can't blame Avril for this.' He lifted his other hand from his coat pocket, displaying between two fingers a transparent plastic bag, like an item of police evidence. There was a something small in the bag: a bright aquamarine piece of fabric.

Ash swallowed. I knew what the blue scrap was, but I still didn't understand what Michael was doing with my old knickers. The ones I'd last seen in Ash's possession.

'A threshold enchantment,' Michael mused, 'is just the sort of primitive shit I'd expect you to pull, Ash. But *love magic*? That's a bit low for you, isn't it?'

Ash cleared his throat. 'I was only levelling the playing field.'

'Hold on,' I squeaked. 'You cast a love spell on me?'

He didn't look over. 'Don't bitch if I try to take your tools off you, Deverick.'

'You tried to *make* me love you by magic? You . . .' I said, then words failed me. Nothing could have expressed my feeling of betrayal.

A smile licked up the side of Michael's face. 'Oh, Ash, how you've misjudged us both. She wasn't my tool; I've never worked anything on or through her. Any problem you have with Avril is your own. I knew nothing about your . . . budding relationship. And her larceny this morning took me entirely by surprise.'

Ash went from pale to green. I'd never seen that before. His eyes met mine and I read in them depths of horror, but it made no difference to me: I wanted to kill him.

'You did make a mistake trusting Miranda though, Avril,' Michael continued. 'Once I knew where you were headed it was easy to get in touch. Miranda and I have been ... familiar ... since that wedding last year. She came to my hotel room rather late that night, and extremely drunk.'

'Bet that didn't stop you,' I mumbled, my voice seeming to come from someone else. I was watching the sweat ooze from Ash's temples.

'It did not. Miranda, it turns out, has a predilection for being tied up and pissed on. It's my pleasure to indulge her need. And she'd do anything for me, including betray you and your boyfriend, it turns out.' Michael hitched a shoulder. 'Now, Ash, give mc the book.'

Ash slipped the grimoire from the rucksack then flipped it open, holding it at chest height, his fingers knotted around the covers. He took a very deliberate pace backwards.

'Don't be stupid,' said Michael, his voice tightening audibly. The muzzle of the gun jutted forwards and we heard the click as he cocked the hammer. 'You do recognise this, don't you?'

Ash's lips twisted. 'Well, I did have my back turned the last time you pulled the trigger.'

Michael had the grace to laugh, baring his teeth. 'Think I won't pull it in your face? Put the book down.'

Ash's eyes narrowed. From somewhere he had found new focus, new obstinacy. 'The death of a magus is a powerful thing. You're taking a big bet that the grimoire will escape unscathed.'

'You're playing dirty.' Michael's eyes narrowed. Then he

swung the barrel round to point straight at me. 'Let's both play.'

I was too stunned to react.

'Now put the fucking book down.' Michael crossed over and put his arm around my shoulders, hand in my hair, jamming the barrel up into the angle of my jaw. 'Or I kill her.'

It was weird, I thought, the gun didn't seem real to me. Ancient sorcerers trapped in oak boles, holly wolves, pond spirits dissolving into my carpet – all those things I could take in my stride. They made a primitive sense to me. The gun didn't. Handguns were objects in American cop shows and on the news. I'd never seen a real one; they weren't part of my world. My head spun. The muzzle was cold and painfully hard on my throat.

Ash believed in the gun though, and I saw the defeat in his face as he dropped the book onto the bed. 'Deverick ...'

'Good. Now put your hands on the floor and kneel on them.'

I could smell Michael's familiar aftershave. Was this man threatening to blow a hole in my skull the same man who'd held me so tenderly in bed? It seemed a world away, but then I'd always managed to compartmentalise my relationships with Michael and Ash, tucking one tidily away as I concentrated on the other. Refusing to think about anything but what I wanted, right at that moment. Finally I was paying the price. And not just me either. 'Don't,' I whispered.

Reluctantly Ash went to his knees. Michael, satisfied, pushed me aside and walked slowly over to stand behind him.

'Please don't,' I repeated. 'Michael, please.' Both men looked at me: Michael appraising, Ash with a great regretful sorrow. I thought of the stag with the golden antlers, gazing with trust into the face of the huntress. 'You need him alive,' I gasped. 'You can't get back into the wood otherwise.'

Michael tilted his head. His thumb slid over the hammer. Then he lifted the gun and smacked the wooden stock hard on the rear of Ash's head. The kneeling man swayed violently, then the second blow crumpled him against the footboard of the bed. I had to turn away, and I swallowed the sob in my throat by sheer willpower. I watched as, ignoring me, Michael ransacked a drawer. He seemed to know exactly what he was looking for: silk scarves with which he tied Ash's wrists behind his back. Then he plundered his pockets, finding among other things the fallen man's knife and mobile phone, which he stuffed into his own pockets. The numbness of repeated shocks was wearing off and I was starting to tremble. When Michael strolled back over I forced myself not to shrink from him. He looked me right in the face. 'Go on, Avril. Just what the hell did you think you were doing stealing my book?'

I'd been trying to do the right thing, I wanted to say defiantly. Was that true, though? Hadn't I just been trying to hurt him? Hadn't I just been trying to get into Ash's pants? There were no straight answers here, and I offered up the one that condemned me least. 'I thought I was in love with him.'

'And now?'

I couldn't answer.

'Was he a good fuck, Avril?'

'Yes.' Even skirting the memory took my breath away.

Michael nearly spat. 'Well you've had a busy twenty-four hours. I'm amazed you can stand up straight.' Under the sneer and the pose he was genuinely angry and, to my amazement, I thought that I saw hurt there too.

'You were the one who said there were no rules. You can't blame me if I take you at your word.'

Ire flashed in those blue eyes, but he controlled it. 'I'm simply surprised,' he said thickly, 'that you managed to hide your feelings so well. You're quite the actress. I could have sworn your tendencies were in another direction altogether.'

'I'm not in love with you,' I told him. 'You're just an addiction.'

'The very definition of love, I'd have thought.'

'Then you know nothing about it.'

His lips tightened. 'Maybe. But I know what goes on here.' He cupped my pussy in his hand; I jerked away from him. With a sneer he returned to the bed, stepping over Ash's body, to pick up the grimoire. He riffled through it, then tucked the gun into his coat pocket. 'OK, we're leaving.'

'Where?'

He returned the book to its satchel. 'Back to the wood, like you said. It's all over bar the cigarette, Avril.' Stooping, he carefully manoeuvred Ash over his shoulder and hoisted his limp form. The weight was obviously awkward but bearable as he straightened, legs braced. The rucksack hung from his free hand. 'Get the door.'

'You'll be seen.'

'I doubt it. Try anything funny, Avril, and I will take it out on your boyfriend.'

The corridor beyond the door looked just the same as it had done when we arrived. I led the way to the lift and summoned the clanking cage. I hoped that someone would spot us on the way down, but the building might as well have been deserted. The wet street was no better. Even London's notorious clamping crews had let me down; Michael had left his vehicle parked on the double-yellow line right before the entrance, but it hadn't been touched. Michael unlocked the 4x4 and offloaded Ash into the front passenger seat.

'You're driving, Avril.'

By the time I'd gone round to the other side of the car my employer was ensconced in the back. He passed the keys to me over my shoulder. 'This is how it's going to be,' he told me. 'You're going to drive us back to the Grange. I'm going to sit quietly here. And if you do anything stupid – if you flash a police car or ram a wall or jump out at a light, or even go over the speed limit – I'm going to put bullets first into Ash and then into you. And before you start arguing, technically all I need from him is his blood. If you want it to stay inside its present convenient container then I'd suggest you do what you're told.'

'You promised me I'd always have a choice,' I said hoarsely.

'That is a choice. It's a choice between life and death. How much more could you ask for?' Michael settled back into his seat, drawing his coat over his lap so that he could handle the gun in the pocket.

I saw to it that Ash was buckled in securely. He didn't seem to be bleeding, and his breathing was regular though shallow. Then, cautiously, I slotted the car into the traffic flow and we set off through the night streets. Michael gave terse directions. The padded steering wheel absorbed the cold sweat off my hands. Neon street lamps flashed across the windscreen in an endless hypnotic procession.

We were on the motorway and heading west before Ash's breathing suddenly grew harsher and he awoke. He rolled his head against the seat rest, taking a long time to come back into focus. His shoulders twisted as he discovered and tested his bonds. 'Where are we going?' he asked at length.

I glanced in the rear-view mirror but Michael, watching us with an alert and sardonic smile, said nothing. 'Back to the wood,' I replied.

Ash tried to look round into the back seat but winced and abandoned the plan. 'Avril,' he said after a long pause. 'I'm sorry.'

'Forget it.' I didn't want him to talk, least of all in front of Michael, who'd raised one scornful eyebrow.

'You should understand. When I met you . . .'

'I said forget it.'

'I fell for you so hard. Awake all night sweating sort of hard. Unable to get my mind off you and concentrate on anything else. The dreams . . . Oh, I wanted you so much. And it made perfect sense. You were Deverick's employee; there was no attempt to hide that. It was obvious you were part of his push into the wood. It was obvious that he was working some sort of enchantment through you, to get a hold on me.'

'Obvious, huh?'

'Why else would you be so keen on me?'

I goggled slightly at this. 'It didn't occur to you that any of it might be . . . natural?' My voice came out ragged.

'No. Not once. You were too perfect. It had to be a trap.' The air left his chest in a sigh. 'I panicked, Avril. I didn't know what else to do. I couldn't stop what I felt, and I didn't understand why, and I wanted to take some measure of control back. I fucked up, Avril, big time.'

'Yeah,' said I bitterly.

'There's no excuse for using magic on you the way I did. I just need you to know . . . that I love you. Whatever happens.'

I didn't reply and I didn't look at him; I just stared straight ahead at the road, my knuckles white on the wheel, tears welling up and running down my face. Because I loved him. If I was honest with myself, that was how I felt. I was far more afraid for him than for myself. I was desperate to hold him and heal him and feel his embrace and his kiss. I was deeply in love; I just didn't know if any of it was real.

10: Wildwood

We drove back into Devon as the dawn mist was rising from the autumnal fields, and we reached the Wood Gate just as the first touch of sun turned it to gold. I parked up and sagged over the steering wheel. Michael had let me break the journey once at a service station where I'd been permitted to doze off for forty minutes – it was either that or I'd have fallen asleep behind the wheel. I'd been aware of the two men talking as I slept, but had registered none of the words.

The cool air that washed in when Michael opened his door brought me wide awake once more. It smelt of autumn, an inchoate sorrow and yearning.

'Get out.'

I went round to open Ash's door and help him down. In the meanwhile Michael opened the back of the car and retrieved the tiny maquette of his cage, which he pocketed. He looked us over with satisfaction. I shivered a little, and blamed the fact I'd left my coat in Miranda's flat. Ash looked towards the wood, the set of his jaw betraying his tension.

'First thing,' said Michael, 'is that you get rid of them.' He was referring to the tribe of protesters who stood silently in array behind the gate. Their blank eyes watched us. Perhaps it was just the result of their scrutiny, but Grange Wood seemed to throb with awareness behind them.

'I can't just –'

'Do it.' The shape of the gun muzzle showed clearly against the taut fabric of Michael's pocket.

With a sag of his shoulders Ash turned to the protestors. 'Go down onto the bridle path,' he said flatly. 'Wait by the farm gate. Do nothing.' We watched as, without a word, they turned obediently away and set off through the trees.

Michael settled himself against the front of his car and pulled the gun into plain view, resting it casually in both hands. 'You'll enjoy this bit I don't doubt, Avril. I want you to untie his hands. Ash, get your clothes off.'

I exchanged a lingering glance with my fellow prisoner as I went up behind him, hoping that he might whisper me some vital instruction, but Ash's eyes held no hope. The silk scarf was tightly knotted and I had to work at it for some moments. His fingers were cold when I brushed them. The two magi kept a steely watch on each other. Once he was free Ash undressed slowly, throwing each garment, as instructed, at Michael's feet. And he in turn, keeping the gun carefully trained upon us, shed his own clothes, until both men were naked. Ash stood rubbing his wrists. I rammed my fists into my pockets, biting my lip. Some witless part of my mind that wasn't concerned with the fact that Ash and I were at the mercy of a vengeful bastard with a deadly weapon and no conscience, was flipping cartwheels with glee at that sight and I couldn't drag my eyes away. My two lovers, bollock-naked on the dewy grass, so much in common and so different. My heart was tying itself in knots. Ash looked pale gold in the diffuse light, Michael like he'd been drawn in black ink lines against the mist. Ash was my raspberries-and-cream lover, sweet and sharp and so irresistible that I wanted to gorge myself upon him. Michael was more like bitter chocolate – impossible to take in more than tiny quantities but with a taste that ravished the senses and kept me coming back for more.

'Tie his hands again.'

I hesitated. The gun jerked.

'As has been pointed out, I could use him in the wood, so I'm not set on killing him right now. But I will check the knots, Avril.'

There was no choice but to obey, though I wasn't quite so cruel with the binding as he'd been. My fingers trembled. I wanted to press my face to the smooth skin of Ash's back and feel his warmth, smell his sweetness.

'Now get on your knees,' Michael commanded, opening the other man's knife.

Slowly, Ash knelt, and the long wet grass clasped his thighs. I put my hand on his hair and he turned his face to my palm. Even his lips felt cold.

'Normally I'd be reluctant to resort to your crude blood-and-shit mechanics,' Michael commented, approaching with the knife and Ash's shirt. 'But you've rather forced my hand, you two.' He squatted and grinned wolfishly at the other man, clearly conscious of the striking picture they were presenting, bared to the golden meadow and the looming wood and the rising sun. 'Takes us right back to the 60s, doesn't it?' Running the knife-point down the bound man's inner arm, he selected the precise place and twisted the tip, indenting the skin over a narrow blue vein. 'Except,' he added with a sneer, 'that you never left.' Then he pushed the point home, deep. Blood began to run out at once – alarmingly quickly.

Ash drew in a sharp breath through his teeth. I felt sick.

Michael planted the knife in the earth at his side, making sure it was out of my reach. Then he laid the shirt to the wound, soaking up the blood. Ash leant away from him against my leg, pressing his face to my thigh. When the cloth was bright red and sodden Michael sat back and wiped it over his chest.

I couldn't watch. I held Ash tightly and looked at my hands in his hair or at the grass or at the dark oak canopies bulking out above the mist or at the car that stood ticking as the engine cooled – anywhere but at Michael Deverick painting himself in his enemy's blood. The world seemed to spin. I wondered if I should make a grab at the knife, but I couldn't believe it would be successful and I knew Michael was ready for me. My mouth seemed filled with glue.

He was thorough. Every inch of his skin, front and back, got baptised, including face and hands and scalp and crotch. I saw it from the corner of my eye. Then he threw the red shirt at my feet. 'Your turn, Avril.'

'No.' Ash sounded hoarse. 'It's not necessary.'

'Afraid it is. She's my guarantee you're going to behave yourself, Ash.'

Ash hesitated. In the gap I grabbed the shirt and pressed it to the cut, ignoring the wetness under my hands as I tried to close the wound by pressure alone. He winced. 'No. No need. I've already sealed her.'

'Oh?'

'Cunt and mouth and arse. On the first day of the waxing moon.'

'Jesus.' Michael sounded partly amused, partly scathing. 'You fucking Neanderthal.'

'What's he done?' I demanded.

Ash didn't answer, so Michael spoke for him. 'He marked you as his own for the duration of the month, Avril. He laid claim.'

I met Ash's pain-filled gaze, sickened and hurt yet again, and asked, 'D'you ever do anything without some creepy magical reason behind it?'

'Avril . . . I thought we might have to run back here. I was trying to ensure you'd be safe.'

He'd screwed that one up then, I thought. But I held on tight to the wadding. 'I just thought you wanted me,' I whispered.

'Do you doubt that?'

Michael cleared his throat. 'Sorry to interrupt you sweet young things, but time is money. Get him shipshape, Avril. We have some walking to do.' He turned away to the pile of Ash's discarded clothing, which he began to put on. I nearly lost it then. He'd been a grisly red like a pantomime demon, but even as he stooped for the first garment I saw the blood streaks on his back fading into nothing, soaking into his skin.

He always was vain, I thought dizzily. Then he pulled on my old white jumper and my gut clenched in anger.

'Avril,' Ash whispered, recapturing my attention.

I took my own T-shirt off to make a bandage, twisting it and tying it tight around his arm. By the time I was done and sure there was no serious leakage, Michael was dressed in his stolen clothes, had thrown his own into the car and locked it and there was no sign of blood on him.

The three of us made a strange posse as we faced the wood. Michael looked so out of character in Ash's cast-offs, with the rucksack hitched over one shoulder and those long trousers crumpled up around boots that were slightly too big for his feet, but possession of a gun does tend to mute criticism. I was shivering, only a Lycra sports bra between my chest and the damp breath of the morning. Ash was barefoot and naked but for his bandage and the scarf binding his hands at his back, though he tried to hold himself with grace. I had to help him over when we climbed the gate.

Grange Wood had changed; I felt it within the first few paces. No rooks flew up clamouring this time – in fact there was total silence from the birds that should have been bustling about the leaves all around us. The silence was thick, like another manifestation of the golden mist. I felt it pressing against my eardrums like a held breath and I cringed, sure that the exhalation would be an unbearable roar. The ground felt strangely taut beneath my feet, as if it had been heaved up by pressure from below, and the soles of my feet itched with discomfort.

'Michael...' I wanted to say that this was not a good idea, to ask whether he couldn't feel the intent regard of the wood turned on us, but then I saw how pale he'd gone and knew I would be preaching to the choir. His jaw was set, his lips pressed into a narrow line, and he was looking about him with undisguised mistrust.

'Lead on.'

Ash obeyed and we turned uphill towards the centre of the wood. He moved slowly, stumbling every once in a while; his tied hands impeded his balance and I think he'd lost enough blood to make him dizzy. I walked close behind him, ready to grab his arm if he really lost his footing, and Michael brought up the rear. Our feet stirred the leaf mould and with every step I felt the pulse of the wood beat up into my bones, filling my skull with its thick surge. A sweet farmyard aroma wafted around us then vanished as we began to climb.

Ash didn't take the same route as the last time he'd led me to the Green Man, nor the one we'd come back by. I wondered if he was stalling for time or whether the routes themselves changed, but said nothing. My mouth had grown dry. Brambles caught at my trousers and I welcomed the clinging stab of the thorns in my skin as relief from the oppressive build-up of pressure all over my body. I wanted to scratch my nails down my arms and sides. I wanted to tug at my hair. I wanted to rub myself between the legs.

We'd been walking long enough and the incline was steep enough to have us all breathing hard when Michael, stubbing his boot against a root, lurched against me and grabbed at me to steady himself. The gun clipped my hip and his open hand slapped hard against my buttock. I stopped dead, paralysed by the shock waves. As Michael caught his breath his palm lingered where it had landed. He did not miss the fact that I didn't shrug him off and I saw the rise of his eyebrows before I looked away again, flushing. 'Still…needy?' he enquired. 'You're unbelievable, Avril. How many men would it take to wear you out?'

I'd hardly have believed it myself, except that I knew what was going on; I'd felt it before. This time, though, it was much stronger. The pulse of the Green Man was throbbing in my blood, plumping tired tissues and making nerve endings itch.

'He's awake,' said Ash, who'd turned to look at Michael's hand fondling my arse. 'He knows his book is here and he's fighting his bonds. You're out of your mind, Deverick. You can't control him. You can't even keep your mind on the job.'

Michael released me to run his hand over his crotch, squeezing what was already a notable bulge. His mouth quirked wickedly and he leant in to breathe in my ear, 'Looks like I've got wood.' Then the humour snapped out of his eyes and they became glittering sapphires once more. 'Get a move on.'

It was warm now we were walking and the golden mist seemed more like steam. There were no trolls this time, no summer stags. Nothing dared stir in the wood, nothing but the power of the Green Man that bled through soil and rocks and bark and flesh: the power of green growing things and red running things and dark devouring things, all the power of a primeval world seeping out from that prison, sending the wood into panic. I saw trees that were only just turning yellow for autumn already brandishing bright green sprays of new leaves from the same twigs, and white blossom springing out on branches of Midland hawthorn eight months ahead of its true time, and I smelled the garlic reek of spring-flowering ramsons. It was a power that surged in me just as surely, making me wanted to dance, to run, to fight, but above all to open my legs to a thick hard cock. That's what the life force is about after all. As a species and as individuals we will risk pain and ruin and death for the chance to fuck. We live to fuck. Now I was squirming with discomfort, and hiding it badly. My clit felt like an overripe berry swollen with juice and ready to burst.

Ash led us to a steep rocky defile, and I had to go ahead to help him balance, pulling him up the steepest bits. Weakened by blood loss his muscles felt cool under my hands, and as we got right to the top he swayed against me. Gasping, Ash and I struggled to steady ourselves. Our lips nearly met; our gazes did, and I saw him fighting to regain focus. I slipped my arms about his waist and our bodies brushed together. Though I was hot enough that my tanned skin was glazed, my nipples stood poking up against the Lycra that bound them, the rubbing of the fabric almost painful against those stiff points. He couldn't push me away, not with his hands tied behind him. He couldn't shield his crotch from me. I looked down between us, belly to belly.

Then suddenly he swayed, staggering in my arms, and I knew his legs were giving way. I backed him hurriedly against a tree trunk and for a moment it seemed to give him support, but then he slithered to his knees, head sagging. A crimson runnel had worked its way from under the bandage and was sliding down his inner arm.

'Give me your belt!' I demanded, turning to Michael who stood breathing hard at the top of the rise. He looked askance and I barely held on to my temper. 'I need to tourniquet his arm!'

'Come and get it then.'

Even though it meant coming right up in front of him I did, uncinching the webbing belt and drawing it out through the loops about his waist. The familiar scent of his aftershave made the skin on my neck prickle. Michael didn't trouble to hide his amusement. He couldn't have hidden his arousal if he'd wanted to; the thick cylinder of his erection was pressing up against the fabric of Ash's stolen trousers. In my dizzy state it was nearly enough to distract me from my task and I hesitated, my fingers drawn involuntarily towards it. Michael hooked his hand in the front of my pants and pulled me up against him, hard. 'Slut,' he said.

'Let me see to Ash,' I whispered. My pulse was nearly choking me.

With a nod of his chin he let me go. I wobbled over to Ash, grateful for the chance to fall to my knees myself. Binding the cloth belt about his arm was a welcome task, forcing my trembling fingers back into use. Ash sat quietly, eyes shut and lips parted, his breath ragged. I stroked his face but got no reaction. When I stood again Michael was glowering at me and cradling his groin.

'This is crazy. I can't even think straight. Avril, get your pants down; I'm going to have to make use of that beautiful arse of yours.'

I stared.

Michael's mocking gaze flicked sideways. 'You don't mind, do you, Ash? Gives you a chance for a bit of a rest.'

A blush of rage darkened my cheeks. 'And me?'

'You?'

'Cock or bullet – that's my choice now?'

Michael grinned. 'Avril, if I offered you cock or the riches of Solomon's treasury you'd choose cock. If I offered you cock or eternal life you'd choose cock. You'd always choose cock because cock's what you love and what you want and what you need. You need it right now. Mine – his – doesn't matter, does it?' He lifted the gun negligently. 'If it makes you feel better about it then, yes, that's your choice. Now drop them.'

It isn't a pretty thing to admit, but I was glad he had the gun. I kicked off my trainers and walked over to where a fallen tree made a support. Then, turning my back on both men, I lowered my trousers, stepped out and bent over, hands on the bark, presenting Michael my backside wrapped in Miranda's lacy white knickers. I was sure he must be able to see the darkened fabric of the damp gusset, and even as I braced my trembling legs another warm trickle of moisture escaped my inner clasp. I felt so open. He wasn't wrong about me being a slut, either; he was going to fuck me at gunpoint in front of the man who loved me – and I welcomed it.

Michael's hand brushed my sex. I could hear the harshness of his breathing. 'Very pretty,' he commented, running his fingers up the inside of the lace edge, across the curve of my bum, back down into the deep cleft beneath.

'No.' It was Ash's voice, hoarse but forceful. 'You can't.'

A red-hot wave of shame washed me from head to toe, but I pressed back against Michael's hand anyway and I'm not sure he even heard the protest. 'Take them off,' he said, as he had done in my living room weeks ago, but this time it was unequivocally an order and I hooked my fingers into the panties and drew them down to my thighs. The taut fabric dug into my flesh as I spread them further for him. 'Oh, yes.'

'No, you'll kill her!' That got our attention at last. 'If she leaks afterwards, Deverick, she dies. We're in too deep – you mustn't do it!'

Michael looked at him coldly.

'Put it in her mouth,' Ash concluded bitterly. 'It's safest.'

Michael picked me up, turning me to face him. 'You hear that, Avril? Your boyfriend wants you to give me a blow job. He wants me to fuck your mouth and shoot my come down your throat.' He pushed me to my knees and rubbed my face roughly against his groin. 'D'you like that idea?'

I loved that idea – though my bereft pussy ached in protest. The crotch packeted in those old army trousers smelt like Ash but felt like Michael. I pressed my hands up the inside of his thighs, seeking his balls.

'Good girl,' he said. 'Now, undo my flies. With your teeth,' he amended as I reached with my hand.

I took the metal tag between my lips and drew it down, feeling every individual tooth of the zip strain and then part. With a grunt of satisfaction Michael helped me by popping the buttons and hefting his cock out into the light. Thick and flushed dark, it stood up and swayed like a drunk – a mean drunk, because when he grabbed the back of my head and shoved my face in, the hard shaft jabbed my eyes and bruised my lips. Michael's anger at my betrayal had not been forgotten and he used me cruelly. 'Kiss it,' he growled, and I kissed the hot shaft fervently. He pulled my lips up to the swollen glans. 'Again.' I tried to, but he angled it past my lips and shoved in hard, all the way to the back of my throat, as if wanting to choke me. 'Take it,' he hissed, his hand knotted in my scalp.

I did, blocking out the pain. I made my mouth and my throat a shrine for his cock, a place where it was worshipped. My tongue worked frantically about it, slicking the thick meat. I knew exactly how much Michael loved oral and I knew he could not resist the wet squirm of my tongue about the head of his cock, however much he might want to punish me in other ways. In moments I felt his grip relax, his stance shift, his thighs tremble. 'Ah, God,' he muttered under his breath. I slid my hand down between my thighs, sinking my fingertips into my own wetness as I sucked and licked him. I wrote eulogies with my tongue on his flesh, declaring how much I loved his heat, his strength, his hardness, the taste and the bulk of him. The slithering friction across my lips seemed to connect directly to my clit; I was hardly aware of my own fingers, just him fucking my mouth and sending me higher and higher.

I heard Ash groan.

Dizzily I eased myself from Michael's shaft – not fully, just enough to be able to turn my head. Ash still knelt at the foot of the tree, his shoulders thrown back and chest straining, his gaze fixed upon us and his expression one of torment. His prick stood erect and glistening. I wouldn't have thought it possible after the amount of blood he'd lost, but the Wildwood must have had its claws in deep. I knew just how he felt.

Carefully, my tongue still dancing on the helm of his cock, I lifted my eyes to Michael's and saw no fury any more, only enthralment to the pleasure of my mouth. Only need. Wrapping my hand firmly about his shaft, I pulled away, wriggling my arse, drawing him after me. For a moment he frowned, and then he made the connection between my splayed retreating backside and his helpless captive twisting against the silk bonds and I saw realisation dawn. His eyes widened. I licked him, pleading as much as teasing, promising as much as placating. His eyelids fluttered and with the faintest bemused smile he let me have my way. Step by step he advanced across the leaf mould while I retreated on my knees before him with wide-splayed cheeks, leading him by the cock, until I'd closed the gap between us and Ash.

My poor, naked Ash. Against his better judgement and flying in the face of all his scruples, the one thing he wanted right now was to slip his aching prick into my pussy and fuck me from behind while his mortal enemy shafted my throat. His anguish was clear, but it was entirely overridden by the demands of his erection. A standing prick has no conscience, as they say. In the depths of the Wildwood Ash was as enslaved to the sexual imperative as was Michael or I. He surged towards me, unable to tear his gaze from the wet crack I was presenting him.

Michael licked his dry lips, as if not quite believing what was happening.

Pulling my panties down to my knees, I wriggled into Ash's lap. He rose to meet me, pushing the head of his member up the slippery folds of my furrow and embedding it deep in me. I gasped to feel the penetration I wanted so much, my breath pulled up around the solid cylinder of meat in my mouth, and Michael pushed deep into my throat as if to remind us who was in charge. I took him gratefully in both hands, delving for the ripe fullness of his scrotum. Ash ground against my backside, gasping with effort, his thighs rock hard.

That was how I paid my toll to the Wildwood, with both men fucking me. I became the bridge between them: between magus and magus, captor and captive, victor and loser. They co-operated to fuck me, finding a rhythm that suited them both and nearly split me in half, rattling my mind clear out of my body, filling me and plundering me and taking everything. Michael had both hands on my head; I held onto his thighs to support myself. Ash had pushed me forwards onto my knees and was leaning hard into me, his hips shuddering as he thrust, his balls slapping my pussy as his shaft worked my wet cunt. I'd never been used from both ends like that. I'd never been so full. I grabbed my clit and held on tight as orgasm took me from arse to head, an electric arc connecting their two cocks. It kept coming, bolt after bolt. I cried out and my scream was muffled by Michael's tool buried deep in my throat. Then he pulled back just enough, his pelvis jerking, to fill my mouth with his spunk.

Ash froze. I had just enough sense left to swallow hard and fast, gulping it down, salty and burning. Michael held my face as I sucked him clean, his fingers slackening, his thumbs tracing the planes of my cheeks and brushing my swollen lips. His eyes were unbelievably blue, like pieces fallen from a summer sky. I think my heart stopped for a moment, looking into them.

Then Ash pulled out of me and somehow managed to stagger to his feet. 'Avril,' he said thickly.

I turned to him and took the wet cock proffered into my mouth, scenting the sharp tang of my shameless want. I sucked those juices off, yearning for his own taste that lay beneath. From the corner of my eye I saw Michael take a step back, running his hand up and down the length of his penis, which showed no sign of flagging yet. Ash leant into me, breathing down his nose. He was far more at my mercy than Michael had been and I seized the chance to get my breath back, taking it slow and teasing. I cupped his balls, tickling the soft skin behind until he groaned. As I fell into the rhythm that would bring him off I shut my eyes, revelling in the smooth sweetness of his cock.

Without a word, Michael's hand cupped my chin and drew me gently off Ash. I opened my eyes and his cock was there in my face, still flushed and shiny and thick with unspent lust. Both of them were there, both men standing so close that with a turn of my head I could take either in my mouth. So I did, in turn. I treated them both with absolute fairness, licking like a girl with a melting ice-cream cone in either hand. I tasted them both and warmed each in turn down my throat. Hey, there are worse combinations than raspberries and cream and bitter chocolate.

Ash seemed to be swimming in and out of consciousness at times; I had to wrap my right arm around his thigh to support him. But his cock wouldn't stop. I felt him gather towards his crisis and I lavished more attention upon him, but Michael wouldn't stand for that and this time he didn't try to distract me from Ash, he simply thrust his own prick between my lips alongside his. Oh, I have a generous mouth, but it's not *that* big – it felt as if my cheeks were splitting, and the shock nearly knocked me over. Ash's eyes shot wide open, but I think he was at the point where he was incapable of withdrawing, in fact I think he wasn't capable of anything by then except fucking to climax. Both men looked glazed, almost drunk.

It took some readjustment before I could handle this new situation and I could take neither of them very deep, but take them both I did: both cocks in the burning crucible of my mouth, transmuting darkest rivalry to pure gold. My tongue laved the two smooth bulbs, explored both seeping slits. They stood hip to hip. Michael ran his hand through my hair, supporting my head as the two of them rubbed and slipped over one another and I licked and kissed and sucked them. Ash came noisily, groaning with effort, and I opened with gratitude to the thick wash of his semen. Then straight away, to my utter surprise, so did Michael. Not so copiously, but then it shouldn't have been able to happen at all. I think it hurt him too; his muscles were clenched so hard I was sure he would go into cramp. Their jism mingled on my tongue and my heart was pounding and I felt like I was about to melt. I held them and held them and would have held them forever, like that, kneeling between them with my lips wrapped about their pricks. What had happened had turned my world inside out. I looked up at Michael with tears in my eyes.

Then Ash slipped away from me and collapsed to the floor.

Slowly Michael withdrew. For once he had nothing to say for himself. We just stared at each other, me kneeling in the damp woodland litter, he hunched and pallid, the rucksack with his precious book lying disregarded against a rotting log.

I think there was a chance then that everything could have changed. If so, then it was my fault it didn't; I turned away to check that Ash was all right, that he wasn't bleeding out. By the time I'd done that Michael was properly dressed and had retrieved the rucksack, his expression closed off and sardonic.

'You enjoyed being spit-roast, didn't you, Avril?' His voice was a little hoarse. 'Who'd have thought it when you handed in your résumé?'

'Michael...'

'Is he still with us?'

Ash's eyes were partly open when I looked down, but unfocused. 'I'm not sure he can walk.'

'Then you'll have to help him, won't you?'

'Give him a chance –'

'No!' For the first time Michael raised his voice, his black brows knotted, but when he spoke again he sounded calm once more: 'He had his chance a long time ago, Avril. And you...' He shoved his sleeves up to his elbows irritatedly. 'I really thought there was hope for you.' He snorted. 'Get him up.'

When I'd dressed I helped Ash to his feet, supporting him against me. His bare feet were bleeding I noticed. For a second I caught another whiff of that sweet bovine aroma, but it was a fugitive scent gone as soon as I sought for it. 'Which way?' I asked, unsteady under his weight. Ash nodded forwards. His face looked haggard. We set off and Michael brought up the rear silently once more.

The last part of the journey was through the boggy woodland I remembered with such distaste. This time it was much worse. I slipped and staggered under Ash's shoulder, my fingers biting into his ribs as I kept a grip on him. He did his best to walk straight but his weakness came in waves and sometimes I had to stop to let him get his feet back beneath him. The water and mud came up to our ankles, sucking with every step, and once I lost my balance too and we both fell to our knees in the ooze. The mist had risen to form a haze that made the sky above invisible. At least the throb of the Green Man's power was less of a distraction now – not because it had diminished, but because my internal pressure felt now equalised with the external. The wood was in trouble though: everywhere black-ened leaves were falling to scab over the surface of the sludge, and bark was peeling off the trunks in necrotic sheets. It was like an acid-rain nightmare or a glimpse of a post-apocalyptic wasteland, except that glimpses from beneath my brow told me that instead of wood beneath the fallen bark the timber of these trees was variously bone or glass or gleaming silver.

By the time we pushed through the ring of yews Ash and I were mired and panting. I didn't look directly at the stump; I didn't dare. I let Ash slide to the floor and rest, his head against my thigh. Michael came through, bent double under the branches, and got his first look at the goal of all his endeavours here.

'Oh shit,' he said softly, recoiling a step.

It was good to know that something could dismay him, but he recovered quickly enough. He pulled out the book, throwing the bag aside, and opened it. Onto the vellum he laid the wire maquette and, after opening it, Ash's clasp knife. Then, setting his jaw, he approached the ancient remnant of the oak. I couldn't look at him straight on, my eyes were watering so much, but I saw him stagger and set his legs as if bracing himself against a high wind. His outline looked smeared, but that might have been a fault of my vision. That arcane pulse was making my skin crawl and a red pain dance at the back of my head. I was glad we'd stopped to pay our dues sexually; I think if we hadn't we might have torn one another apart here.

'Avril,' said Michael bleakly, 'move away from him. Over there.' A jerk of his head indicated the other side of the clearing.

I put my hand on Ash's hair. The ground was trembling beneath my feet and the air vibrating. I didn't like the look of that open knife at all. 'What are you going to do?'

His lips tightened. 'There's the small matter of the binding ritual. It requires a sacrifice.'

'You can't take any more of his blood,' I protested. 'It'll kill him.'

Michael tilted his head, still looking at the tree. 'Not your decision, I'm afraid.'

'For God's sake –'

'Out of the way.' He swung to face me, lifting the gun. 'I mean it. Move.'

I moved in front of Ash. 'No chance.' Then it dawned on me that I'd just discovered something about the reality of my love, and the shock left me dizzier than the fear. 'Oh God, Michael, don't. Please.'

'This is the man who used magic on you, remember? He made you fall in love with him.'

'So did you,' I said, my heart in pieces. 'It doesn't take magic to do that.'

I watched him grimace. I still didn't completely believe he would put a bullet in me, not even when he aimed the gun between my breasts and cocked the hammer. And, God help me, Michael did hesitate. At that moment the yew branches heaved and into the clearing lumbered Bull Peter, snorting and wild-eyed. Michael jerked back. The changeling looked from me to him.

'Peter!' I cried, thrusting my hand out at Michael. The bull man charged him, head lowered, roaring.

I think he managed to fire twice before Bull Peter hit him, but it did nothing to slow his attacker down. Michael was thrown back across the clearing, the naked changeling on top of him, and the two rolled over in a tangle of kicking limbs. Bull Peter was still on top when they came to a halt, but Michael was still conscious and in possession of the revolver. He heaved it from under the bull man's bulk, shoved it to his neck and fired three times up under the heavy jaw, the reports ringing round the clearing. Bull Peter shuddered and stopped moving.

Slowly Michael managed to crawl out from under the steaming chestnut bulk. He was clutching his hand to his side as he sat up, and blood was seeping out into the white wool of his jumper like a scarlet poppy blooming. There was blood on one of Bull Peter's horns, sticky and glistening, blood all the way down to the base. Michael tried to get to his feet but sat back down with a bump, staring around wildly. He looked down at his hand and made a little noise of disbelief. Finally he looked over at me. It was only then that he noticed that I was holding the grimoire.

'Avril?'

Bull Peter spasmed, a groan issuing from his lips. Michael lifted the gun again and pulled the trigger in a single reflex motion, but the hammer fell on an empty chamber with a snap. Michael's chest was heaving as he scrabbled away across the bare earth, but he needn't have worried, the changeling did not move again.

When he looked up at me his eyes were bright, his voice razor-edged. 'Give me the book, Avril.'

'Avril,' groaned Ash, 'run. Run!'

I didn't do either. I took a step backwards, towards the Green Man's oak. The look of panic that shot across the faces of the two magicians was identical. Michael pointed the gun at Ash but his wrist was trembling and his heart was not in the bluff.

'You're out of bullets,' I croaked. My heart was trying to climb out of my throat.

'Avril, for God's sake, run!'

'Avril, listen to me.' Michael heaved himself onto his knees, jamming his hand against the seeping hole beneath his ribs as hard as he could. A little blood spilt out from his lower lip. 'Give me the book. I will give you anything you want if I have the book. Anything. You have no idea what it makes possible.'

'Don't listen to him.'

'I can save the rainforests, Avril. Would you like that? I can make the Amazon a no-go area for loggers and trappers. I can save the redwoods and the Taiga and the orang-utans in Borneo. I can sink every whaling vessel on the planet in its harbour. I can turn back global warming, for God's sake! Isn't that worth it?'

I stared at him, tears running down my cheeks. I could feel the split in the ancient trunk yawning at my back like a slavering mouth. I could feel the guilt of Bull Peter's death clawing at my belly. I could feel my instinctive longing to believe Michael; to believe that I mattered to him, that he could be honourable, that there was more to him than power and charm and good looks. I wanted to believe that he deserved what I felt for him – feelings that were in their own way as elemental and irreducible as were my feelings for Ash.

'Just give me the book, Avril. We can do it together.'

'Yes,' I said sadly, 'and all I'd have to do is trust you.'

Turning, I flung the grimoire into gaping fissure, down into the dark. There was just time enough for me to hear both men scream 'No!' in unison before the tree exploded.

The blast engulfed us. For the briefest moment I felt shards of wood and splinters of corroded bronze punching through my flesh, and then I was suspended in a place where the power of the Green Man roared through me like a tide, invading every orifice, boiling the flesh from my bones. I lost my body altogether, swept away in the flood of atavistic memory. I was a bee swarm, a hundred thousand butterflies rising on crumpled wings made of soul silk, a blizzard of dust motes caught in the sunlight and turned to gold. I was a swan maiden tumbling in a gale over a black loch; I was Pan ravishing the moon; I was Culhwch in wild pursuit of the boar Twrch Trwyth; I was Meroudys returning joyfully to the arms of King Orfeo; I was Black Annis cutting the throats of children with my famine knife. They rode through me, all of them, a host of fallen angels, a wild hunt.

Then the storm dropped me. When I finally returned to my self I was on hands and knees on the woodland floor and I was facing, where once there'd been a huge dead oak stump, a shallow crater scooped from the raw earth. The light was no longer gold. The sun must have risen above the mist and the stripped trunks of the ruined yews, blasted clean of foliage, stood out black against the grey vapour. It was chilly.

I ran my hand down my torso, seeking blood. There were no wounds though my clothes were in tatters, no protruding splinters, not so much as a scratch on me. I felt shaky but unhurt.

Looking around me the first thing I saw was Ash, who'd been thrown back against a tree and lay with head and one shoulder shoved up against the base, the rest of his body buried in rotted leaf litter and torn up moss. I crawled over to him and nearly knelt on his hand, limp in the dirt. When I picked it up there were shreds of a silk scarf still knotted around his wrist. Then his fingers closed around mine and he reached up with his other arm to touch me, and in a moment we were clinging together and he'd taken my face in his hands and kissed me. I wrapped my arms round him and we hugged the breath out of one another, frantic with relief that we were both still alive. When I pulled away it was to examine his arm. The bandage and tourniquet had worked loose, but there was only a crust of dried blood on his arm and no hole. 'You're OK?'

'Yes. You? You're sure?'

Further round the clearing something stirred. I turned just

in time to see Michael rise unsteadily to his feet. His clothes were shredded too. He lifted the unravelled edge of the jumper to check the skin on his left side; the puncture wound had disappeared. It was only then that I noticed that so had the body of my poor Bull Peter. I knelt up straighter, my heart thumping. Michael blinked, let the piece of fabric drop from his fingers and met my gaze. I think it was at this moment that Ash really remembered; his hands moved from my arms to close about my wrists. For a moment there was dead silence.

'Avril . . .' said Ash, painfully.

'Do you have any idea what you've done?' demanded Michael.

I pulled out of Ash's grasp and stood.

'You've let them out.' Michael's voice was jagged with emotion he was trying to keep under control. 'All the dreams and the nightmares of an island that's been sleeping for sixteen hundred years: you went and let them out, Avril. *Why?*'

I heard it all in that word: the anger; the fear; the awe. I set my jaw. 'Because I had a choice.'

They both stared. Then Michael took a pace towards me and Ash scrambled to his feet, moving to my side. There wasn't any real call for it; I knew that I'd no need to fear Michael any more. But I liked the feel of his hand on my shoulder. Right at that moment it seemed to be the only thing connecting me to the earth.

'Too late, Deverick,' said Ash. 'Too late for that.'

Michael's eyes flashed but he halted.

'This isn't your wood,' Ash added. 'And not your world any more either, I think. Things are going to be tough for you.'

'I'll adapt,' Michael growled. His gaze dismissed Ash and returned hotly to me. 'That was your decision, was it? Well, let's hope you can live with the consequences, Avril.'

I couldn't answer.

'And you'd better hope you picked the right man.' For a moment something bleaker than anger burnt in his eyes. 'That he can keep you safe long enough for you to learn how to handle your wonderful new world.'

'She'll learn.' Ash took my hand and turned it over, displaying my palm on his, his long fingers haloing mine. 'Can't you feel it? She was there. Ground zero. She's part of it now.'

'What's going to happen?' I asked, looking from one to the other.

'Oh, don't you know?' Michael asked.

I turned to Ash. His expression was hardly kinder than Michael's but he held his peace.

'Don't bother asking him,' Michael rasped. 'He doesn't actually know. And I don't either. You've gone and changed everything, Avril. *Everything*. The world isn't going to be the same from now on. Nor are we.'

'I know that.' I had to whisper because of the lump in my throat. Somewhere in the woods the first blackbird had started to sing, already forgetting the oppressive presence of the Green Man and the explosive resurgence of legend, living in the now.

Michael shook his head and turned away, too overcome to find words. He ran his hands through his hair. I watched Ash lift my fingers to his lips and it seemed to me that he was not only giving reassurance but seeking it too. I laid my head against his shoulder, trying to soothe my hammering heart, grateful for the arm he slipped around me. Beyond the soft everyday sounds of the wood there were others I could hear, others less familiar. Singing as if of a distant choir, and the winding of a hunting horn, and – in the distance – the beat of impossibly mighty wings.

Visit the Black Lace website at
www.black-lace-books.com

**FIND OUT THE LATEST INFORMATION AND TAKE ADVANTAGE OF OUR
FANTASTIC FREE BOOK OFFER! ALSO VISIT THE SITE FOR . . .**

- All Black Lace titles currently available
  and how to order online
- Great new offers
- Writers' guidelines
- Author interviews
- An erotica newsletter
- Features
- Cool links

BLACK LACE — THE LEADING IMPRINT OF WOMEN'S SEXY FICTION

TAKING YOUR EROTIC READING PLEASURE TO NEW HORIZONS

LOOK OUT FOR THE ALL-NEW BLACK LACE BOOKS – AVAILABLE NOW!

All books priced £7.99 in the UK. Please note publication dates apply to the UK only. For other territories, please contact your retailer.

ENCHANTED
Janine Ashbless, Olivia Knight, Leonie Martel
ISBN 978 0 352 34195 2

Bear Skin
Hazel is whisked away from her tedious job and humdrum life by the mysterious Arailt, to be his lover. The only problem is there is more to Arailt than meets the eye – much more.

The Three Riddles
The elves, they say, know the secrets of events – but the queen has no time for superstitions. As her kingdom crumbles, she longs for her lost love, but can she risk her country on a whim?

The People in the Garden
Strange things are happening in the grounds of Count and Countess Malinovsky's Gothic manor house. Local people tell of fairies, goblins and unnameable creatures, and there are stories about a ghostly girl with an uncanny resemblance to the decadent couple's beautiful servant Katia.

ODALISQUE
Fleur Reynolds
ISBN 978 0 352 34193 8

Set against a backdrop of sophisticated elegance, a tale of family intrigue, forbidden passions and depraved secrets unfolds. Beautiful but scheming, successful designer Auralie plots to bring about the downfall of her virtuous cousin, Jeanine. Recently widowed, but still young and glamorous, Jeanine finds her passions being rekindled by Auralie's husband. But she is playing into Auralie's hands – vindictive hands that drag Jeanine into a world of erotic depravity. Why are the cousins locked into this sexual feud? And what is the purpose of Jeanine's mysterious Confessor, and his sordid underground sect?

To be published in September 2008

THE STALLION
Georgina Brown
ISBN 978 0 352 34199 0

The world of showjumping is as steamy as it is competitive. Ambitious young rider Penny Bennett enters into a wager with her oldest rival and friend, Ariadne. Penny intends to gain the sponsorship and the very personal attention of showjumping's biggest impresario, Alister Beaumont. The prize is Ariadne's thoroughbred stallion, guaranteed to bring Penny money and success.

Beaumont's riding school is not all it seems, however. Firstly there's the weird relationship between Alister and his cigar-smoking sister. Then the bizarre clothes they want Penny to wear. In an atmosphere of unbridled kinkiness, Penny is determined to win the wager and discover the truth about Beaumont's strange hobbies.

IN TOO DEEP
Portia Da Costa
ISBN 978 0 352 34197 6

Librarian Gwendolyne Price starts finding indecent proposals and sexy stories in her suggestion box every morning. Shocked that they seem to be tailored specifically to her own deepest sexual fantasies, she begins a tantalising relationship with a man she's never met. But pretty soon, erotic letters and toe-curlingly sensual emails just aren't enough. She has to meet her mysterious correspondent in the flesh.

To be published in October 2008

THE DEVIL AND THE DEEP BLUE SEA
Cheryl Mildenhall
ISBN 978 0 352 34200 3

When Hillary and her girlfriends rent a country house for their summer vacation, it is a pleasant surprise to find that its secretive and kinky owner – Darius Harwood – seems to be the most desirable man in the locale. That is, before Hillary meets Haldane, the blond and beautifully proportioned Norwegian sailor who works nearby. Intrigued by the sexual allure of two very different men, Hillary can't resist exploring the possibilities on offer. But these opportunities for misbehaviour quickly lead her into a tricky situation for which a difficult decision has to made.

ALSO LOOK OUT FOR

THE NEW BLACK LACE BOOK OF WOMEN'S SEXUAL FANTASIES
Edited and compiled by Mitzi Szereto
ISBN 978 0 352 34172 3

The second anthology of detailed sexual fantasies contributed by women from all over the world. The book is a result of a year's research by an expert on erotic writing and gives a fascinating insight into the rich diversity of the female sexual imagination.

Black Lace Booklist

Information is correct at time of printing. To avoid disappointment, check availability before ordering. Go to www.black-lace-books.com.
All books are priced £7.99 unless another price is given.

❏ PACKING HEAT Karina Moore   ISBN 978 0 352 33356 8   £6.99
❏ PAGAN HEAT Monica Belle   ISBN 978 0 352 33974 4
❏ PEEP SHOW Mathilde Madden   ISBN 978 0 352 33924 9
❏ THE POWER GAME Carrera Devonshire   ISBN 978 0 352 33990 4
❏ THE PRIVATE UNDOING OF A PUBLIC SERVANT   ISBN 978 0 352 34066 5
   Leonie Martel
❏ RUDE AWAKENING Pamela Kyle   ISBN 978 0 352 33036 9
❏ SAUCE FOR THE GOOSE Mary Rose Maxwell   ISBN 978 0 352 33492 3
❏ SPLIT Kristina Lloyd   ISBN 978 0 352 34154 9
❏ STELLA DOES HOLLYWOOD Stella Black   ISBN 978 0 352 33588 3
❏ THE STRANGER Portia Da Costa   ISBN 978 0 352 33211 0
❏ SUITE SEVENTEEN Portia Da Costa   ISBN 978 0 352 34109 9
❏ TONGUE IN CHEEK Tabitha Flyte   ISBN 978 0 352 33484 8
❏ THE TOP OF HER GAME Emma Holly   ISBN 978 0 352 34116 7
❏ UNNATURAL SELECTION Alaine Hood   ISBN 978 0 352 33963 8
❏ VELVET GLOVE Emma Holly   ISBN 978 0 352 34115 0
❏ VILLAGE OF SECRETS Mercedes Kelly   ISBN 978 0 352 33344 5
❏ WILD BY NATURE Monica Belle   ISBN 978 0 352 33915 7   £6.99
❏ WILD CARD Madeline Moore   ISBN 978 0 352 34038 2
❏ WING OF MADNESS Mae Nixon   ISBN 978 0 352 34099 3

BLACK LACE BOOKS WITH AN HISTORICAL SETTING

❏ THE BARBARIAN GEISHA Charlotte Royal   ISBN 978 0 352 33267 7
❏ BARBARIAN PRIZE Deanna Ashford   ISBN 978 0 352 34017 7
❏ THE CAPTIVATION Natasha Rostova   ISBN 978 0 352 33234 9
❏ DARKER THAN LOVE Kristina Lloyd   ISBN 978 0 352 33279 0
❏ WILD KINGDOM Deanna Ashford   ISBN 978 0 352 33549 4
❏ DIVINE TORMENT Janine Ashbless   ISBN 978 0 352 33719 1
❏ FRENCH MANNERS Olivia Christie   ISBN 978 0 352 33214 1
❏ LORD WRAXALL'S FANCY Anna Lieff Saxby   ISBN 978 0 352 33080 2
❏ NICOLE'S REVENGE Lisette Allen   ISBN 978 0 352 32984 4
❏ THE SENSES BEJEWELLED Cleo Cordell   ISBN 978 0 352 32904 2   £6.99
❏ THE SOCIETY OF SIN Sian Lacey Taylder   ISBN 978 0 352 34080 1
❏ TEMPLAR PRIZE Deanna Ashford   ISBN 978 0 352 34137 2
❏ UNDRESSING THE DEVIL Angel Strand   ISBN 978 0 352 33938 6

BLACK LACE BOOKS WITH A PARANORMAL THEME

- [ ] BRIGHT FIRE Maya Hess — ISBN 978 0 352 34104 4
- [ ] BURNING BRIGHT Janine Ashbless — ISBN 978 0 352 34085 6
- [ ] CRUEL ENCHANTMENT Janine Ashbless — ISBN 978 0 352 33483 1
- [ ] FLOOD Anna Clare — ISBN 978 0 352 34094 8
- [ ] GOTHIC BLUE Portia Da Costa — ISBN 978 0 352 33075 8
- [ ] THE PRIDE Edie Bingham — ISBN 978 0 352 33997 3
- [ ] THE SILVER COLLAR Mathilde Madden — ISBN 978 0 352 34141 9
- [ ] THE TEN VISIONS Olivia Knight — ISBN 978 0 352 34119 8

BLACK LACE ANTHOLOGIES

- [ ] BLACK LACE QUICKIES 1 Various — ISBN 978 0 352 34126 6 — £2.99
- [ ] BLACK LACE QUICKIES 2 Various — ISBN 978 0 352 34127 3 — £2.99
- [ ] BLACK LACE QUICKIES 3 Various — ISBN 978 0 352 34128 0 — £2.99
- [ ] BLACK LACE QUICKIES 4 Various — ISBN 978 0 352 34129 7 — £2.99
- [ ] BLACK LACE QUICKIES 5 Various — ISBN 978 0 352 34130 3 — £2.99
- [ ] BLACK LACE QUICKIES 6 Various — ISBN 978 0 352 34133 4 — £2.99
- [ ] BLACK LACE QUICKIES 7 Various — ISBN 978 0 352 34146 4 — £2.99
- [ ] BLACK LACE QUICKIES 8 Various — ISBN 978 0 352 34147 1 — £2.99
- [ ] BLACK LACE QUICKIES 9 Various — ISBN 978 0 352 34155 6 — £2.99
- [ ] MORE WICKED WORDS Various — ISBN 978 0 352 33487 9 — £6.99
- [ ] WICKED WORDS 3 Various — ISBN 978 0 352 33522 7 — £6.99
- [ ] WICKED WORDS 4 Various — ISBN 978 0 352 33603 3 — £6.99
- [ ] WICKED WORDS 5 Various — ISBN 978 0 352 33642 2 — £6.99
- [ ] WICKED WORDS 6 Various — ISBN 978 0 352 33690 3 — £6.99
- [ ] WICKED WORDS 7 Various — ISBN 978 0 352 33743 6 — £6.99
- [ ] WICKED WORDS 8 Various — ISBN 978 0 352 33787 0 — £6.99
- [ ] WICKED WORDS 9 Various — ISBN 978 0 352 33860 0
- [ ] WICKED WORDS 10 Various — ISBN 978 0 352 33893 8
- [ ] THE BEST OF BLACK LACE 2 Various — ISBN 978 0 352 33718 4
- [ ] WICKED WORDS: SEX IN THE OFFICE Various — ISBN 978 0 352 33944 7
- [ ] WICKED WORDS: SEX AT THE SPORTS CLUB Various — ISBN 978 0 352 33991 1
- [ ] WICKED WORDS: SEX ON HOLIDAY Various — ISBN 978 0 352 33961 4
- [ ] WICKED WORDS: SEX IN UNIFORM Various — ISBN 978 0 352 34002 3
- [ ] WICKED WORDS: SEX IN THE KITCHEN Various — ISBN 978 0 352 34018 4
- [ ] WICKED WORDS: SEX ON THE MOVE Various — ISBN 978 0 352 34034 4
- [ ] WICKED WORDS: SEX AND MUSIC Various — ISBN 978 0 352 34061 0

To find out the latest information about Black Lace titles, check out the website: www.black-lace-books.com or send for a booklist with complete synopses by writing to:

Black Lace Booklist, Virgin Books Ltd
Thames Wharf Studios
Rainville Road
London W6 9HA

Please include an SAE of decent size. Please note only British stamps are valid.

Our privacy policy
We will not disclose information you supply us to any other parties. We will not disclose any information which identifies you personally to any person without your express consent.

From time to time we may send out information about Black Lace books and special offers. Please tick here if you do not wish to receive Black Lace information. ❏

Please send me the books I have ticked above.

Name ....

Address ....

....

....

....

Post Code ....

Send to: Virgin Books Cash Sales, Thames Wharf Studios, Rainville Road, London W6 9HA.

US customers: for prices and details of how to order books for delivery by mail, call 888-330-8477.

Please enclose a cheque or postal order, made payable to Virgin Books Ltd, to the value of the books you have ordered plus postage and packing costs as follows:

UK and BFPO – £1.00 for the first book, 50p for each subsequent book.

Overseas (including Republic of Ireland) – £2.00 for the first book, £1.00 for each subsequent book.

If you would prefer to pay by VISA, ACCESS/MASTERCARD, DINERS CLUB, AMEX or SWITCH, please write your card number and expiry date here: ....

....

Signature ....

Please allow up to 28 days for delivery.